JEB

LIGHTHOUSE SECURITY INVESTIGATIONS WEST COAST

MARYANN JORDAN

Cover by: Graphics by Stacy

ISBN ebook: 978-1-956588-62-0

ISBN print: 978-1-956588-63-7

❀ Created with Vellum

ABOUT THE AUTHOR

I am an avid reader of romance novels, often joking that I cut my teeth on historical romances. I have been reading and reviewing for years. In 2013, I finally gave in to the characters in my head, screaming for their story to be told. From these musings, my first novel, Emma's Home, The Fairfield Series, was born.

I was a high school counselor, having worked in education for thirty years. I live in Virginia, having also lived in four states and two foreign countries. I have been married to a wonderfully patient man for forty-two years. When writing, my dog or one of my cats can generally be found in the same room if not on my lap.

Please take the time to leave a review of this book. Feel free to contact me, especially if you enjoyed my book. I love to hear from readers!

Facebook

Join my Facebook group: Maryann Jordan's Protector Fans

Sign up for my emails by visiting my Website!

Website

Author's Note

Please remember that this is a work of fiction. I have lived in numerous states as well as overseas, but for the last thirty years have called Virginia my home. I often choose to use fictional city names with some geographical accuracies.

These fictionally named cities allow me to use my creativity and not feel constricted by attempting to accurately portray the areas.

It is my hope that my readers will allow me this creative license and understand my fictional world.

I also do quite a bit of research on my books and try to write on subjects with accuracy. There will always be points where creative license will be used in order to create scenes or plots.

DON'T MISS THE OTHER LIGHTHOUSE SECURITY INVESTIGATIONS BOOKS!

Are you ready for Logan, the start of the Lighthouse Security Investigations Montana series?
Click here! Logan

And for Leo's brother's story, click here!
Oliver's story: Time for Home (LSIWC crossover novel)

You do NOT want to miss these other Lighthouse Security Investigations books!

Lighthouse Security Investigations West Coast

Carson

Leo

Rick

Hop

Dolby

Bennett

Poole

Adam

Jeb

Chris's story: Home Port (an LSI West Coast crossover novel)
Ian's story: Thinking of Home (LSIWC crossover novel)
Oliver's story: Time for Home (LSIWC crossover novel)

Lighthouse Security Investigations

Mace
Rank
Walker
Drew
Blake
Tate
Levi
Clay
Cobb
Bray
Josh
Knox

At the end, you'll discover all the Maryann Jordan books!

JEB

LIGHTHOUSE SECURITY INVESTIGATIONS WEST COAST

MARYANN JORDAN

1

Beneath the velvet cloak of night, the water was a canvas of inky blackness. The night sky had the benefit of moonlight and stars, but immersed under the surface, the only illumination was through his underwater light.

Jeb Torres's movements were fluid and synchronized, his form blending seamlessly with the others swimming alongside him. The presence of his fellow Keepers, who were also former SEALS—Rick Rankin, Chris Andrews, and Frederick Poole—was a silent comfort as they glided through the waters at his side. They hadn't served on the same SEAL teams but understood the needs of the mission just as they would have in their former military lives. The weightlessness of the water belied the seriousness of their mission. If he could see the expressions behind their masks, he knew they would mirror his own—focused and unyielding.

In his neoprene dry suit, he felt a connection with the sea. The suit hugged his body like a second skin, bending and flexing with each deliberate stroke he made. The rash guard and leggings provided a barrier against the cold that threatened to penetrate and seep into his bones. Glad they were closer to the surface than deeper, he knew the water temperature was forty-five degrees. The gloves, hood, flippers, and mask kept him comfortable. This was a far cry from the discomforts he experienced in frigid waters during his SEAL training days. Those memories were now distant echoes, a stark contrast to his current mission. This was a leisurely swim compared to that training.

But those days were over. Now, as a civilian working for Lighthouse Security Investigation West Coast, he not only had the latest military-grade equipment to use but also had the opportunity to take on a personal mission. And this was personal.

For months, the LSIWC computer programs had suffered interference from an elusive nemesis. He'd been stymied as to who was perpetrating the intrusion. Granted, the tampering hadn't hindered the effectiveness of the programs, but it had remained an irritating mystery. One he'd pledged to investigate and mitigate. In the silent depths of the ocean, Jeb felt the weight of this mission—not just a task to be completed but a challenge to be fought and won.

His boss, Carson Dyer, started the West Coast branch of LSI after joining forces with Mace Hanover from Maine. Mace brought former Special Forces members together to create the original Lighthouse Security Investigations. The success of the two branches meant they considered expanding and were already in talks with another leader Mace had served with years before.

They embarked on assignments that ranged from security designs to individual security and investigations, often involving governmental contracts. Each member of LSIWC, while having their own specialties, worked together on most missions, but Jeb was particularly adept at their computer security programs. He often worked in the field but supplied support when the others were on assignment. He'd taken it as a personal affront when his programs were hacked and hadn't discovered the cause.

The interference started slowly… initially, he noticed another signal coming in with a security system they had designed for a house that wasn't yet occupied. It struck him at the time that none of the programs for currently lived-in houses were affected. The problems continued but never in a way that was detrimental to a current mission or the danger of a Keeper. But someone was fucking with him, and he'd been determined to discover the cause.

Finally, he'd narrowed the signal to a tiny, almost uninhabited island off the Canadian coast. Kunghit Island, a fifteen-mile-long island, was in the province of British Columbia. The only inhabitants were at the northern tip, where a few houses stood, offering lodging to touring kayakers.

But they were interested in the southernmost tip, where someone had taken up residence. His fellow Keeper Natalie had captured satellite images of a helicopter hovering over a small building that had once been a lighthouse. Now decommissioned and, from all appearances, crumbling and in poor condition, it didn't even capture the attention of anyone seeking shelter while on a boating excursion.

Due to her years as an Army Delta support team member, Natalie was more adept at pulling up and interpreting satellite images than any other Keeper. She had discerned the helicopter lowered a basket to the island, disengaged the device, and then flew away. She'd grinned with glee when announcing that *someone* must be there, and that was how they obtained supplies. Not only was someone there but they also had connections with others who were able to assist them in their lonely existence.

But when Natalie tried to ascertain the helicopter's owner, she was furious to find that the trail was obliterated. Realizing it was luck that they were able to have the snippet of the satellite image, it appeared the island's occupant had finally made a mistake.

With that information, Carson had commissioned them to discover the secrets of the island and why the hell someone targeted them for computer interference.

As Jeb and the others neared their destination, their formation tightened. Brief and precise hand signals were exchanged and used to coordinate the next moves, a silent language that spoke volumes, defining their brotherhood and commitment to the mission. His heart maintained its steady rhythm, but a current of excitement pulsed through his veins, aiding in keeping him warm.

Above them, the moon hung like a silver medallion,

casting a faint glow over the choppy waters as the group rose to the surface. The dark silhouette of the island loomed ahead, a shadowy sentinel. Jeb's gaze remained locked on the terrain, his razor-sharp focus fixed on the shadows. His fellow Keepers moved with a fluidity that belied the roughness of the waters, moving to where their feet could gain purchase on the underwater rocks. The sound of waves crashing against the rocks reached his ears now that his head was above water. The rough and unwelcoming shoreline was exactly what was needed—a natural cover for their stealthy approach.

Whoever was on the island, Jeb wanted their approach to be undetectable. Thanks to Natalie's abilities, she'd jammed the security set up for that area of the island. The fact that there was security told the Keepers that whoever was there wanted their privacy protected. Lips curving, Jeb couldn't help but grin at the surprise the inhabitant was about to receive.

Jeb's muscles stretched as he reached the rocks with a final, powerful stroke, and his gloved hand found purchase on the rough surface. Burying the grunt, he hoisted himself upward. His keen eyes scanned the immediate area, seeing nothing unexpected as he made his way onto the small island. The other three Keepers emerged from the ocean like silent shadows next to him.

Once safely on the shore, they deftly shed their fins and masks, stowing them in their tactical waterproof packs before shoving their feet into lightweight wet-shoe boots. Now snugly settled on their faces, the night vision goggles illuminated the path ahead as they climbed farther onto the craggy rocks. A dense forest of towering trees lay ahead, but they traversed through it with practiced ease, forging their own path as they made their way toward the small building on a crest that had once served as a lighthouse many years ago.

The night was shrouded in uncertainties, but a quick glance at the others assured him they were in their element. Whoever had dared to fuck with LSIWC's computer systems would soon realize their grave mistake.

They clambered over the uneven terrain where tree roots and undergrowth replaced the rocky shoreline. Drawing closer to the dark building, he took his first look at the exterior. The stucco was in a state of decay, crumbling patches exposing the bare brick underneath. It was hard to fathom that anyone could endure living here for an extended period. A tiny crack near a second-floor window sent a sliver of yellow light toward them, drawing Jeb like a beacon. The window was covered with wooden boards nailed in place. It kept out prying eyes but also kept the interior dark.

The others fanned out around the small square building and reported that the main door was the only entrance into the old lighthouse besides the small window. The low hum of a generator on the backside of the building proved that a resident needed electricity. Two rainwater barrels were stacked onto a small wooden platform against one side, with PVC pipes disappearing into the weathered wall of the building.

After confirming their presence was undetectable with

Natalie, he turned the doorknob and slipped inside, quietly removing his night vision goggles. The softly illuminated room came into focus. His gaze swept over the tiny interior, noting where the paint had peeled off the brick walls and the bare and well-worn wooden floor. As he assumed, the wooden slats covering the window kept most of the light from seeping out while also keeping the sunlight from entering. Whoever lived here must have had a preference for darkness. Or to keep out curious eyes.

But puzzling incongruences also met his gaze. There was undeniable evidence of someone living here even though the building seemed uninhabitable. A small bed was pushed into one corner, adorned with a handmade quilt neatly tucked over the mattress. A bright blue pillow was propped against the wall. His chin jerked back slightly at the sight. Someone with military training might continue to make their bed with tight corners, but the aesthetics of a colorful quilt and pillow hinted at a more personal touch.

His top teeth bit into his bottom lip as he inhaled but made no noise as he continued to scrutinize the interior living space. A small refrigerator and hotplate perched on a tiny counter in another corner near a table with a lone chair pushed in place. A metal sink stood alone, with a pipe leading from high on the wall, and he assumed it was connected to one of the outside rainwater barrels. To the side of the pipe was a shelf that offered a view of a few dishes and pots, all clean and precisely stacked. Several wooden crates filled with dry goods were stacked meticulously along the wall. Jeb couldn't help but raise an eyebrow at the abundance of ramen noodle packages filling one crate.

His brow furrowed at the sight of the meticulously organized living space. A door near the foot of the bed was open, exposing a compact bathroom. Stepping closer, he observed a small camping toilet and a shower head that was attached to a pipe leading outside. Assuming the water also came from the rainwater collection, he could only imagine how cold the shower would be.

In the other corner, a wooden staircase beckoned to a second level. He stealthily moved to the bottom step and peered upward, signaling his intent to the others. A faint bluish glow came down the stairwell, casting shadows, but no noises were heard or movements detected.

Making no sound while ascending, he felt Poole at his back. At the halfway landing, he paused before continuing. Before his head could rise above the flooring, he slid a small tube with a camera on the end to peek just above the step leading to the next level. From the screen on his wrist, he spied several portable tables set up around the room with multiple wires leading downward to three uninterrupted power supplies. Shifting the camera, he saw the tables laden with computer equipment and monitors. The chair's bottom rollers were visible, along with two legs ending in thick socks, but the lone resident remained out of sight. With their back to him, he pulled back the camera and let the others know he was proceeding with hand signals.

Jeb bounded up the final steps with a sense of urgency, his earlier concern for stealth abandoned.

Poole moved to his left while Chris stationed himself at the top of the stairs, leaving Rick downstairs to cover any escape routes they hadn't discovered.

The room erupted with a screech as the lone occupant abruptly swiveled around in the chair. A long braid whipped over their shoulder. One hand flew to their chest as the other jerked off their headphones.

A woman stared back, eyes wide and mouth open. *A woman?* Staring in return, Jeb struggled to grasp why a solitary woman resided on the inhospitable tip of an island, working on computers that were fucking with LSIWC's programs.

"Damn," Poole whispered, his voice filled with astonishment.

"Damn," Chris breathed softly from his position behind Jeb.

Dragging his hand over his nearly shorn head, Jeb inhaled deeply as his gaze roved over the woman. A neat braid cascaded over her shoulder, the ends reaching down her chest. A few stray tendrils framed her face, and with the computer monitors behind her, the backlight created a halo effect. Her dark hair glowed with a blue-black hue. Her face was in shadow in the absence of other light sources in the room. Her lips had initially parted as she cried out but now pinched together. In the dim illumination, her eyes appeared too large for her heart-shaped face, but the thick black eyeglasses perched on her nose may have made them appear wider than they really were.

Clad in an oversized sweatshirt and pants that concealed her body, it was obvious from her exposed wrists that she was thin. Her chin lowered as she slipped her glasses down her nose and pulled them completely off, laying them on the table. Her chest heaved as she breathed heavily, and then she pushed to a stand. The room had little available space, with the computer tables lining the walls and the three large Keepers standing nearby. As she stood, he realized just how petite she was. She'd barely come to his shoulders if she were to stand closer to him.

"What the fuck is going on?" Rick asked, his footsteps suddenly halting on the stairs.

Jeb had no doubt that as soon as Rick had seen the woman, he'd been stunned by the unexpected sight… like the rest of them. Never taking his eyes off her, Jeb threw out his hand toward the bank of computers. "Not a bad question to start with. What the fuck is going on here?"

She remained quiet, and he pressed, his tone becoming more assertive. "Let me make it perfectly clear to you. We're here to put a stop to whatever you're doing. You've fucked with our programs for the last time. You might as well start talking because there's no getting out of this for you."

Her tongue darted out to moisten her bottom lip. He dragged his gaze from her shadowed face to the computer screens behind her and around the room. Some displayed lines of code, while others held maps, and one in the corner was paused on an old movie. A soft snort escaped at the evidence of her need for entertainment.

She flinched ever so slightly at the noise he'd emitted. Remaining quiet, he stepped closer to the computer screen filled with lines of code. Given time, he felt sure he could decipher what she was working on and how it tied into LSIWC. But at a quick glance, it appeared to be code hacking into one of the largest search browsers. Cocking his head to the side, he asked, "You aren't doing this on your own, nor for yourself. Who the fuck are you working for?"

She started to speak, but the words were barely audible. Her voice was scratchy, as though not used recently. She swallowed, then licked her lips again. Trying once more, she managed to speak. "Thank God you finally came."

Jeb glanced at Poole, who offered an imperceptible shake of his head. Staring at the woman, Jeb hardened his voice. "You were expecting us?"

"I hoped." Her words were barely a whisper.

"Maybe you finally just made one mistake too many," he bit back, not willing to admit she had lured them there.

Her head tilted to the side as she appeared to study him. "Maybe it just took you a long time to recognize the clues I was leaving." Her words were biting, but her soft voice continued to give evidence of unuse.

"Are you a prisoner here?" he asked.

Her lips pressed together again, but it was Chris who replied. "Who the hell would voluntarily agree to work under these conditions?"

Jeb stepped closer and to the side, no longer willing to stare at the shadows covering her face. As she turned to face him, the darkness was chased away, and her face became awash with the monitors' lights.

He noted the pale skin, almost translucent in the light, and wondered if she spent any time in the sun. Her eyes stayed on him. As he stared at her icy-blue eyes, he detected a violet ring around the blue. Pale blue eyes with a purple ring. He'd seen those eyes before but could hardly process the significance of what he was seeing.

"Hello, Jebediah," she whispered.

The oxygen left the room as he gasped, his eyes wide. "Holy fucking shit. What the fuck?"

"You know her?"

Jeb was barely aware of Chris's question as he continued to stare into the eyes he had never expected to see again. Waves of memories crashed over him, each one more assaulting than the last.

"Jeb?" Poole's sharp voice cut through the fog, filling Jeb's mind.

"Uh… yeah…" His gaze tore from the woman's face over to Poole, seeing his teammate's brow-lifted expression of concern. Jerking his eyes back to the room's occupant, he noted her stance. Her arms crossed over her stomach as though to ward off any unpleasantness. It was a stance he remembered well. Her name fell from his lips. "Skylar."

2

TWENTY YEARS AGO

Jebediah Torres stood on the sidewalk, his gaze fixed on the nondescript two-story brick home in a neighborhood that appeared achingly familiar. As he glanced to the side, the neighbors' houses mirrored the one in front of him. The neighborhood he'd lived in with his parents was very much the same—houses that all looked alike. But inside, he knew that was where the differences came into play.

His mother had loved what she liked to call soft colors. Pale blues, gentle yellows, and soothing greens had adorned the throw pillows, his parents' bedspread, and the bath towels. His room, however, was a stark contrast, filled with posters of cartoon heroes brought to life. Superman. Captain America. Thor. Wolverine. All the things he loved.

But that was all in the past before his world shattered. Now, he stood in front of another house, wondering what it would be like inside.

In the six months since his parents' tragic accident, he'd been shuffled between three temporary foster placements. Now, Mrs. McKenzie, his social worker, led him to this new destination with a hopeful smile. Looking over her shoulder, she called out, "Come on, Jeb. Remember, I told you this is where you get to stay from now on. You're going to love the Bakers! They're one of our best foster families!"

Jeb was only eleven years old, but in the past few months, he'd been forced to accept life's harsh realities. Parents didn't always survive. Kids didn't always get to stay in their homes. And foster homes didn't replace what he'd lost.

With no other choice, he sighed heavily as he trudged behind her up to the front porch.

The door swung open, and he was taken aback by the sight of a small girl standing on the other side of the screen door. She was tiny, with long, black hair accentuating her fair skin. But what struck him most was her pale blue eyes. He'd never met anyone with eyes so light in color.

A voice from inside the house interrupted his captivation. "Skylar, sweetie. Step back and let me welcome our new guest."

Reluctantly, he tore his gaze from the entrancing eyes. *Skylar.* He'd not only never seen eyes so light, but he'd never met anyone named Skylar. Looking up at the approaching woman, he was met with a smiling face staring down at him. Her hair was brown with a few streaks of silver. She wore jeans and a bright red sweatshirt, beaming warmth as she opened the screen door when Skylar scampered back.

"Hello! You must be Jeb. I'm Marlene Baker, your new foster mom. I can't tell you how excited we are to have you join us, Jeb."

He followed Mrs. McKenzie inside, his gaze quickly taking in the neat interior. Glancing to the left, he saw blue and green pillows on the dark green sofa. The weight on his chest lifted slightly at the sight.

Mrs. Baker ushered him and Mrs. McKenzie toward the back, where she invited them to sit at the kitchen table. She set a saucer with two chocolate chip cookies and a glass of milk in front of him. Staring at the treat, he was flooded with memories of his mother offering the same snack when he'd get home from school in the afternoons.

Swallowing past the lump in his throat, he blinked back the tears that threatened to spill. He didn't want to cry all the time, but it was a struggle to accept that he'd never see his mom again.

He distracted himself by munching on the cookies and drinking the milk, pretending not to eavesdrop on the conversation between the two women. In reality, he hung on every word they uttered. He'd learned to do that in the last six months. He knew to listen for phrases such as, "This is only temporary," "We don't have room right now," and "He may have to sleep on the sofa."

Yet the exchange between Mrs. Baker and Mrs. McKenzie didn't sound like any other foster home he'd been in. They talked about his school, and his chest eased a little more to learn that he wouldn't have to change schools again. Mrs. McKenzie spoke of his love of sports and computers. Mrs. Baker wanted to know what his favorite foods were. So far, this home was different from the others.

Relaxing slightly, he glanced around the kitchen, noting the large refrigerator and lots of fruit piled high in a bowl on the counter. Plastic crates filled with rain-boots and hats were against the wall by the back door. Names were on each crate, and he easily found the one labeled Skylar, seeing small pink boots. A strange warmth filled him at the thought of the little girl wearing pink boots. There were four crates, each with names on them. He pressed his lips together. Four. I'll make five. He blew out a long, silent breath. That seemed like a lot of kids in one house. Only three kids were in his last house, and the foster mom complained that it was too crowded. He shot another gaze toward Mrs. Baker, but her smile was still in place. *Maybe five kids won't be too many for her.*

By the time Mrs. McKenzie left, the air moved in and out of his lungs easier. With a smile, Mrs. Baker picked up his suitcase, and he followed her upstairs. She explained that she and her husband had a bedroom on the first floor, and the three bedrooms upstairs were for the children they fostered. The room she ushered him into had bunk beds. "This will be yours," she said, pointing at the bottom bunk. "Randy will be here after school and has the top bunk. He's twelve, so the two of you are close in age. He's a sweet boy, and I'm sure you'll be good friends."

Jeb didn't hold out any hope that he and Randy would be good friends from what he'd seen in his other foster homes. But if Randy would at least not try to steal his things or beat him up, his situation would be an improvement.

"This door leads to the bathroom, and on the other side is another bedroom. We have one older boy, John, who is sixteen. He'll be with us a few more years, but he's involved in lots of after-school sports and activities, so you might not see him as much."

Following her back into the hall, he caught sight of an open door across the hall. That bedroom also had bunk beds, both covered in pink bedspreads.

"The two girls are across the hall and have their own bathroom," Mrs. Baker explained. "You met Skylar, and the other girl is older. Carol, like John, is in high school."

Over the next couple of weeks, Jeb slowly adapted to the Baker household. Mr. and Mrs. Baker were friendly, loving, and determined to ensure each child who passed through their door was met with kindness and understanding.

The school was a large complex, with the elementary school on one side and the middle school and high school just one block over. Each morning, the five children walked together, splitting when it came time for John, Carol, and Randy to head to the upper schools, leaving him and Skylar to walk to the elementary school.

For the first weeks, they said little to each other. That was fine with him since he hated to try to think of things to say. She rarely spoke, but sometimes he'd find her pale blue eyes on him, then she'd quickly look away when he turned to stare. He was shocked when he found out that she was only one year younger than him. With her diminutive size, he'd expected her to be no more than nine or ten. With him in fifth grade and she in fourth, he was fascinated by her and determined that he had nothing in common with her. After all, she was just a little girl.

One day, Skylar shifted closer to him when they walked past a group of boys who snickered. Once past them, he asked, "Do they bother you?"

She hefted her thin shoulders. "Sometimes. They just call me names."

Incensed, he asked, "What names?"

"Skinny Skylar. Alien Eyes."

Her voice held a touch of sadness, tinged with anger. She kicked a little pebble on the sidewalk, then swiped her hand over her cheeks. Without thinking, Jeb whirled around and stalked to the boys, his hands clenched into fists. "No more. No more name-calling. You'll have to answer me if I hear you've picked on her again."

His words must have struck a chord because they ran away. Maybe it was because he was taller and broader even though there were more of them. Whatever the reason, he didn't care. All he knew was that a protectiveness he had no idea was in him had roared to life. He hated that she had to live in a foster home and put up with idiots who thought it was funny to call her names. He stomped back to where she watched.

As they fell into step again, she asked, "Why'd you do that?"

"I don't know."

"Oh." After a moment, she turned her pale-eyed gaze up to him. "Thanks all the same. That was really nice."

"Sometimes I get called names," he said, surprised that he'd admitted that to her.

Her eyes widened. "Really? But you're… you're not like me. You're big and strong. Why would anyone call you names?"

Now, it was his turn to shrug. "Because of my skin color."

Her nose crinkled. "Huh?"

"It's because I'm so tanned. My dad was Spanish, and my mom was Italian." He shrugged as a memory floated back. One kid in his first-grade class had called him Beaner. Jeb had gone home that day and asked his parents why someone would say that. His mother had cupped his jaw and said, *"Oh, Jeb, honey. Some people are afraid of anything different from them. But you hold your head up high. You have a blend of my Italian and your father's Hispanic blood in you. What a heritage you claim!"*

The memory stung, but not because of what the kid called him. Remembering his beautiful mother and gentle touch made everything seem so much better.

"Jeb." Skylar's soft voice brought him back to the present.

"Yeah?" He looked down to witness her blue eyes ringed in purple staring up at him.

"If anyone calls you a name here, I'll punch them in the nose," she vowed, her words sounding fierce despite her diminutive size. Smiling as they reached the doors to the elementary school, she whispered, "You can be my friend."

He watched her go inside, and he stood for a moment, his hand rubbing his chest. He felt just like he did when his mother touched him. Finally, he entered the school, his chest now expanding with pride that he'd stopped Skylar's bully. And just like she did, he vowed to be her protector.

Several days later, Jeb found the energetic Baker household to be overwhelming. Having been an only child, he occasionally felt the hustle and bustle of all the family members to be too noisy. Seeking a respite, he headed upstairs to his bedroom. Once at the top of the stairs, he spied Skylar slipping through a door and quietly closing it behind her. He had assumed it opened to a closet. Curiosity overtook him, and he slowly opened the door, surprised to see a set of stairs leading upward.

He followed the stairs and discovered an attic storage room filled with boxes and plastic tubs, some containing Christmas ornaments. He looked around but found no sign of Skylar. Wondering where she had disappeared to, he walked toward the end of the small room and spied an open window. His heart skipped a beat as he rushed forward, catching sight of her perched on a wide ledge with a rail around it outside the window. His initial instinct was to run and tell Mrs. Baker, but seeing Skylar sitting with her legs bent, her arms wrapped around her shins, and her chin resting on her knees, she appeared peaceful.

Drawing closer to the window, he saw that the wide ledge created the perfect perch and that she wasn't close to the edge. He crept nearer, thinking he was being quiet, when she suddenly said, "You can come out here, too, if you want."

He was gripped with uncertainty but reasoned that if it were safe enough for her, it would also be safe enough for him. Crawling over the windowsill, he settled onto the wide ledge. "What are you doing out here?"

"Sometimes it's nice to have a place of my own."

He couldn't see her eyes since she faced out over the neighborhood. Twisting his head around, he spied the other rooftops, the large trees, and the neighbors' yards. He could even see the school several blocks away. Turning back to her, he said, "You're not alone if you invited me to come out here with you."

"Sometimes it's nice to have a place you can share with someone," she quickly responded.

It was his experience that girls chattered a lot. At least, they did in school. But the more he was around Skylar, the more he realized she didn't speak much. And now that he thought about it further, he realized that when she did, she was very precise in what she said. Uncertain what to say, he finally nodded. "Thanks for sharing it with me."

She turned to face him, and her gaze held his for a prolonged moment before a faint smile graced her lips. It also dawned on him that most girls laughed, smiled, and giggled a lot. But a smile from Skylar felt as though she'd carefully and thoughtfully given a gift. His lips curved in response. The movement of facial muscles felt odd and unfamiliar, and it hit him that he hadn't smiled one time since finding out his parents had been killed in a car accident.

But staring at the enigmatic little girl brave enough to climb out an attic window and kind enough to invite him to join her private place had made him smile.

Together, they turned their attention back to the neighborhood below. Neither spoke, and that was all right with him. From the little sigh he heard slip from Skylar's lips, he assumed it was all right with her, too.

After a comfortable silence, she slowly reached over and placed her hand on his resting on the ledge. His fingers twitched briefly at the unfamiliar contact but quickly settled. He wasn't sure if he should acknowledge her touch but finally turned his hand upward, his palm now pressing against hers. Again, neither spoke as they watched the neighborhood's activities from their rooftop perch, but words weren't necessary.

Finally, Mrs. Baker's voice echoed from below, calling them to dinner. They exchanged glances and grinned. He inclined his head toward the window, indicating she should go first. Once she had crawled safely back into the attic, he followed, shutting the window behind them.

Skylar stood nearby, making no move to go downstairs. She wrapped her slender arms around her waist, holding tight. Lifting her intense gaze to his face, she remained silent, but he waited, assuming she would speak when ready.

"You won't tell anyone about our secret place, will you?" she finally whispered.

He had a feeling that if the Bakers knew that their two youngest foster charges were sitting on an attic ledge, they'd be horrified and quickly stop it. Jeb didn't want anything to happen to Skylar, but she was safe from what he'd seen. But then, he also wanted to make sure she was protected.

"No, it can be our secret." As relief escaped her lungs with his assurance, he quickly added, "As long as you promise to be careful and let me be up here with you."

Skylar furrowed her brow for a few seconds, and he realized he was taking away her private place. Pinching his lips together, he tried to think of a compromise. "Let me know if you ever need to be here alone. I just don't want anything to happen to you."

He must have spoken the magic words because her hands slowly unwrapped from her middle, and a small smile slipped across her face. Nodding, she agreed. "Okay. I'll only go out there if you know where I am."

Mrs. Baker called from downstairs again.

"We better go, or she'll come looking for us," Skylar said. She reached her hand out toward him in silent invitation.

He hesitated, staring at her outstretched hand, uncertain what to do. Her fingers finally drooped, and just as her arm lowered, he reached out and clutched her hand. Giving a squeeze, he exhaled heavily, acknowledging how nice it was to feel her small hand in his. "Come on. I'm hungry."

With a soft giggle, she nodded, and they hurried

down the stairs, slipping through the door before making their way to the kitchen. He didn't know any other almost twelve-year-old boys who would hold hands with a ten-year-old girl, but he didn't care. At that moment, for the first time since his parents died, he felt a glimmer of hope bloom in his chest.

3

PRESENT DAY

"Get your shit," Jeb ordered, staring down at Skylar.

"What?" Her voice was still soft as when she'd first spoken. It made him wonder when she last spoke to anyone.

"You heard me. Get your shit. Or leave it. It doesn't matter. We need to get out of here."

"Jeb," Poole said, stepping closer. "We need to radio for backup if we're going to try to get her to the boat."

"Fuck!" So thrown by her presence, he'd forgotten that he had no way to get her to the boat safely at the moment. Scrubbing his hand over his face, he sighed, feeling stupid.

"We can call for Hop to bring the helicopter in. We can get her out safely that way," Chris suggested.

"How long will that take?" Jeb asked.

"Not long," Rick said, now fully standing with the others in the small space.

Skylar recoiled, taking a step back. Her arms wrapped around her middle again like a protective shield in the looming presence of the four large men. She tilted her head to the side, her eyes piercing Jeb with a defiant glint. "Don't talk about me like I'm not here. And just because you're barking the order for me to pack my shit hardly means that's what I'm going to do."

"Well, you need to get the fuck out of here. That's for sure," he argued.

"I can't do that," she retorted, her voice a mixture of resignation and challenge.

"Why the hell not?" Jeb's patience was fraying, something that never happened on a mission.

"My absence would be noticed. I assume you've managed to jam the security around here, and that's why you were able to slip up on me. That's all well and good, and quite frankly, what I hoped for. But I have no chance of getting out of here undetected."

Jeb opened his mouth, ready to unleash the frustration filling his entire being. His cool head and calm demeanor were hanging on by a thread when a heavy hand landed on his shoulder, squeezing slightly. Whipping his head to the side, he stared at Rick.

"Focus, Jeb. We need to find out what the hell is going on. The mission's parameters may have changed since you obviously know who's here, but the overall purpose is the same."

He knew his fellow Keeper was right, but his thoughts were twisted and tangled as if his extensive training had evaporated in her presence. Facing her again, he growled, "You wanted me to find you. You've been fucking with my system for months, reeling me in.

Why? If not to discover you and rescue you from this high-tech prison, then why?"

She swallowed deeply, her gaze flitting from his face to the other Keepers and then back to him, a silent battle raging in her eyes. She slowly turned, releasing one of her arms from around her waist, and waved it toward the bank of computers behind her. "This," she rasped. "All of this is why I can't leave."

Jeb's confusion was palpable. His brows rose, and he shook his head. "What is all this? We know you get supplies brought in. Someone's got you here, and it sounds like they're not letting you leave. So what the fuck is all of this? What's the endgame?"

"Let's move this downstairs so we can get more comfortable," Rick suggested.

Jeb's head swung around, incredulity seeping into every cell until he caught the expression of concern on his comrades' faces. Planting his hands on his hips, he dropped his chin and stared at his boots for a moment before nodding. Something was obviously going on… something big. And whatever it was, Skylar was at the core and couldn't walk away. And maybe the only way she had to reach out was to find him and tweak him just enough to come looking for her.

Lifting his head, he said, "That's a good plan. Is that okay with you, Skylar? Can we go downstairs and get comfortable and talk this out?"

Her shoulders rose in a heavy sigh, her nod almost imperceptible. "Yes. But, um, there's only one chair down there."

Poole's warm smile broke through the tension. "Wouldn't be the first time we sat on the floor."

Jeb knew Poole was trying to ease the tension radiating from her. *That should be my job.* He had no idea where that idea came from—it had been many years since he'd taken on that role. Glancing behind her, he inclined his head toward her chair. "We can take your chair down with us. We'll manage just fine."

The men shifted slightly, creating a space between them. Rick went down the stairs first, and then they allowed her to follow. She wasn't a prisoner, but they weren't about to give her a chance to escape before they had their answers.

"Go on, I'll get the chair," Chris said.

Jeb trailed Skylar down the narrow staircase to the first floor. The air was thick with tension as he gestured toward the old rustic table. She chewed on her bottom lip but walked past him to slide onto the wooden chair. Chris set the computer chair down and rolled it toward Jeb.

Jeb settled into the seat, his hands resting near hers on the table. Rick leaned casually against the wall near the window, his stance belying his alert gaze. Chris mirrored Rick's stance at the door. Her gaze once again darted around to the men, but she didn't voice a protest on their strategic positions of obvious entrapment.

Jeb's thoughts drifted momentarily. When he first entered the old lighthouse earlier, he'd been struck by the unexpected warmth someone had created, the orderliness with which they lived, and the smallness of the space. The room seemed to shrink even more with four imposing men and one small woman downstairs. It was as though every molecule of space had been claimed.

It was fine by him. He was used to intimidating a person of interest, but he could sense Skylar's discomfort. He recalled how she hated crowds, often escaping when she could. Jeb shook his head slightly to dislodge the unnecessary memory.

Letting out a long sigh, he turned his attention to her, waiting until she finally lifted her head and met his gaze. "Skylar, I'm sorry that I haven't introduced my coworkers. This is Poole, Rick, and Chris. Gentlemen, this is Skylar White." Murmurings of greetings were made.

Continuing, Jeb said, "I'm at a loss here." He leaned forward. "Please, try to see this from my perspective. We expected to confront an adversary interfering with our programs, only to discover that it's a single woman living out here all by herself. And to top it off, you're someone who I know from my past. And if that wasn't crazy enough, then to find out that you were specifically trying to contact me..." His palms lifted upward as he added, "I want to help you, Skylar. I need to understand. But I can't do that unless you're willing to share what's going on."

Poole caught Jeb's attention from the side. "We need to let Carson in on this."

Nodding, Jeb agreed. "Skylar, my boss and coworkers need to hear what's happening."

Her face creased with uncertainty, but after a

moment of hesitation, she acquiesced with a whispered, "Securely?"

"Absolutely. Just like they're here in this room. We're jamming any signal other than ours leaving this place."

Her head jerked up and down in agreement. Jeb glanced over to see Rick speaking on his secure line. Once the others at LSIWC were on speaker, Rick nodded toward Jeb, and he turned his attention back to Skylar.

Her hands rested on the table, clasped together. Driven by an impulse bridging years of distance, he slid one hand over to place over hers. He had no idea how it would be received after all these years. She flinched, and her head lifted, spearing him with her pale-eyed, otherworldly gaze. Her head nodded in jerks before she dragged her tongue over her bottom lip.

"I… I don't really know where to start."

"The beginning isn't a bad place," Poole proposed.

Her laugh was short, tinged with irony. "I'm afraid there's not enough time in the world for that kind of story." Sighing, she continued, "I'll at least explain the short version. But first, please sit. I'm not going to run outside and try to escape. Believe me, if there were a chance I could have done that before now, I would have. At least use the bed."

Poole nodded, then moved to the bed and sat on one end while Rick sat on the other. Chris pulled up a few empty wooden crates and made a seat out of them. Once they were seated, she released a long sigh.

"My specialty is in computer coding and cybersecurity. Eventually, I became particularly gifted in circumventing cybersecurity." Her voice held no pride, but regret bled through.

"The dark web?" Jeb interjected, his brow lowering.

She nodded, her eyes reflecting a complex mix of emotions. "I never saw it as anything other than just coding. My work was neither right nor wrong... just coding. I was given a task, and coding for a solution was just a puzzle to be solved."

Shrugging, she added, "But the company I worked for soon had me work in more and more isolation and delving into different ways of subversion and manipulation. I was given seemingly unrelated tasks and never put them together as a whole."

She pressed her lips together and rubbed them back and forth, betraying more of her inner turmoil. "The paycheck was lucrative." Her eyes sought Jeb, and she whispered, "You know where I came from. I was proud to have a job and career that paid me well. I had no idea I was being... groomed to be the perfect tool for their schemes."

Jeb's grip on her hand tightened involuntarily. Her intense gaze searched his. He internally cursed, hating that he revealed his emotions so easily in her presence. *Just like so long ago.* He had no idea where his ironclad military training had fled to. As a SEAL and recently as a Keeper, he'd maintained professionalism in the face of all missions and assignments. But hearing her use the word *groomed* had his blood racing through his veins. "Groomed?"

Tension radiated from her shoulders, and his fingers

twitched to reach over and rub the crinkle from her brow.

"Groomed to do the work they required." Her mouth twisted. "I had no family. Few friends. No coworkers who I hung out with. I was an ideal candidate for manipulation. I was lured into doing whatever was asked of me. I never suspected that anyone wanted me to do anything wrong… until it was too late. By then, my name was all over everything I'd worked on. I'd go down if I stopped or reported what was happening to anyone. Only me." Dropping her chin to her chest, she slowly shook her head. "God, I was so stupid."

"And this place? How did you get out here?" Jeb prompted, his tone deliberately neutral. He had a fuck-ton more questions he wanted to ask but was finally letting his cautious demeanor take over, willing to guide her to keep talking.

"I was told that someone needed to be willing to separate from everyone else to work on a critical project. I thought they just meant I would be in another room or building with no one else around. When I asked for more details, I was told that I would be staying on a remote island in a place all my own." She snorted and looked around. "Here's my great *resort* location."

"How did you get here?" Jeb probed further.

"I was brought out by a boat and then shown to this location. I couldn't believe it, but I was told it was only for a couple of months."

"And you agreed?" Rick asked, his voice managing to mask his incredulity.

Her gaze jumped over to him. "I didn't have much choice." Her composure crumpled, and she blinked rapidly, then swiped under her eyes. "I know it's hard for you all to imagine what it's like for me. I'm not six feet tall and built like a tank. I don't know how to fight. What could I do? I was told this was where I had to be. They had the computer equipment necessary and brought plenty of supplies." She looked away and sat straighter, stiffening her spine before bringing her gaze back to Jeb. "I once went to a summer camp as a kid… it looked kind of like that, so I figured I could handle two months."

Jeb sucked in a quick breath. He remembered the camp. And he remembered her at the camp, awed by nature and thrilled to sit by the campfire to toast marshmallows. Their gazes held for a long moment as memories slid between them.

"And they helicoptered in food and supplies?" Chris asked.

She nodded. "When the supplies were running low, they sent more."

"How long have you been here?" Jeb asked.

Her lips pressed together again. "Almost six months."

"Fuck," Jeb cursed, anger once again running through his veins. "Six months in isolation," he muttered.

"Skylar, haven't you been able to talk to the ones who hired you? Ask them to get you out of here?" Chris asked.

She slowly shook her head. "After numerous supervisors over the years, I now just have one contact. I'm sure the reason is to keep me working here until the end goal is met."

"What are you working on?" Jeb asked.

She hesitated, pressing her lips together before taking a deep breath through her nose and slowly releasing.

"My initial job was to build and maintain websites that disseminate information that can't be traced. At first, my job was working for government contracts. Slowly, I moved to the private sector, yet the information appeared to be coming from government sources. Then when I came here, the job was to create programs that could change various orders. Later, I realized I was being used to change government or military requisition orders."

"And you're trapped here?" Poole asked. "I mean, I realize that you are physically stuck, but with your knowledge, couldn't you have sent a signal to someone for help?"

"That's what I was attempting with Jeb," she said, her gaze once again on him. Her hands trembled. She pulled her hand from Jeb's and, with her elbows on the table, dropped her head into her palms. Her fingers dragged along her scalp as though in agony.

He cast a hasty gaze at the others but could tell by their concerned expressions that they were just as mystified as he was.

She lifted her head, her face now filled with fierce determination. "I need just to blurt it all out and stop beating around the bush! I was brought here under false pretenses by my employer, and when you called it a prison, you were right. But why haven't I tried to contact someone? Get out? Because I'm being watched. My communications are being monitored. I have no phone. I only have the computers upstairs, and they're surveilled. And who would I tell? As I said… no family, hardly any friends, and no one to wonder where I'd gone."

"What about me?" Jeb asked, his soft inquiry breaking through her impassioned revelation. "Why did you start trying to reach me?" His voice was tender, tinged with a regret that had simmered for years. They hadn't seen each other since she was seventeen years old. And they'd fallen into a silent chasm between them. He'd searched for her long ago, only to resign himself that she'd moved on with her life. There was so much that he'd given up by not talking to her years ago. Now kicking himself, he hated that she'd had no one to miss her. And he wasn't about to have that conversation in front of the other Keepers. The history they'd shared and how he'd fucked it all up was a discussion that would have to wait. *Again.*

"I had followed you over the years," she admitted with candor. Hefting her thin shoulders in a shrug, her intense gaze held him captive. "Even though you stopped… um… we lost contact over the years… I knew you'd left the Navy and started working for a private security firm." Shrugging again, she averted her eyes. "That's when I got the idea. I couldn't contact you directly, so I hacked in and tried to mess with your systems just enough to catch your attention without drawing undue attention to those watching me." A little snort slipped out. "It finally worked."

Jeb absorbed her words, recognizing the depth of their shared past and her current situation. There was a lot to unpack with what she'd confessed, but now was not the time. The room fell into a tense silence. When it seemed she wasn't going to volunteer any more information, Jeb leaned closer so that his face was just in front of hers. "Skylar… with all this incredible story you've told us, you've never mentioned who you work for. What are we up against?"

Her pale eyes dimmed slightly as her pupils widened. He could smell fear oozing from her and hated she felt trapped.

She cast her gaze about the room, looking into the faces of the other Keepers before turning her attention back to Jeb. Swallowing deeply, she replied in a barely audible whisper, "Alistair. Alistair Montague."

The name hung in the air, casting a shadow over the room. The Keepers barely contained their looks of shock and disbelief as the gravity of her revelation sank in.

4

Alistair Montague. Alistair fucking Montague. The name reverberated through Jeb's head with a sinister echo, a sentiment he was certain his fellow Keepers shared.

Alistair Montague—a name synonymous with wealth and influence. A billionaire several times over if the press was to be believed. While he'd never sought a political career, he was the money behind many politicians in the country, ensuring that legislation would always go his way. And his way appeared to be simply making more money. He was rumored to stir up political unrest, use resources to plant false stories and theories, and manage to sway voters in the way that he wanted. The fact that he'd been born in France was probably the only reason he didn't run for president himself, but then, as the ultimate puppet master, even the president danced on his strings.

It was rumored that he also interfered in the elections in Canada, France, and several other smaller countries. His pockets were deep, allowing him to float above the common man, easily skipping over having to abide by the laws that govern everyone else.

Nothing had ever been pinned on him, although after the last major election fiasco, he had come under more and more scrutiny. And if Skylar were caught in his web, then extricating her would take more than the four of them could accomplish in one night.

She excused herself and disappeared into the bathroom. The Keepers huddled near the tiny kitchen counter.

"What the fuck do we do now?" Chris's question cut through the tense air.

Jeb scrubbed his hand over his head, his mind racing for answers.

Before he had a chance to respond, Rick shifted into personal territory. "Look, man, I'm only asking this if it pertains to what's happening now, but what's the story between the two of you?"

Jeb shook his head, filled with reluctance. "I haven't seen her in years. This situation has nothing to do with me, but for transparency, we were close as kids. Close until I graduated and joined the Navy." His reply was guarded, keeping unspoken memories hidden—the ones he wasn't ready to face.

"You two must have been more than just close for her to keep up with you." Poole's voice held a softness that cut through the steel wall Jeb was trying to erect around his mind.

Jeb's gaze shot to Poole, but no twinkling eyes indicated mirth or teasing from his friend. "We were close. But when I left for the Navy… I walked away from my past." It was only a partial answer, bordering on untruth, but close enough that he felt it was sufficient for now. At least until he had a chance to talk to Skylar more. Preferably alone.

Carson's voice came across their ear radios, keeping Skylar from hearing anything. "I have to get ahold of Landon about this situation. But this is way above his fucking pay grade."

Jeb winced, knowing what his boss said was correct. Landon Summers was their FBI liaison, but dealing with someone like Alistair Montague would take LSIWC into a dangerous zone that could have far-reaching implications.

Carson continued, "It's taking all of our resources to keep your presence on the island under wraps. And Ms. White is correct. If she were to leave suddenly, then it would be noted by the computer programs set up."

"I'm not leaving her here alone," Jeb said. "Chris, Poole, and Rick can get back to the boat, and we can work on what we need to accomplish."

No one disputed his claim, and the tightness around his chest eased slightly. The bathroom door opened, and Skylar emerged. Her gaze shot to the group, and her arms wrapped around her middle again.

Stepping away from the others, Jeb moved to her. "You okay?"

"Yeah," she replied, her head jerking up and down. "I just needed… a moment."

"I'm sure." His hands itched to reach out to pull her into a hug, but battling the desire, he remained in place. "We're going to get you out of here—"

"You can't! It would be too dangerous—"

"We'll worry about that. But I agree that it won't happen right now."

Her chest heaved, and her arms tightened even more. "I understand. That makes sense. I'll see what I can do on this end, and if there's anything you can do on your end, then that'll be good—"

"You don't understand. I'm staying here with you, and the others will go back to see how we can get you out of here undetected."

Her eyes widened for a few seconds, then narrowed as she shook her head. "But—"

"No buts, Skylar. I'm not leaving you here alone."

"How can you do this? How can you hide out here without detection?" she pressed, stepping closer, her gaze never wavering from his face.

"It won't be for long," he promised, not knowing if it was a lie. "You're here alone and only get supplies from a helicopter drop. No one will know I'm here."

She glanced around the tiny room, nerves pouring off her. "There's no room, Jeb—"

"I've slept outside, in the rain, in the desert, and on rocks, so believe me, the floor will be fine."

Pressing her lips together, she sighed. "I don't know how to help us get off. Hacking into some of your programs on the side flew under the radar of the person using my programming. But setting up something so I can escape… I have no idea how to do that."

"We'll cross that bridge when it comes to it. Plus, you're not alone anymore."

Her gaze leaped to his as her breath caught in her

lungs. Memories threatened to assault him, and from her wide-eyed expression, she was hit with them, too. After holding his gaze, she glanced at the others, a blush rising over her cheeks.

"Before we do that, we need a bit more information from you to help my people get started."

Wondering if fear would keep her from agreeing or if she would protest, he smiled at her encouragingly when she easily acquiesced with a simple, "Okay."

They settled around the room again, and Carson came over the speaker. "Ms. White, I realize everything that's happened today has been a surprise to you, yet something that you hoped would happen. We have many unanswered questions, but most can wait until another time. Right now, I need to let you know that you were also on speaker with an FBI liaison of ours, Agent Landon Summers."

A quick intake of breath hissed, and Jeb carefully watched as Skylar's expression morphed from interest to terror.

"Mr. Dyer, Agent Summers, I just hoped to be able to contact Jeb. I had no other thoughts beyond wondering if he could help me. But FBI? You have no idea what Alistair Montague is capable of—"

"Ms. White, this is Agent Summers. I can tell you that the Department of Justice, the FBI, and even the CIA are looking into Alastair Montague. What he has you working on has been suspected for several years. Believe me, agents are chomping at the bit to be able to finally nail him."

"And you need me to be able to provide the proof."

Skylar's words were a statement, not a question. Yet as Jeb looked at her resigned expression, he recognized strength mixed in with her fear. If he could help her harness more of the strength, she'd be able to escape whatever tentacles Alistair Montague had out toward her.

"I won't lie to you, Ms. White," Landon said. "You have inside knowledge that could be key to taking him down."

Her top teeth worried her bottom lip. "What do you need from me?"

"For now, give us as much detail as possible about what you're working on and how someone can monitor your actions. All of this will help us know how to reroute the signals going out so that it appears nothing has changed on your end, but the reality is that you and Jeb will be backing up any files that you have."

Skylar began to talk hesitantly at first, almost as though fearful that someone would break into her abode, guns blazing. Except for the lack of weapons, Jeb supposed that was exactly what did happen today. He was one of the good guys, and she knew that. The past two hours had shocked him, but the more he stared at the adult version of Skylar White, the more the memories threatened to pull him back. Shaking his head to dislodge the musings of the past, he focused his attention on what she was saying.

"I received instructions on what to code but wasn't told what it would be used for. It took a while for me to build these secure networks and systems. I eventually realized that some of it was to hide Alistair's hand in politics… or rather, the back door of politics. Suffice it to say, it has taken what I thought was a dream job and turned it into a nightmare."

"So let me get this straight," Landon said. "Various political and non-political groups rely upon Alistair Montague for untraceable information and misinformation?"

"Yes. But as I built the links to some of these groups, I realized how dangerous he is. Some of these groups are on the FBI hate list. Others are neo-Nazi groups operating here in the United States. Others are white supremacists, and I sometimes wonder if they don't hate women as much as they hate anyone who doesn't look like them. There are criminals on the Interpol lists, as well as on the FBI lists."

Jeb noticed how her fingers tapped on the table, and his mind flooded with memories of how she would tap her fingers when overly nervous. Something was off, but he hesitated, uncertain if he should question her further in front of everyone.

Carson interjected. "If we can get this information from Skylar, then that would be the link between Alister Montague, the politicians he funds, and the people already on the FBI wanted list, right?"

"That's exactly right," Landon said. The spark of interest he'd expressed was easily heard to have flamed.

"I have the evidence of his tie-in to these groups and the politicians," Skylar said. "On the outside, everything is well hidden, but the connections are there at the deep level that I function in." She sighed heavily, her shoulders slumping. "Of course, by the time I got in this deep,

I was told that if I ever tried to get out or let anyone know what was happening, my life would be worth nothing."

A growl erupted from deep in Jeb's chest at the threats made toward Skylar. He might not have seen her in years, but a relationship like theirs transcended time and distance.

"Here's my plan," Jeb said. "Rick, Poole, and Chris can swim back to the boat where Dolby waits. I'll stay here with Skylar. I can protect her and coordinate with you all on getting the information from her computers to a safe backup location without detection. But I have to let it be said right now that my number one concern is getting her to safety."

"Completely agree," Carson said.

"Absolutely," Landon added. "Alistair Montague has politicians, judges, and probably federal agents in his back pocket. With his billions, that's easy. Whatever we do, we want to ensure Ms. White is safe. Everything else is icing on the cake."

Jeb was thrilled and relieved to hear the Keepers' agreement.

With a final burst of strategic planning, they were ready to begin the next phase. Clapping Rick on the back, he turned to Chris, repeating the gesture of camaraderie. Again, with Poole, they pulled together for a bro hug, fists thumping each other's backs in a rhythm of solidarity and strength.

He turned just in time to see Skylar gazing up at the three Keepers. The soft light cast a glow on her delicate features. Her hands were clasped in front of her, and her voice trembled. "I can't thank you enough for coming. I can't begin to repay you for what you're doing for me."

Poole stepped forward, reached out, and took her hand in his much larger one. "Believe me when I say it's our pleasure." The sincerity in his tone caused her to blink rapidly as she nodded her appreciation.

With a smile that reached his eyes, Chris said, "The next time we see you, you should be in California with Jeb, and you can meet the rest of the team, including our wives."

Rick threw his head back and laughed before focusing his gaze on Skylar. "Believe me, when my Abbie gets ahold of you, she'll be thrilled to have someone else to talk computer programming with. The two of you will get along immediately."

With a final meaningful glance between the Keepers, they offered a quick two-fingered salute toward Jeb, then slipped back into the night. The door shut behind them, and Jeb double-checked the lock. For a long moment, he and Skylar said nothing, their gazes simply staring at the closed door. Then slowly, they pivoted toward each other, their eyes meeting. The world seemed to pause as the only sound came from their whispered breaths.

5

Jeb's mind filled with unasked questions. His gaze searched hers with a fierce desire to know about her life now. He yearned to delve into the chasm of years lost but knew the timing wasn't right. But her trust was slow to give, and the cocoon she kept tightly around her would only slowly release. Pushing would only chase her away. She would open up when she was ready. He just needed to get her ready.

A large ball of guilt lodged in his throat, making it hard to breathe. Guilt that he should have done more to keep up with her over the years. *But I assumed...* He dropped his chin to his chest. Assumptions were a feeble excuse. He knew all too well what assumptions were worth—exactly nothing. Standing in the old lighthouse, he vowed to forge a new bond... one based on understanding. He had no idea how long they'd remained silent, but her words jolted him back to the current situation.

"So... um... there are things I need to get back to,"

she said, her gaze now looking everywhere except at him.

As she turned toward the stairs in the corner, he rushed, "Skylar!"

She stopped and twisted to look at him, remaining quiet.

"I…" The tangled thoughts refused to unravel. "I'll fix something for us to eat, then I'll come up."

Her gaze shot over to the crates holding food items. "There's not much to fix."

"No worries. I'm a simple eater."

Her gaze held his for a long moment, then she nodded before turning. Her shoulder slumped before she looked back at him. "I'm sorry, but I will need my chair back upstairs."

"Of course." He picked up her chair and, without waiting, carried it up the narrow stairs. Once it was in place in front of the desk filled with computers, he jogged back down, stopping just in front of her.

"Thank you." She hesitated for a moment, opened her mouth as though to say more, then turned and hastened up to the second floor.

As she disappeared from sight, he sighed heavily, shaking his head. So far, the day had unraveled into a tangled shitstorm. From the moment he set foot on the island, ready to confront a perceived cyber adversary, his expectations had been upended time and again. In the span of a few hours, he'd been perpetually stunned. He couldn't remember the last time he'd ever felt so out of his element.

Of all the Keepers, he was the calmest. The rock. The

most methodical. The one determined to research every rabbit hole until he could come up with the necessary information to make every mission as successful as possible.

And now, he was so thoroughly caught off guard he barely knew which way to turn. Scrubbing his hand over his head again, he glanced toward the crates holding the food. A flash of anger hit him as he looked at the modest supplies. The idea was that while they were still sending in supplies, she was only having her barest needs met. *That stops fucking now, and I guess I know where to start...*

He found cans of vegetables and a tin of cooked chicken along with the ramen noodles. As a former SEAL, he'd learn to eat off the land when necessary, and with these supplies, he was in a much better position to create a dinner that he hoped would be well received.

It didn't take long to fix a one-pot meal with ramen noodles boiled in the water she had filtered in the refrigerator. Adding mixed vegetables and pre-cooked chicken, he had a meal. Not fancy, but filling. Glad she had more than one bowl, he filled them and decided to join her upstairs.

When he arrived, she glanced over her shoulder, her gaze landing on his face and then dropping to the steaming bowls in his hands. She sniffed, appreciation filling her expression.

"I didn't expect you to fix me something to eat," she said softly. "But thank you, all the same."

He dipped his head in acknowledgment and walked over, placing one of the bowls in front of her.

"With only one chair downstairs and this one upstairs, don't feel like you have to eat with me," she said. "This place was very much designed for one person."

With his back against one of the walls, he slid down until his ass met the floor. Balancing the bowl on his bent knees, he took a hefty bite. After swallowing, he said, "It makes you wonder who would've lived out here as a lighthouse keeper."

She nodded, then glanced up toward the wooden ceiling. "When I was first brought out here, I was caught up in the romanticism of the history." She nodded toward the far corner where a metal ladder was attached to the brick walls. It led to a trapdoor. "The third floor is unusable. The only thing up there was a light, but some of the glass had broken out."

She pressed her lips together as she held his gaze with a palpable longing. He could have sworn she was about to share something personal, but then she dropped her gaze to her bowl. After taking a bite, she shrugged as she continued, her voice flat. "But I used to wonder the same thing about who would live here. I couldn't find a lot of research, but I guess in the 1800s, there was a keeper. He lived here by himself."

"Lonely existence," Jeb commented, his words heavy with meaning.

"It's an existence I understand."

Again, the silence stretched between them, and he wondered if he'd ever faced a deeper chasm in all the missions he'd worked.

As she delicately spooned another bite into her

mouth, little murmurs of contentment hummed through the room. "It's funny," she mused. "I've made this simple meal countless times, but food always tastes better when someone else makes it."

His grin spread across his face, and he savored another bite himself. It didn't take long for him to scrape the bottom of the bowl, and he watched as she ate carefully and deliberately. There was no rushing through the meal for her. Each bite was savored. Revered. When she finished all the noodles, vegetables, and chicken, she gently tilted the bowl and drank the broth, ensuring no drop was wasted.

At that moment, a rush of memories surged through Jeb. Memories that hit hard, making the food sour in his stomach. Pushing those thoughts down, he waited until, finally, her bowl was back in her lap, and a little smile of satisfaction curved her lips.

The need to escape for a moment pressed on him, and he stood. Reaching out, he collected her bowl with his. Forcing down all the personal questions he wanted to ask, he let out a slow exhalation, trying to recenter his thoughts. "I didn't bring up anything to drink. I assume you usually have the water from the filter in the refrigerator?"

"Yes. The water comes from the rainwater catch, and I run it through the filter."

"That's smart. I'll bring you some."

She glanced toward one of her computer monitors, then looked back at him. "Everything is set for this evening's runs. I don't have to do anything else."

He cast his gaze around the room before settling it

on her. "What do you normally do when you finish your work?"

She leaned back, her gaze now following the same trail as his had. "I read books online or stay up here and watch a movie. I've been able to stream almost anything I might want to watch." Her brow furrowed, and she shook her head. "It's weird, but I realize that I've been fortunate in many ways."

A jolt of tension coursed through him, and his body tightened. His chin jerked back in disbelief. "How the hell do you figure that?" His jagged words were harsher than he meant, but seeing the resigned expression on her face made him want to lash out.

Her pale gaze penetrated as she met his squarely. "Jeb, a lot of people in the world don't have enough food to eat, books to read, and certainly not movies to watch. While I have been stuck out here longer than I was told, I've been earning a paycheck because I can see it going into my bank account. And while the food isn't gourmet, I haven't gone hungry. And it may be in an ancient, somewhat crumbling lighthouse, but at least I have a roof over my head."

His muscles vibrated with anger. "You do realize that what you're saying would only make sense if being here was your choice? If you had decided to eschew the trappings of the world and come live out here on your own, that would be one thing. But you were coerced out here under false pretenses, and now you're essentially being held hostage. Don't turn this into something that it's not, Skylar. This is a fucking prison, and you're being treated as a prisoner, even if you have been given some privileges and a fat paycheck."

His body still shook with rage, but he remained steady, his gaze not wavering. Her tongue darted out to moisten her bottom lip, but she continued to be quiet. And as though the years had dropped away, he could see how she carefully pondered his words the way she used to.

Everything about the moment between them was new… yet hauntingly familiar.

6

EIGHTEEN YEARS AGO

Jeb sat in the bustling cafeteria of the middle school, surrounded by his classmates. Some he would call friends, yet as a loner at heart, he knew not many were good friends. He played baseball and felt a closer bond with a few of his teammates, but he was acutely aware of his preference for being alone once he stepped off the field.

As the laughter and chattering cacophony rose around him, his eyes were magnetically drawn to the corner of the noisy room where Skylar sat. She unwrapped her sandwich with meticulous care and then ate each bite slowly. When finished, she would do the same with her apple and cookie. Every bite was savored, and nothing was wasted. She rarely filled her plate at dinnertime but always made sure to eat every morsel.

Other students were nearby, but she existed in her own bubble, occasionally offering a polite smile or appropriate nod in response to the laughter or a question from the other girls at the table. Surrounded yet alone. Much like him.

Occasionally, her gaze would move toward him, and the instant her pale eyes locked on his, a smile curved his lips, as it always did. She would send a tiny smile his way. His chest swelled, knowing they shared that secret moment.

He hadn't admitted to anyone, not even her, that last year had felt odd when he'd gone to middle school, and she still had a year left in elementary school. He'd worried about her, hoping she wasn't being teased or shunned. When he'd ask her about school during their time sitting on the attic window ledge, she would simply shrug and say she was fine. He could never ascertain if she told the truth.

Now in middle school together, their paths seldom crossed during the day. That was what made their time together in the attic so important. When the weather had become too cold to sit on the ledge during his first winter at the Bakers' house, he and Skylar had started meeting in the attic, just sitting on the floor underneath the window.

It dawned on him that when she talked about school, it was always the subjects she liked learning but never about other classmates, friends, or even if she had a boy she liked. Suddenly, as he held her gaze, he wanted to know what she was thinking and wondered if she would tell him if he asked.

That afternoon, when he got home after practice, he noticed Mrs. Baker and Skylar in the kitchen. Mrs. Baker wore a wide smile, but whatever they had been talking about, Skylar simply shrugged as though it wasn't very important.

After he finished his homework, he hurried up to the attic, knowing she would be there. The chill of late fall nipped at the air, but he wasn't surprised that she had slipped outside anyway. A thick sweater was wrapped around her, and she sat with her knees tucked up, the sweater providing cover for most of her.

Climbing out the window, he sat beside her, accepting the smile she sent his way. Not willing to wait for her to decide whether she would mention it, he blurted, "What were you and Mrs. Baker talking about?"

Skylar's shoulders lifted slightly in the familiar shrug she often gave before speaking. "The principal had called her in for a meeting. They want to move me up to a higher-level math class."

Jeb wasn't surprised, considering he knew how smart Skylar was. But he couldn't tell from her mannerisms what she thought about the change. "I take it Mrs. Baker was happy. What about you?"

"It's okay, I guess. It just means I won't be with the same kids I'm used to during math. And I don't think some older kids will be glad to see me in their class." Her voice was soft, and he could hear her nervousness.

"Maybe you'll be in my math class."

Her gaze darted over to him, hope flickering in her eyes. "Would you mind?"

"Why would I mind if you were in my math class?"

"Because I would be the odd one. Always different." She sighed and shrugged again. "I never seem to fit in anywhere. Girls my age don't like me because I'm not into the same things that they are. And because they don't like me, the boys don't either. I'm just weird to them. And if I'm the little one who shows up in the older math class, I'll still be the weird one."

"You're not weird to me," he said with emphasis. "You're just... um... you're special."

She laughed, and her hand flew up to cover her mouth. But her beautiful eyes twinkled, and he loved that he was the one privileged to see that side of her.

"Maybe that just makes you weird, too," she said, still grinning.

Now, he was the one who chuckled. "That's cool. We can be weird together."

Her hand slipped out from the long sleeves of the sweater, and she placed it on the ledge between them. And just like each time she made the offer, he reached over and placed his palm on hers. They didn't make that connection every time they chatted in the attic or on the attic window ledge. But whenever she did, he found he was more than glad to reach out and hold her hand.

That evening before bed, he found a quiet moment to approach Mrs. Baker.

"What's on your mind, Jeb?" she asked.

"Skylar told me about going into a higher-level math class. I thought that if you talked to the principal, they might let her be in my class."

Mrs. Baker held his gaze for a long moment. "Do you think that would be a good idea?"

"I just thought that it would be easier for her to go into a new class with older kids if she had someone she already knew in there." Feeling the need to keep giving reasons, he added, “And if we had questions about our homework, then we could help each other.”

Mrs. Baker nodded slowly as she continued to peer deeply at him. “I think your idea has merit, Jeb. It’s also a generous suggestion, considering that many people your age wouldn’t want to have anything to do with someone younger.”

He jammed his hands into the pockets of his jeans. “She’s only a year younger. But since she’s kind of small for her age, I’d hate that she might get picked on or made fun of. If she’s in my class, I can watch over her.”

Mrs. Baker continued to nod as her face eased into a gentle smile. “You’re a good friend, Jeb. And you’re growing into a good man.”

Embarrassed by the praise, he simply shrugged and mumbled, “I just thought it might be a good idea.”

“I happen to agree, and I’ll talk to the principal first thing in the morning.”

He started to turn away when Mrs. Baker called him back. “Jeb, your parents would be proud of you.”

He sucked in a hasty breath, his chest both warm at her words and aching at the thought. Nodding, he hurried back upstairs.

The next day, as he sat down in math class, he saw Skylar standing near the teacher's desk.

“Who is she?”

“What’s that shrimp doing in here?”

“Is she skipping up?”

Ignoring the comments from the others in the class, he stood and caught her attention. He could discern terror in her eyes, but she hid it well. As much as he hated bringing attention to himself, he jerked his chin and said, "Hey, Skylar. There's an empty seat over here."

The teacher nodded his acquiescence, and Skylar slipped past the other students in the room, who stared until she sat in the seat next to him. His classmates now had little to say, but he knew he'd take some teasing later. For now, the curiosity of the other students seemed to wane.

He didn't understand his reasons, but the familiar urge to protect her had roared to life. Sitting back in his seat, he swallowed his smile and opened his math book. Glancing to the side, he spied her doing the same with much less tension. And he smiled to himself.

7

PRESENT DAY

Once downstairs, Jeb rinsed out the bowls and the pot in the cold water. Looking over his shoulder, he watched Skylar stand awkwardly in the middle of the small room. It struck him that he'd invited himself into her abode and remembered how she'd always cherished her personal space. His presence would surely feel intrusive. "I'm sorry."

She jumped, then immediately wrapped her arms around her middle.

"Sorry," he repeated, chagrined.

"What are you sorry for?" she asked.

He opened his mouth, then chuckled. "Well, the last apology was for startling you."

"And the first?"

He turned to face her fully. "For just taking over your life here. I didn't ask if I could stay. I just announced that I was."

She snorted. "Why do I have the feeling that you and your coworkers usually just take over situations?"

He lifted his arms to the side, palms upward. "You'd be right. We're trained to see what needs to be done and step in to mitigate the situations."

Her brows lifted. "Is that what I am? A situation to be mitigated?"

He wiped his hands on the dish towel, then turned and closed the distance between them in just two steps. At only six feet tall, he was one of the shorter Keepers, but he towered over Skylar. He dropped his chin as she leaned her head back, and their eyes locked on each other.

He extended his hand, letting it hang between them with the unspoken invitation. Her gaze flickered down to his outstretched hand, and a crinkle formed between her brows. Time stretched, creating a bubble around them. Finally, with a tentative move, she placed her palm against his. Their contact was like a spark, bridging years and memories. Looking up, her chest heaved with a great sigh.

Closing his fingers around her small hand, he shook his head. "You're not a situation to mitigate, Skylar."

"Then what am I?"

"An old friend. Once a good friend. The best I ever had."

She nodded slowly, and in a voice barely above a whisper, she agreed. "Yes. Me, too. You were the best friend I ever had."

He yearned to ask more… talk more… delve into every aspect of her life now. But staring, he spied the dark shadows underneath her eyes that had nothing to do with the poor lighting. Her translucent complexion now held a ghostly pallor. Fatigue filled her expression, and he knew there would be time for conversations later. Now, he just wanted to take care of her. "Listen, I know you're exhausted. Why don't you just do whatever you normally do at night? I'll get ready to camp out on the floor."

The crinkle between her brow deepened. "You can't sleep on the floor!"

"It'll be no problem. Honest. Remember, a lot of people don't have a roof over their heads, so this will be fine."

"Are you making fun of me?"

He shook his head slowly, his lips twitching. "I'd never make fun of you, Skylar. It was just a poor attempt at levity."

Pressing her lips together, she held his gaze and smiled. "It's okay. Anyway, you're in luck. I have an extra blanket and pillow."

"Then I'm in luck," he agreed, squeezing her hand again.

Their hands released, and she moved to kneel at the bed, reaching under to pull out a long plastic tub. She opened the top with a soft pop and pulled out two blankets and a pillow. Shoving the tub back under the bed, she stood and handed them to him. Glancing toward the bathroom, she said, "I'll be honest, Jeb, the facilities are an upgrade from someone just camping on the land, but they're still fairly primitive. The generator runs for the computers. I don't shower often, usually just washing off at the little sink." Her nose crinkled, and a delicate blush painted her cheeks. "Since it was just me, it didn't really matter."

"Don't worry about it. Just keep remembering my military background. I've gone days without a shower and used toilets in the ground. I'll be fine. Anyway, it won't be much longer until we get out of here."

She opened her mouth, then snapped it closed, and nodded. She turned and headed into the bathroom and closed the door.

While she was gone, he checked his phone for the messages he knew were coming in. Rick, Chris, and Poole had made it back to the boat, and they were now ashore, meeting with Hop, who would fly them back to California. Carson reported that LSIWC and Landon had been working with his FBI superiors. They had more questions but would talk to Skylar tomorrow. Carson assured him they were already working on the computer programs necessary to make her disappearance from the island undetectable.

By the time he'd finished with the messages, the bathroom door opened, and Skylar walked out. His gaze raked over her, seeing her now in leggings and a long-sleeved T-shirt. Her curves were more evident than in her baggy sweatshirt, but she still seemed too thin. Anger at her forced existence flared once more, but he tamped it down. There would be time to learn more about what happened to her later.

He stepped to the side, giving her room to move to her bed. "I'll be just a moment, then I'll be back." Once in the tiny room, he used the chemical toilet, then washed his hands and face in the sink. Looking in the mirror, he was glad for his short hair, just scrubbing his hand over his scalp.

Back in the room, he smiled at the sight of Skylar snuggling under the covers. Even though the bed was small, she didn't take up all the room. Her eyes were on him, and as he dropped his gaze, he saw that she had made a bed on the floor with the blankets and extra pillow.

She leaned up and frowned, peering down as he lay on the floor. "Jeb, I feel so bad—"

"Nope," he said, pulling the top blanket over him and laying his head on the pillow. "I'm good. Now go to sleep. Tomorrow will be busy."

She sighed but settled once again. They lay in the dark, neither speaking. Finally, she said, "Are you asleep?"

"Do you hear me snoring?"

A giggle slipped out. "No, but then I didn't know if you still snored."

"Were you just checking to see if I was asleep, or did you want to talk?"

She was momentarily quiet, then said, "I just can't believe you're here."

"I'm glad I'm here, Skylar. And I promise, if I'd known you were in trouble, I would've already been here."

As he lay in the dark, another thought filled his mind. *I should have never walked away and stayed away.*

8

SEVENTEEN YEARS AGO

Skylar perched on the attic window ledge, her knees bent as she hugged her legs. Pretending to relax while looking out over the neighborhood, she couldn't lie to herself. She was waiting for Jeb as her heart betrayed her composed exterior.

Her life had changed drastically in the three years she had known him. His quiet strength had become an integral part of her existence.

The details of his life before arriving at the Bakers' home remained shrouded. It was a common trait among children in foster homes, each harboring their own hidden reasons as to why they were *in the system*. She hated that term, but it was what the social workers and teachers would use.

Every story of a foster kid was different but personal, and the one thing she and Jeb had never shared was the *why* they were there. That was fine with her—the last thing she wanted was to have him know.

She was only nine when she first arrived at the

Bakers'. Several girls rotated through, sharing the bedroom with her, each coming and going as their situations changed. But for her, there was no going back, so she stayed.

The Bakers were nice, and she liked the cookies Mrs. Baker always seemed to have on hand. God knows, her mother had never made a cookie in her life. As nice as everyone had been, it wasn't until she first discovered the attic and then the ledge outside the attic window that she felt truly comfortable. She'd always found safe hiding places when needed, even before she was taken from her home. Though the Bakers were good people, she still desperately craved a safe hiding place.

She felt sure Mrs. Baker knew she disappeared to the attic and equally as certain her foster mother had no idea that she actually slipped out of the window. And none of the other kids ever followed her upstairs to the attic.

At least no one had until Jeb.

She'd noticed him the first day he arrived. Though he was only a year older than her, he was so much larger. And he was quiet. She'd liked that about him. And a few weeks later, she wasn't upset when he appeared at the window. In truth, she'd almost hoped that he would search her out. He seemed to be the one person she didn't mind sharing her secret hiding place with. After that first day, when he sat, listened, and pressed his palm against hers, she felt safe.

He'd become her champion. Walking her to school each day, making sure no one made fun of her or called her names. And the next year, when he'd gone to the middle school, and she was still in elementary, he walked with her to the elementary school door before saying goodbye and heading to his own school entrance.

And now that they were both in middle school, she had the chance to see him more often during the day. Last year, she'd even been placed in his math class. She'd been so scared of the change, but he'd made it easy.

Now, he was in his last year of middle school, and some things had changed. She heard the way girls talked about him. How cute he was. How much they hoped he would ask them to the eighth-grade dance. At least, he rarely smiled at the girls when they were walking down the hall, seeming to save his shy smiles for her.

And as much as she hated to admit it, she was jealous when the other girls tried to gain his attention. Jeb was *her* friend. Her special friend. Yet it seemed she would lose him eventually. After all, everyone eventually leaves.

Next year, he would be in high school, and she'd still be stuck in middle school. She was terrified that year would change everything between them. He would be the cool teenager, and she would just be the foster kid who shared a home with him.

She sighed heavily, shivering slightly as a cool breeze blew.

A sudden noise behind her caused her to jump, and she swung her head around to see Jeb climbing onto the ledge. Her heart leaped, as it always did.

He laughed. "You jumped like I startled you. You must've been lost in thought."

"A little bit, I guess," she said, shrugging. "I wasn't sure if you were coming or if you had something to do after school."

"Our baseball practice was short today since we have a game tomorrow."

She nodded, hiding a secret smile that he came straight up to see her.

"So what were you thinking about so hard?" He gently bumped her shoulder.

"I was thinking about next year. You'll be in high school, and I've gotten used to seeing you at school again every day."

"It'll just be for one year," he replied. "After that, we'll be in the same school again. Anyway, you'll be at the high school for part of the day since you're in advanced classes."

He was right. She had moved up again in math and was already taking high school-level English as well as science. There was a program where middle schoolers could spend part of the day at the high school taking advanced classes, and Mrs. Baker had already talked to her about that possibility. She wasn't concerned about the classes but now wondered if seeing Jeb in his high school glory while she was still a kid would be painful.

She hadn't grown much in the years she'd known him. Her body had matured a bit, but thirteen was still so in-between. And Jeb had gotten taller and broader. At only fourteen, he was definitely the kind of guy who captured and held attention, even if he didn't seem to notice.

The silence between them was always comfortable,

and today was no different. That was one of the things she loved about him. He never made her feel stupid for staying quiet. He spoke when he had something to say and gave her room to speak when she was ready.

Suddenly, she blurted, "Do you ever think about life after this?" She kept her gaze forward but could tell his head had swung toward her, feeling his penetrating gaze.

"After we graduate?"

She nodded but remained silent, now wondering why she'd asked.

He shrugged. "Yeah… sure. Sometimes. I guess I'll join the military. It'd be a good thing to do."

"Oh…" The single word came out on a breath, barely heard.

"My dad had been in the military," he continued.

She tried to stifle the hasty intake of air. His comment was the first time she'd heard him speak of his parents. *Military. That sounds good. Honorable. Like maybe he came from somewhere nice.* Keeping her gaze out over the neighborhood, she pressed her lips together to keep from asking him more, battling the curiosity that threatened to overspill.

"He was out by the time I started first grade, but I still remember seeing him in his uniform."

Now, her breathing shallowed, worried he would stop talking. And even more terrified that he would start asking questions.

Jeb continued, "He got out of the service, so we didn't have to keep moving. At least, that's what Mom always said."

Heart pounding in her chest, she barely breathed as she waited, and he didn't disappoint.

"Holidays were the best. Dad and I would get the tree, and Mom would bake all kinds of goodies." He sighed heavily, swiping at some of the leaves that had blown onto the wide ledge. "Mrs. Baker is a good cook, but even her holiday treats aren't as good as what my mom made." Shrugging, he added, "Anyway, I kind of like the idea of joining the military one day, just to feel like I could be closer to my dad." After a silent moment, he shook his head. "I haven't told anyone that."

Skylar lifted her face to the sun and closed her eyes, realizing the gift Jeb had just given her. She'd been privileged to receive a rare glimpse into where he'd come from and what made him so awesome. The sting of tears pricked behind her eyelids, and she kept her eyes tightly shut, pretending it was just the sunlight that affected her. "What happened?"

The words were past her lips before she had a chance to halt them or pull them back. Her heart seized, and she knew he must hear its erratic staccato. But he didn't appear offended by the question.

"Car accident. Ice on the road. They were coming back from a school program. I was going home with a friend or would have been with them."

Her gasp could not be contained as her eyes flew open and her head swung around. "Oh… Jeb… I'm so sorry." Her heart ached with the sorrowful expression on his face.

"I had no living relatives, so it was foster care. The first ones were just temporary, but then I landed here."

"Yeah, me, too," she blurted.

"Your parents are gone, too, Skylar?" he asked, his voice wrapping around her.

She couldn't hold his gaze. The pain in her chest was too sharp. "Yeah. They're gone." She swallowed deeply, so wanting to be like him. "I remember the first day you came," she whispered. "I saw you from the window and wanted to answer the door."

"Why?"

Shaking her head, she shrugged. "I don't know. Something about you standing on the front path made me want to open the door to see you."

A small grin curved his lips at her confession, and knowing she had given him that moment of happiness made her chest ache less. Pushing her luck, she added, "I was really glad you wanted to come to the attic to see where I was hiding."

His smile widened, and they sat in comfortable silence once again. She didn't ask more about his pre-foster care situation, and she didn't want him to ask any more questions. Just as she started to slide her hand toward him, he reached his arm over and lay his hand, palm up, between them. Without hesitation, she placed her palm on his. His hand had gotten larger with his growth spurts, and his long fingers curled around hers.

9

PRESENT DAY

Skylar woke abruptly, her senses immediately alert. The bed was familiar, but an unusual noise caused her to awaken. Turning her head, she spied the origin of the sound… Jeb snored as he lay on the floor in his makeshift bed. A smile tugged at her lips, and she held her hand over her mouth to stifle a chuckle. Rolling to the edge, she stared at him sleeping. She couldn't believe that he was here. That he had come and stayed.

It didn't matter that he'd arrived expecting a confrontation, ready to defend against an unknown hacker. When he discovered it was her, his demeanor shifted, enveloping her in the familiar cloak of his protection.

Rolling onto her back, she stared at the ceiling as she had done countless times. But this time, the gentle snores from the floor created a completely different environment. One that she'd hoped for but hadn't dared believe would happen. Something was so strange about having someone else here… yet with tinges of familiarity.

Her mind wandered to the past, remembering that when sitting in the warm attic, Jeb and she would pull out an old blanket and take a nap. She would usually drift off first but then wake up to see Jeb, his mouth slightly open with a soft snore escaping his lips.

Never thinking she'd have that sight again, she was determined to commit it to memory. His coworkers didn't give an estimate of when they thought they could help her escape, but she had a feeling it wouldn't be long. And while she was desperate to escape Alastair Montague's clutches, she was determined to commit being with Jeb again to memory. And that included savoring each second.

Suddenly, the vibration of Jeb's phone shattered the quiet. She flinched, and he was instantly alert, answering his device. She marveled at his ability to quickly transition from sleep to complete readiness.

"Jeb here. What have you got?"

He'd answered the call with a focused intensity, keeping his responses brief and to the point. His gaze cut over to her, and his brows lowered as he stared. She battled the urge to squirm, knowing she must be the topic of conversation, hating the scrutiny. Yet she couldn't help but feel an emotion coming from him. Uncertainty. Disappointment. Disbelief.

Nerves coursed through her, but she refused to leave the warmth of her bed and hide in the bathroom or upstairs. Whatever his coworkers were discussing, she was determined to meet his questions head-on. Perhaps she wouldn't be in the current situation if she had done that to begin with.

Jeb disconnected the call and scrubbed his hand over his face as he sat on the floor facing her. She waited, not speaking, determined to have him ask whatever questions raced through his mind.

"How did you sleep?" he asked.

That was not the question she expected from him. If he wanted to play it cool, that was fine with her. "Okay. And you?"

"Surprisingly good." He glanced toward the kitchen. "I thought I'd get some food going this morning since you probably have to get upstairs."

"I'm an early riser, so they expect me to log in soon. But there's not much for breakfast. Powdered eggs and toast."

He laughed as he stood and stretched. "Powdered eggs and toast were a staple when I was a SEAL."

His calm and casual demeanor was the same as last night. Perhaps she'd only imagined the questions she thought ran through his mind when he was on the phone. *And maybe I'm just paranoid from being away from people for so long.* She watched as he snagged the blankets off the floor, his muscles bunching and stretching underneath his smooth skin. He flicked his wrists, snapping the linen before folding them carefully. Dragging herself out of her Jeb-drooling stupor, she climbed from the bed and quickly made it, tucking the covers in.

"You always did like things to be neat," he said.

Looking over her shoulder to find him smiling gently toward her, she nodded, then turned back to the bed. Her hands glided lightly over the already taut quilt. "I guess it gives me a little control in a chaotic world."

"Nothing wrong with that." He laid his blankets and pillow neatly at the foot of her bed. He jerked his head to the side, and she took his silent invitation to use the bathroom first. Grabbing her clothes, she hastened into the small bathroom, used the toilet, washed her face, then quickly dressed.

Once out, she fixed a pot of coffee while Jeb was in the bathroom. When he came out, she smiled. "Coffee is already made, so I'll head upstairs. I can just grab breakfast later. I don't want you to feel like you have to cook for me."

His eyes narrowed on her as he shook his head. "You better believe I'm going to fix food for you. You look like you've skipped too many meals as it is."

She jerked slightly, his words hitting her insecurity. She had always been petite, but having lost her appetite a month ago, she knew she'd dropped a few more pounds. She turned to go up the stairs when her progress was halted when he reached out and wrapped his fingers around her arm.

Gently turning her back toward him, he bent so that his face was right in front of hers. "I'm sorry, Skylar. I didn't mean anything by that. You look perfect. It's just that you seem a little pale."

She forced her lips to curve upward and nodded even though it felt like her head was simply jerking up and down randomly. "I don't get outside as much as I used to." She glanced at the small kitchenette behind him. "But I promise that whatever you fix, I'll eat."

He let go of her arm, and she ascended the stairs with her coffee cup firmly held in her hands. She logged into her computers, checking each one to see the new daily password they required. It was one of her *employer's* precautions to ensure she was still in front of the bank of computers in the lighthouse each day.

Sighing, she worked for several minutes, checking to make sure that all programs were functioning correctly. From downstairs, she could hear the noise coming from the hot plate and smiled at the thought of Jeb fixing her breakfast. Even though the food would be the same as what she had every day, having it fixed by him seemed special.

A few minutes later, he walked upstairs, carrying two plates. He handed one to her and set the other down on one of the tables. Then he went back down the stairs, and a few seconds later, she could hear him coming back up. Her heart squeezed at the sight of him with a coffee cup in one hand and the kitchen chair in the other.

He placed the chair close to hers, and they ate in companionable silence. She couldn't remember the last time she'd had a nicer breakfast, and that included the time before she had been brought out to the lighthouse. *It's all because he's here.*

Once he was finished eating, he moved his gaze over the bank of computers. "My people are working on ways to read the login passwords without you actually being here. Anything you can do to help us would be appreciated."

She nodded her agreement. "I hadn't worried about

it before because I had nowhere to go. No way to get off the island by myself. But I have already looked at the kind of program I would need to write and then embed to make this work."

She turned toward her computers and, for a while, worked silently, aware that his intelligent and analytical gaze watched over her shoulder. As soon as he understood the coding she created, he pulled out his phone and began sending the information to his coworkers. They continued this way for several hours while she maintained an eye on the programs she monitored.

"I know there was more to the story than you were able to give yesterday," he said, breaking their silence. "Skylar, for the life of me, I can't understand how you agreed to come out here alone."

She turned in her chair and looked at Jeb. His face appeared closed off and hardened, yet she swore she could still see the young boy she had known many years ago. She understood he had learned to be wary… always waiting for the other shoe to drop. Once he confided how his parents had been killed, she realized that it wasn't as though he couldn't trust other people. He just couldn't trust that life would always make him happy.

"I understand how difficult this is for you to grasp, but you have to think of the situations from my perspective. I had been working at offices, one cubicle after another. I finally worked up to where I was given my own office. It might seem silly to you, but I took that as a sign of acceptance. They valued my work, and they valued me as an employee. And like a child starved for attention, I ate it up."

She grimaced. "I should be embarrassed that I was so naive. But I was the most adept computer programmer they had. My supervisors realized I did not have supervisory talents, and I did not want other people working under me. I worked best alone. That worked for me, and it obviously began to work well for them. I was given tasks and projects no one else was working on."

"Did you ever suspect what was really happening back then?"

"What the Montague Industries were up to? I assume that's what you're asking."

He nodded, and she set her empty coffee mug to the side. "Not at first. You see, I was hired by one of his subsidiary companies… I had no idea Montague owned it." She shrugged and sighed. "Not that it would matter. You know that he's involved in multinational, multibillionaire corporations. He has legitimate businesses all over the world. And I'm sure that law enforcement knew he had many nefarious business dealings, but I certainly didn't. Maybe I am naive, but even when I realized who I was truly employed by, I just worked diligently, sure that I had a dream job."

"And by the time you realized what they had you working on wasn't legitimate…?" His question hung between them.

"By then, the threat was over my head that my programming had allowed things to happen. Political donations could be traced back to the sites I had created. Even then, I kept telling myself that he wasn't all bad. And what I was doing couldn't possibly be all bad either."

He was quiet for a moment, and she felt unasked questions hanging heavy between them. Finally, he tilted his head to the side and speared her with an intense gaze before he spoke. "You didn't mention all of the programs he had you working on yesterday when talking to me and my coworkers."

She wasn't surprised. She knew she hadn't mistaken the feeling that as he talked to his coworkers this morning, more information was coming in. She hadn't planned on keeping any secrets, but somehow, the shock of seeing him yesterday and trying to confess everything she'd been roped into working on had been too overwhelming. And now, Jeb would know the worst. The fear that he wouldn't want to help her now since shivers throughout her body. But the fear that he wouldn't want to know her anymore sent ice through her veins.

"They didn't anticipate how much digging into the dark web I would learn, even about Alastair Montague. I knew I had stepped into a different world when I uncovered his arms deals, even selling to both sides of a conflict. It was one thing to kid myself that his disinformation on the political front would change elections. Suppose I pretend that was how politics have been running for a long time. But when I discovered he was in the black market sales of our own weapons using some of his military contacts, I knew the world I'd been forced into wasn't one I wanted to have anything to do with."

Jeb sucked in a deep breath, then let it out slowly. Rubbing his hand over his jaw, he never dropped his gaze from her. "Were you scared? Were you threatened?"

"Yes, to both. The instant I made those discoveries, I knew my life would be in danger."

"Why do you think they didn't… um…"

"Kill me immediately?"

He jerked, a wince distorting his face. "Yeah," he growled. "I hate like fuck to even think this, and I sure as hell am glad that they didn't, but it makes me wonder why, considering you could be a liability."

"There's no way Alister Montague deals in the black market by himself. He has his own army of trusted minions to do his bidding. In all honesty, I was nothing more than one of those. Plus, threats go a long way. In my case, I think what saved my life was that I had a commodity they needed. No one else was coding and programming the way I could or as fast as I could. This gave me a certain value. I think it was worth more for them to threaten me to keep me in line and keep me alive than for me to have a fatal *accident*."

"And you being brought out here?"

She barked out a rueful laugh. "I was told I needed to work in isolation so no one else would find out what I had. I was told it was too dangerous for me to work in an office with a lot of other people around. In my naivety, I believed them. I was told that there was a remote location where I would be safe, have the computers needed to do my job, and my needs would be taken care of. When I asked about the location, I was told it would be on an island, and I would have room and board, and supplies would be brought to me, but that I would have the isolation required to do the job without distraction. When I asked how long this would last, I was told no more than two months."

"And they brought you out here." Jeb's voice held incredulity.

Dropping her chin to her chest, she stared at her hands clasped in her lap. Slowly shaking her head side to side, she said, "I was so fucking stupid. I was brought by boat and showed to the lighthouse. I was mortified that it was as rough as it was. It seemed that all the work and upgrades were to keep the computers functioning at their best ability. Everything for me was an afterthought. Money was deposited into my account, and it was four times my regular salary. So I thought I could do this for two months and then return to an office."

"Six months ago."

She nodded. Slowly, the sting of tears hit her eyes. "Yes. Six lonely, fucking, miserable months ago."

"And you never thought of escaping?"

She jerked as though slapped. "Seriously, Jeb? You think I've just been sitting here in my *rustic AirBnb*, enjoying my escape from society's solitude?"

He winced and shook his head. "Sorry! That's not what I meant."

Snorting, she looked down at her clasped hands again. Sighing heavily, she said, "I understand how crazy all this is. Believe me, I didn't come to the full understanding until I was here almost two months." He remained quiet but attentive, so she continued. "Someone monitors everything I do on the computers here. To be honest, I was curious whether I was being watched, but I couldn't find any evidence."

"We searched. Or rather, Chris did when he was here. There are no bugs or cameras on you. So it appears that it's just the computers that keep track of what you're doing as far as the programming."

Nodding, she agreed. "It wasn't until the second month, when a helicopter dropped a supply box, that I realized no one was coming to check on me or take me away. I tried to contact a supervisor but was given the runaround. *My work was too important to risk anyone finding out what I did. I needed to ensure that the websites were undetectable. National security depended on what I was doing.* Believe me, Jeb, it soon became evident that whatever they had me working on, I needed to be hidden away. But what I couldn't understand was why out here? Why couldn't I just be in a basement office by myself somewhere?"

"And did you figure out why?"

"Any signal from the mainland could be traced. But out here? Even though this island is part of Canada, if anyone discovered the signal, it wouldn't be traced back to Montague Industries. It would just look like I was a crazy hermit doing my own thing. You see, I realized they could change the programs at any time to blame me. I was their fall girl. They hijacked my programming, kept me out of the way in a place where I couldn't escape, and ensured I kept working for them."

"Then you started digging into more of what you could find?"

"I figured the only way I could have any leverage was

to gain more information. And what I discovered was the arms deals. Then I realized that just made me more expendable. If they knew that I was discovering more and more about what Alistair Montague was into, I'd be killed and never have a chance to escape. I kept writing code that they couldn't trace to try to figure out how to get out of here."

"About that… tell me what made you try to get my attention?"

She sucked in a ragged breath, her gaze holding his before dropping down to her hands again. If ever there was a defining moment in her life, she felt this was it. She hesitated, uncertain what to say. The air in the room seemed to still which only echoed her inner turmoil. She was surprised her childhood traumas had a way of continually rearing their ugly heads, creating painful new memories besides the old ones they left behind. Her past now resurfaced with a sharpness, intertwining with her current reality.

10

Before Skylar could gather her thoughts into words, she was saved by the bell—or rather by Jeb's phone vibrating again. A look of annoyance swiftly crossed his face, but he reached for the phone, giving her a reprieve. She was glad for the temporary escape, allowing a brief pause in the unfolding emotional narrative she had been considering.

He listened, nodded, then said, "Give me five."

He disconnected, but his intense gaze never wavered from her, locking her in a moment thick with uncertainty before he spoke. "It seems there's a connection that you might know of between Alastair Montague and Colonel Robert Spelling." His words came out in a growl but carried an edge of urgency.

A heavy, resigned sigh left her lips, the sound carrying the weight of unshared secrets. While the urge to lie was strong, she pushed it away. She might hide things from Jeb, but she never lied to him. Filled with a sense of inevitability, she nodded. "Yes, there is. And hence the real reason I've been banished."

Jeb's jaw hardened, determination filling his face. Gone was the easy demeanor of earlier. "Skylar, we need to know everything you've discovered."

She hesitated, but he jumped in, his tone now harder. "If you think you're in danger with what you know, you're in more danger by not telling me. I can't protect you fully if I don't know what we're up against."

With weary resignation, she replied, "Everything you know, Jeb, is just going to put you in more danger."

"More danger?" His scoff was a brief, bitter sound. "Skylar, you're in about as much danger as somebody can be. Don't worry about me. The Keepers know how to take care of ourselves. We know how to cover our tracks. And we know how to bring down someone who seems untouchable. You need us, and we need you."

A long-lost desire caused his words to send a shard of pain through her heart. *I need them, and they need me. I used to long for those words. Only they were slightly different. It would've been Jeb saying he needed me, and I needed him.*

She swallowed her sigh, knowing those were not the words she would hear from him. Dragging her thoughts back to the subject, she steeled herself for the revelations to come and the consequences they might bring. "Okay, I'll give you everything."

"Grab a jacket because we're going to go outside."

"Outside? Why?"

"We both need some fresh air. I'll get my people back on a secure line."

She followed him downstairs and grabbed her jacket

from the small closet next to the bathroom. Walking toward him, she halted as he stopped and turned toward her. His gaze moved from head to toe, and he reached forward to grab the edges of her jacket. Fitting the zipper in its slot, he zipped her coat, and she felt the material hug her. A flood of memories poured over her, from when they were young and how he had always watched out for her.

Darting her tongue out to moisten her lips, she mumbled her thanks, then led him outside. The sun was shining, and even though there was a breeze, they walked to a small clearing that held wide rocks that the sun's rays had warmed. Sitting down, she lifted her face to the sky and, for a moment, pretended that she and Jeb were anywhere other than where they were. Hearing him speak into his phone dragged her wandering thoughts back to the matter at hand.

"Okay, Skylar. You're on the line with my coworkers, boss, and our FBI liaison. We need to know what you discovered about Alistair Montague and Colonel Robert Spelling." He leaned closer. "Remember, I can't keep you safe if I don't know what you're up against."

Glancing at Jeb's serious face, she nodded as her shoulders slumped. Leaning down, she picked up a small pine branch that had fallen on the rocks and began plucking pine needles out. "When I realized I wasn't leaving here, I started searching for leverage, foolishly thinking that I could try to gain someone's attention to get me back home. I had no doubt that Montague Industries was into illegal dealings, but I had no idea what I might find. It took a while, but since I had become so adept at using the dark web for my job, I knew how to search deeply without leaving a trace. What I discovered had to do with the Arbors tank hulls."

"What the fuck?" Jeb asked, his brows lowered.

"A factory in Montana makes the military tank hulls. The hulls can be retrofitted onto older model tanks. It's a much cheaper alternative to scrapping the entire old tanks and manufacturing new ones. Colonel Robert Spelling is in charge of the Army's requisitions of the tank hulls. But when I dug into what I might use for leverage against Montague Industries, I discovered that Alistair has a hold on Colonel Spelling. And like so many others, Spelling dances to Alistair's tune."

"What tune is that, Skylar?" Jeb prodded.

"They steal from the stocks and then sell to bidders… anyone with money… even to countries that aren't our allies. And to some who are arming our enemies. Colonel Spelling signs off on contracts, and then Montague Industries provides the shipping of the products to whoever buys them, all under false shipping, of course."

"You have proof of the colonel selling on the black market?"

She wasn't sure of the speaker but thought it was Jeb's boss. "Yes. At first, I was just curious as to why Montague Industries was doing so, but the more I searched, the trail wasn't as hidden as they thought. I had to develop a backup program to save information that I was stealing as I gathered evidence of *them* stealing. The only reason Montague Industries… or my superiors don't know what I've discovered is that I haven't left a trail for them to follow. But I know I'm on borrowed time. Eventually, it'll catch up to me."

"Jesus, Skylar," Jeb cursed, dragging his hand over his face, then pinching the bridge of his nose.

She continued, "There are checks and balances that should be part of any military acquisition. But so often in the military, someone of lower rank won't take the time to question higher-ups."

"How did you discover what was happening?"

"In all honesty, it wasn't me. Or at least, it wasn't all on me. As I dug behind some of the various Montague Industries, I was surprised to see the Arbors since it was listed as military. Alastair Montague doesn't have any companies that actually make a product. So I could only imagine what he had going with the military was some kind of computer program he had sold them. I kept coming up on information that had to do with the tank. After a bit more digging, I realized that something was going on at the military base. Since it appeared that a man named Colonel Spelling was signing off on requisitions that ended up in Montague Industry requisitions, I started looking into him more. Honestly? He was easy. He was ridiculously naive when trying to hide his correspondence."

"And what did you find?"

"Two years ago, a lieutenant sent an email to Colonel Spelling asking about the discrepancy in the requisitions. His reply to her surprised me. It was curt, unprofessional, and downright rude. I know sometimes military personnel can be brusque by the nature of their jobs, but his reply surprised me. It didn't take long to see that she followed up with an email to the base commander. Only that email never got received. The reason? It was trapped in one of the programs I wrote for Montague Industries. The program searched for various words and halted their progress so they wouldn't be delivered until someone had a chance to review it. At the time, I was told that the program would be used to make sure certain threats were identified and neutralized."

"So when creating some of these programs, you had no idea how the result would be used?" Landon asked.

She winced. "I was given tasks, and then I wrote computer code to make the parameters of those tasks. It wasn't my place or, at that time, my interest to question. It wasn't until later that I had a problem with one of my codes, and while searching for a solution, I discovered how some of it was being used."

"Could anyone else tell what you were doing?"

"It would've been possible when I first began checking on things. I wasn't trying to hide the fact that I was attempting to see where my coding might've gone wrong. But the more I found, the more questions I had. That's when I started digging into the backend of my cybersecurity. What was it being used for? How was it being used? And I very quickly realized that I needed to hide what I was doing. But by then, my superiors must've figured out that I was looking."

He nodded as he listened, and she remembered how he always gave his full attention to whatever she was saying. She twisted her head to stare at him as they sat side by side on the wide, flat rock with the gentle breeze and the sunshine warming them. *How many times did we sit together and just talk? Or even remained quiet but enjoyed each other's company with the distant noise of the neighborhood in the background and the other foster kids running around the house.*

"Skylar?"

She blinked and was dragged back into the present, shoving the past behind her where it needed to be. Sucking in a deep breath, she pushed beyond the desire just to sit and remember the time long ago when he was her best friend. She let out her breath and continued.

"My direct boss would come into my office and ask why I was looking into things. I might've been naive at that time, but I could see a hard glint in his eyes. I made sure to keep my face as neutral as possible while I told him that questionable responses were coming back to some of my programming. He would know if I was giving him a bullshit answer, so I showed him a more generic version of what I was looking at. He seemed mollified, but it wasn't much longer that I was told I was being given special privileges to look into their most private programs."

"And you don't think they've caught onto what you're doing now?"

"I haven't been searching on any of the computers they provided. And the codes written for my own are completely secure."

Carson came back on the line. "We've taken everything you've given us and have sent it to the FBI's programmers. Landon is in contact with them, and they are gathering all the evidence they can from it."

"Is that when you decided to try to reach out to me?" Jeb asked.

She was surprised he asked her while on the phone with his coworkers. She tried to think of what to say that would skirt around their former personal relationship.

"Um, yeah. I knew that I needed help. There was only so long that I could gather information to buy back my freedom and would instead be signing my death warrant." Holding his gaze, she forgot about the phone between them. "You were the only person I could think might be able to save me."

Silence filled the space between them, leaving the birds twittering and the wind in the trees as the only sounds. Her words held such meaning, and from his expression, she wondered if he remembered hearing them before.

"We need to work on obtaining that evidence, Ms. White," Carson said. "Jeb will give you the details, and we'll start working immediately. But we need you two to be careful. The last thing we want to do is tip off anyone at Montague Industries that you are on to something bigger than what you've been assigned to work on."

"Yeah… I know," she agreed. She looked down, seeing the stripped bare pine branch, and had no memory of decimating it. Tossing the twig to the side, she wiped her hands on her thighs before looking at Jeb again. "Jeb can tell me what you need, and I'll be happy to give you everything I have."

"I'm sure he's already warned you that you are placing yourself in more danger by giving us this information."

"Mr. Dyer—"

"Carson, please."

She smiled at his offer of familiarity. "Carson, I can't imagine I'll be in any more danger than I already am. By now, it's obvious that this rustic prison would be where I'd spend many more months. If my life is threatened, then I'd rather go down having stopped someone who I truly believe is evil."

"We'll keep you safe, Skylar," Jeb said, his voice low but full of promise. So much so she almost believed him.

After Jeb had disconnected his call with his coworkers, they continued to sit on the sun-filled flat rock. Her fingers twitched, now missing the mindless task of obliterating the small pine branch. In an effort to do something besides stare at him and wonder what he was thinking, she leaned back with her palms on the warm, smooth stone surface and closed her eyes once again while lifting her face to the sun.

"We were interrupted before you had a chance to answer my question," Jeb said.

She replied honestly, "I was hoping you'd forgotten."

"Not a chance."

"Does it matter why I thought of you? All that matters is that I did reach out. And you're here, and we're trying to figure out our next move."

"Look at me," he urged, his voice a gentle command.

The pull of his soft demand stirred something deep within her, his words filling a need that she begrudgingly admitted was still there after all these years. She angled her head as she opened her eyes, and just as she knew he would be, her vision was filled with only him. He dominated her vision, a reminder of past and present intertwining.

Seeing both the familiar and the new, it was surreal to look at him as an adult. Once worn longer in his youth, his hair was now cropped close, illuminating his mature face. He was taller and certainly more filled out. The last time she'd seen him, he was muscular but lean. Now, his body was sculpted as if carved from the dreams of artists. He could have graced a magazine cover, yet she knew he would have scoffed at the idea of such vanity.

But it was his eyes, deep and brown, that captivated her. They had not changed. Intelligent. Seeking. Analyzing. Cautious. He'd been all those things when she'd known him as a child and teenager, but now, he was more so. The warm chocolate-brown orbs pulled her into a depth of ease that was achingly familiar.

Their gazes locked, and neither spoke as if words weren't necessary. It was a moment meant to be treasured, not sullied with meaningless words.

Finally, the spell was broken when a cloud passed over the sun just as another breeze kicked in, and she shivered. He reached out and took her hand, drawing her upward as he stood. "Let's get you in where it's warmer."

At that moment, she would've followed him anywhere. As they approached the old lighthouse, her gaze moved over the crumbling exterior. Her mind flashed back to the first time she'd seen it. A cascade of doubt crept in, questioning her past choices and compliance. *Maybe I am just a compliant follower. Maybe I should've fought harder when they first brought me here. Maybe I never outgrew the little girl who just wanted to be accepted.*

Shame moved through her at that thought. After years of considering herself smart and making the most of her intellect and education, the idea that she had been a follower cut deeply into her identity.

They entered the small room, and she looked around, no longer filled with fear or dread but now with anger that threatened to explode. Her feet came to an abrupt halt, and with their hands intertwined, he was also jerked to a stop. His brow lowered in silent question.

"Why did I just accept this? Why didn't I fight harder? Why didn't I try to run when I was first brought here?" Her voice cracked as her tear-filled eyes sought his.

His fingers tightened before leading her to the bed, where he let go of her hand. "Please, sit," he begged. Her legs gave out, and she plopped unceremoniously onto the bed.

He turned and moved to the kitchen, then began a simple ritual of boiling water, a tea bag, and a spoonful of sugar. The task was filled with a care that spoke volumes. Once finished, he brought the tea over to her.

As her fingers wrapped around the mug and the scent of orange blossom and cinnamon tea wafted past, she felt the band around her chest ease. Uncertain what to do next, she noted he didn't have that affliction. He grabbed the kitchen chair and placed it in front of her before lowering his body so that his knees bracketed hers and his face was dangerously close.

"Drink," he ordered gently.

She blew over the surface and then took a sip. The warm brew's restorative powers were just what she needed to chase away the chill she'd felt, both outside her body and deep inside. Sipping again, she sighed as the tension in her shoulders eased.

He waited quietly as though he had all the time in the world. And the years faded away, leaving only memories that seemed as though they were yesterday.

11

FIFTEEN YEARS AGO

Skylar waited by Jeb's locker at the end of the school day. It was a habit she had formed over the years and secretly loved. Painfully aware that his looks and athletic prowess had deemed him one of the popular guys, she was thrilled that he still walked her home whenever he didn't have practice.

She glanced up at the clock on the wall above the lockers and observed that it was later than usual. Wondering if she had misunderstood his baseball practice schedule, she hesitated, pondering if she should go ahead and walk home alone. The lockers in their school were not just against the walls but located in pods. Hearing a giggle from the other side, she was surprised when she heard a female voice call out his name.

"Jeb, I don't know why you have to walk her home every day," the voice whined. "She's nobody. It's not like she's your real sister."

"I always walk her home when I don't have practice," he replied.

"Then just pretend you have practice today. Or that you have somewhere you need to be." A high-pitched giggle sounded out. "In fact, that's not a lie. I think you need to be with me."

"Skylar is my friend," Jeb said.

Skylar knew she shouldn't eavesdrop, but considering the conversation was just on the other side of the pod of lockers, she was hardly being sneaky. Yet she was torn between wanting to dash away and hearing Jeb's defense of her.

"Your friend! She's such a pathetic nerd."

"She's not a nerd," Jeb said. "She's just really smart."

The female cackle sounded out. "Smart girls are nerds. Smart guys can be hot, like you."

Skylar's breath halted in her throat, and she waited to hear Jeb reply against the words from the interloper trying to insert herself between them.

"You think I'm hot?" Jeb's voice held incredulity as well as a dose of pride.

Just as the other girl began to assure him, all the air rushed from Skylar's lungs. She knew the other kids thought she was a nerd. *The quiet one. The weird one. The loner.* But she'd also reveled in the fact that Jeb was, too. It was a trait they shared. But now, it seemed the idea that all it took to pull him away from her was a giggling girl telling him he was hot.

Tears pricked her eyes, and she hurried down the hall as quietly as she could, flinging open the door to the outside. Stomping heedlessly, she headed home. She kicked a stone on the sidewalk, anger filling her at the unfair societal expectations. She knew there were smart girls in her school who were also popular, but they tended to be more outgoing. Society was harder on introverts. *We're not exciting. We don't always know exactly what to say. People think we're rude when sometimes we're just happy with silence. People think we don't care when we offer quiet, soft support.* It didn't help that she was already taking college-level math at fifteen. Being in a classroom with all seniors simply meant that she had no friends her age there.

She made it home, greeted Mrs. Baker, and then said she was going upstairs to do her homework. Mrs. Baker gave her a kind look and a gentle hand on her shoulder as she walked past. It was too cold to climb out the window, but desiring to be alone, she pushed the button on the doorknob and locked the door behind her.

Stomping up the stairs, she walked over to the window and looked out, sighing heavily. Tears pricked her eyes, and this time, several made their way down her cheeks, dropping onto her shirt.

She hated feeling sorry for herself. She'd learned at an early age it did no good. But all the turbulent emotions of being a teenage girl seem to swirl, creating a maelstrom inside.

I'm not statuesque. I'm not a great beauty. I don't have the gift of knowing exactly what to say in any situation. I don't know how to laugh breathlessly or hang on a guy's arm. I don't brag about what I can do, but neither will I deny who I am.

The sound of the doorknob below had her swirling around, suddenly unsure. She waited, wondering if someone would call out for her or just walk away. But it only took a few seconds for the doorknob to jiggle again, then the click of the lock to give away and the door to swing open. Before she had a chance to blink, Jeb jogged up the stairs, his gaze immediately landing on her.

"Why did you lock the door?"

Placing her hands on her hips, she groused, "Why does anyone lock a door?"

His chin jerked backward. "You wanted to keep me out?"

"You say that as though it's unheard of. It's called privacy, Jeb."

He continued to hold her gaze, but his brows lowered, and his expression could only be described as confused. "If you want privacy, you only have to ask, Skylar. It's just you never have tried to stay away from me before."

A grimace twisted her mouth. As angry as she had been, just staring at him eased her ache and embarrassment. She backed against the wall and slid down until her ass hit the floor. Drawing up her legs, she encircled her shins with her arms and rested her chin on her knees.

He followed suit, mimicking her actions, except he balanced his forearms on his knees with his hands dangling in front of him.

They sat side-by-side for several minutes, the peace of the attic settling around them like a favorite blanket. She knew he wondered what was going on but, as always, gave her a chance to gather her thoughts.

"Do you ever hate being a foster kid?" As soon as the

words left her mouth, she wished she could pull them back. She had no idea where they came from, yet with all the emotion swirling inside her, that was what she blurted out.

"Sure," he said.

Her gaze stared out over the attic, afraid to look at him. Some of the kids that passed through the Bakers' house for shorter stays often talked about being a foster kid, being in a foster home, hating the title, or loving being with others they felt safe. She and Jeb talked about almost everything else except that. He'd shared how he came to be at the Bakers' house, but she kept her story to herself. Not that she didn't want him to know everything about her, but she didn't want him to look at her differently.

Now, hating the direction she'd sent the conversation, she sighed heavily. "I guess right now, I just hate feeling different. I'm not in classes with people my age. The seniors look at me like I'm odd for being in their class. The sophomores barely talk to me because they think I'm just a nerd."

As soon as she said the word, she felt Jeb jerk slightly and could tell his gaze swung over toward her.

"You overheard what Lauren said."

She shrugged. "I don't know who Lauren is."

He leaned to the side and gave her a little shoulder bump.

She slumped in defeat, then tightened her arms around her legs. "Well, I didn't know Lauren was the name of the girl you were talking to. But yes, I heard what she had to say about me."

"You shouldn't let what others say bother you so much, Skylar. You should be proud of who you are and everything you've accomplished."

Now, she jerked her head to the side and gave him a narrow-eyed glare. "Yes, well, that's easy for you to say. She thinks you're hot. After all, smart guys can be hot!"

"I admit I was surprised she said that."

Jerking slightly, she reared back, studying him. "Seriously?"

"I never thought of myself as that. It sounded kind of weird hearing it."

Realizing that he'd been surprised when Lauren called him hot and he hadn't just preened, looking for more compliments from her, gave her pause. Wanting to hold on to her righteous indignation, she said, "At least you get called hot. I'm just the weird one. The nerd."

"Well, if you were listening so closely, then you must've heard me tell her that I thought you were worth more than any of the other empty-headed girls at school."

At that, her mouth dropped open, and her eyes bugged out. "Really?"

Now, it was his turn to jerk. "You didn't hear that?"

"I must've left before then," she mumbled.

"Well, that's exactly what I told her."

They sat in silence for another minute as she turned this new information around in her head. Finally, she asked, "Do you really think that?"

"Skylar, you're the best friend I have. You're smart, kind, and you always make me feel like I'm good enough just the way I am. And there was no way I was going to let some entitled girl put you down."

She wanted to say so much. *Thank you for defending me. Thank you for caring about my feelings. Thank you for making me feel like I'm good enough.* Mostly, she wanted to thank him for protecting her, even from her own thoughts.

From the smile on his face, he already knew all of the things she wanted to say.

So they sat side-by-side in the attic until they heard Mrs. Baker call out for dinner. He stood with his hand extended toward her, and she looked into his face. She knew she loved him, but a part of her wondered if she wasn't falling in love with him. And that was a dangerous place to go. Pushing those thoughts to the side, she reached up and placed her hand in his, allowing him to draw her to her feet.

Heading downstairs, they shared a smile before greeting the others and helping the younger ones as they all settled around the table.

12

PRESENT DAY - LSIWC COMPOUND

After disconnecting the call, Carson looked at his entire staff and Landon. It was one of the rare times when Landon had driven to the compound. He was the only non-employee or contractor allowed inside the inner sanctum. But Carson and Landon had worked together for too long not to have complete trust.

No one spoke, but Carson knew it wasn't because no one had an opinion or an idea about the situation. But it was as though collective breaths were being held to see what might happen next. Landon faced the others, then dragged a hand over his face before returning his attention to Carson.

"What a fucking mess," Landon breathed. "Hell, this is the kind of case every young agent who joins the FBI hopes to crack open and hand to the DOJ. But, Jesus… it's also the kind of case that every experienced agent knows can blow up simply because the person being investigated has more money and influence than God. And Alister Montague will have so many layers of people between him, and whatever the fuck he's got his hands in that he'll never see the inside of a jail cell." He dropped his chin to his chest and let out a heavy sigh.

Carson nodded. "Landon, we have a lot of leeway here. No one says we have to pursue Alistair Montague. For that matter, we know it takes a helluva long time to gather the kind of evidence to bring someone like him down. And I sure as hell aren't suggesting you put your career on the line for this. If we do nothing more than get Ms. White out and to safety, I'll consider it a successful mission."

The entire room of Keepers remained as quiet as a tomb as Landon stared down at the table for a moment. Finally, he lifted and shook his head. "I can't unsee a crime. I can't walk away from knowing what some asshole is doing just because he's rich and connected. If it costs me my career, then so be it. And we might never get enough for a conviction, but if it just slows them down or takes down one of them, it's worth it."

A collective sigh of relief resounded in the room as grins and high fives were given all around. Carson held Landon's gaze, then nodded. "Okay, let's see what Ms. White has for us."

"It might not ever hold up in court, but even if we can get the evidence to stop Colonel Spelling, I'll take whatever we can."

Carson looked around the room. "Then let's get to work. I need a secure way for Jeb to get what Ms. White has collected and see what we need to process it. And then we need to get them the hell off the island."

13

Jeb knew it was only a matter of time before his coworkers and the FBI had what they needed from Skylar to allow them to escape from the island safely. *And then what?* Of course, they would protect her, but it was more than that… he wanted to protect her. He'd walked away once, but that was when they were both young—teenagers bordering on adulthood with no idea what they wanted or needed.

And she still hadn't answered why she contacted him. Of all the people in the world, why had she reached back through time and contacted him? He wanted it to be because she never forgot, as he hadn't forgotten. He winced. He may have walked away, but he never forgot. *But I sure as hell didn't let her know that, did I?* For several minutes, as she drank her tea, he fell into self-flagellation, hating that they had lost contact for so many years.

"Thank you."

Her soft voice startled him, and he looked down to

see the now-empty mug in her hands. With the windows covered in boards and nailed shut, the room was marked with shadows. It made it difficult to tell that the sun was even shining outside. He thought about the months that she had lived this way and had to tamp down his rage that she felt as though she had no choice. Focusing on anything but his anger, he looked back at her mug. "Do you want more?"

She shook her head, her dark hair dancing softly with the movement, and offered a little smile. It wasn't the first time she'd ever smiled at him, but just like with each one, he felt it was a gift. One she didn't give to just anyone or for just any time. Smiles from Skylar weren't dispensed carelessly. They were bestowed with thought. And when they were directed toward him, he felt the honor resonate to his very marrow.

Their gazes held, and time stood still, tethering them at that moment. Past and present intermingled. Need and want melded together. Probabilities and possibilities became one. There was no turning back as their fates were irrevocably entwined. The same question that went beyond his professional persona still haunted his thoughts and broke free in a whisper. "Why me?"

She swallowed deeply before her lips quirked upward on one side. "Kind of like, 'Of all the gin joints in all the world'?"

He chuckled at her Casablanca reference. "Yeah, kind of like that." He allowed the moment of mirth, then pressed, "You must have had other people you could have contacted. So I ask again, Skylar—why me?"

The slight smile fled her lips, and she looked down

at her lap, offering a small shrug. "I knew people, Jeb. It wasn't as though I lived the last thirteen years in hibernation. But it came down to who I could trust. Certainly, anyone working for any of Montague Industries or subsidiaries put them out of the realm of my trust." She closed her eyes and sighed before seeking his gaze again. "Truthfully, probably over ninety percent of the people who work for one of Alastair Montague's companies are honest people doing an honest job and have no idea what he's involved in. But how could I be sure who to trust?"

He nodded slowly but continued to press. "How did you know I could help?"

"I… I knew what you did. After the Navy." She looked down at her hands, her fingers playing with the edge of one of the pillows nearby.

She seemed to need the distraction, and Jeb wouldn't stop her as long as she kept talking.

"I knew you had little social media presence." She scoffed and shook her head. "For that matter, I didn't either. But I also knew that you weren't exactly going to have work pictures up when you were a SEAL. But even though we weren't in contact anymore, I didn't forget about you."

His chest squeezed at her words. He'd never forgotten her, either, but now wished he'd tried harder to stay in contact.

"I set up a program that would alert me if news about you ever came out." Pain slashed across her face as she lifted her gaze. "To be honest, Jeb, I was afraid of you being killed in action, and I would never know. I could handle knowing you were living your life, even if I wasn't in it. But I couldn't bear the idea that you might die, and I would have no way of knowing that."

If he thought his chest squeezed at her earlier words, his entire heart threatened to beat against his ribs at the expression on her face. He reached out his hand, wrapping around her fingers, needing to touch her. To have even the slightest physical connection to someone who meant everything to him when he was growing up.

"When I finally got a notice, I was terrified to read it. I was so scared that it was going to be a news article telling me of your death." She swallowed, a little laugh slipping out. "You can imagine my surprise when it was a notice of employment change. My program had included IRS records, so when you went from receiving a Navy paycheck to one from Lighthouse Security Investigations West Coast, I checked them out."

"I don't know what to say, Skylar. Blown away, but also incredibly grateful that you did that."

She shrugged. "I had no plans of contacting you. But after I ended up here, I knew everything I'd been told was a lie by the third month. They wanted me to keep working for them, but they wanted to keep me trapped and hidden. I knew who you worked for but was afraid to contact you directly. That might seem strange, considering I've spent a great deal of time discerning how to cover my tracks from my own supervisors. But I couldn't take the chance that someone would discover I was trying to contact you. Hacking into LSIWC computer systems, I hoped to create just enough of a nuisance and leave enough breadcrumbs that I simply tried to gain your attention in the only way I could."

At that, his eyes widened, and he reared back. "You were trying to protect me?"

"Is that so surprising? You used to always protect me."

He knew that wasn't true but wasn't ready for that conversation yet. Instead, he continued to dig. "That tells me what you did, Skylar. But it doesn't tell me why?"

"Does it matter why?" she whispered.

"For me or my coworkers to help you? Not at all. But to me? Yeah… I'd like to know," he pushed.

A soft sigh slipped from her lips. She scooted back on the bed until she rested against the pillows. He wasn't sure if she was trying to get comfortable or put some space between them. But he wasn't willing to give her space at the moment. He shifted over onto the mattress, trying not to crowd her but wanting to be close enough to touch her.

She seemed to ponder his proximity but didn't scoot away further or say anything about it. He remained quiet, seeing the pensive expression on her face, remembering how a similar expression always meant she was pulling her thoughts together.

She sucked in a deep breath, then let it out slowly. "When you left… I missed you. I thought you might reach out… or come back to visit. Our parting was… less than civil. But after your naval boot camp, it was as though you had moved on. You didn't come home once during my senior year. The Bakers went to your graduation and showed me pictures they'd taken. I thought you looked harder. Full of purpose. Determined. It was as though I no longer existed as the friend you needed."

"That's not true," he protested. But even as the words left his lips, he knew why she thought that. He spent time during boot camp deciding he wanted to work hard enough to be accepted into BUDS eventually. Still protesting, he continued. "I remember how full of future plans you were. College. Getting out on your own. You were ready to leave the nest, and all the Bakers talked about were your plans to fly."

Silence enveloped them, more suffocating than the darkness. Finally, she whispered, "You were my best friend, Jeb. Flying never meant alone. Finding my future never meant that it didn't have room for you."

"I came back." He realized his words made no sense, and she cocked her head to the side and waited. Swallowing deeply, he explained, "I had to give everything I could to the Navy to prove that I was worthy of being accepted into the SEAL training. I scored high on the computer programming and technical tests and did that training first while working on a degree in computer programming. Once I had that under my belt, I applied and was accepted into the BUDS course. And as a SEAL, I had to give one hundred percent to my job. If I didn't, people could die."

She nodded slowly, indicating she understood, but there was more he needed her to take in.

"I came back to visit the Bakers once after you'd already graduated and were in college. Mrs. Baker gave me your address, and I drove to the university, deciding that I wanted to see you. Make things right between us. I ended up outside your dorm and stood for a long time, terrified of going in. And then I heard your laughter. I turned around, and you walked toward the dorm but weren't alone. There was a whole group with you. Guys and girls. I stepped to the side and into the shadows, wanting to see you yet suddenly terrified to speak to you."

Skylar's gaze intensified as she stared at him with lowered brows. She shook her head slowly, her expression one of uncertainty. "I don't remember. At least, not that specific moment. But I wish you'd talked to me. Let me know that you had come. Because whatever you thought you saw, I assure you it wasn't the real me."

Now, it was his turn to shake his head. "No, it was you—"

"That's not what I meant. I'm sure it was me, but not what you thought it was. I went to college my freshman year, determined to change myself. I was there on scholarship, but had little spending money. I looked at what the other girls wore and went to the secondhand store to try to dress in a similar fashion. I guess I was lucky that it was usually just jeans and T-shirts. I accepted group invitations to go out for coffee, get drinks, or participate in study groups. I laughed at other people's jokes, even if I didn't understand them. Sometimes I even laughed at other people's comments when they were making fun of someone." Skylar shivered. "Those were the times that made me feel terrible. I even had a few dates but never felt comfortable with anyone. I never felt like I could let the true *me* be seen. The foster kid who… well, you know."

"Christ, Skylar. You are worth ten of any of those people. You should never feel like you have to change yourself," he implored in a fervent whisper.

She stared at him, her eyes reflecting a tumult of emotions. Her fingers twitched underneath his hand. She lifted a brow but remained silent.

The condemnation in her expression pierced him, but he didn't recoil from the pain. He deserved all the shards of anger she had to toss his way. But she withheld her wrath. That had always been Skylar's way. Everything that made her who she was also made her take what she shouldn't have to. What life handed her made her feel unworthy when everything about her should be celebrated. Skylar felt she deserved the dregs when, in reality, she deserved the best.

He was acutely aware that he needed redemption, but this wasn't the moment for atonement. He linked fingers with her and prodded, "The night I saw you… you were pretending to be happy when you really weren't?"

"While I don't remember that exact situation, I can unequivocally say yes."

"I'm so sorry, Skylar. If I had only known. If I hadn't been such a chickenshit…"

She shrugged. "Who's to say anything would've changed, Jeb? I might not have been honest with you. I might have lied and told you everything was wonderful. We can't go back and change the past."

Even though she was right, he wished it weren't so.

"Probably not long after you saw me, I finally decided that I had to be happy with myself. I traded an unsatisfactory social life for extra classes. I didn't join study groups because I found that I learned best by myself. I still occasionally went out for coffee or drinks, but only if I felt like it and not just because I thought it was the socially acceptable thing to do. I finished my degree in computer programming and double majored in cybersecurity."

"Cybersecurity?"

Rueful laughter bubbled from deep inside her. "Who would have guessed that my employer would use my knowledge for his own gain?" She shook her head and sighed. "I was so dumb. So incredibly naive."

"I don't think it's dumb to trust people. I don't think it's naive to believe your employer. You should be able to trust them. But you were definitely taken advantage of. And on top of that, you've been abused in this situation. And I promise you, Skylar, we're going to get the fuck out of here, and you will never have to hear of Alastair Montague again!"

14

The afternoon was spent upstairs on the second level of the tiny lighthouse, where time seemed to stand still. Jeb surprised her with a tablet he had stowed in his gear. She plugged one of her keyboards into it, and the setup became their makeshift command center. Buzzing with the urgency of their mission, they were able to work on the programs necessary for her to have the Montague computers keep running while she escaped.

As they worked, Skylar was enmeshed in a network of allies. Jeb introduced her to Abbie, who was married to Rick, one of the Keepers she'd met earlier. Then there was Natalie, who was married to Leo, Carson's second-in-command. With each new name—Hop, Adam, Dolby, Bennett— the list of her clandestine allies grew. But it was Landon, the FBI agent, who scared her the most. After one tense conversation where he suggested the Witness Security Program, Jeb jumped in to argue, leaving a stern Carson to intervene with a curt, "This can be discussed once the two of you are out."

Her gaze drifted to Jeb, his presence a steady anchor in the storm of her thoughts, just like so many years ago. Tentatively, she reached over to place her hand on his leg. "It's not like I haven't considered the ramifications of turning over evidence. I've always known that would make me vulnerable."

He leaned closer until his face was a breath away from hers. "Skylar, I didn't just connect with you again after all these years to just have you disappear again."

His words hung heavy in the air, a testament to the bond that time hadn't eroded, despite the way they'd parted years before.

She pressed her lips together, unable to think of a response as her heart was caught in the gravity of his sincerity. The memories of their past, the pain of their separation, and the shock of his sudden reappearance swirled within her. When she'd tried to contact him surreptitiously, she had no idea he would try to help, much less arrive in person. And she sure as hell had no idea he would volunteer to stay.

She returned to the covert programming she was supposed to be working on. With Jeb's presence so close, her mind continued to rebel against the important work she was trying to complete. She refused to deal with the surging emotions between them as their professional conversations flowed. They discussed the security measures needed and tested the computer programming parameters they set up.

Her gaze often wandered to Jeb as the day moved into the evening. His face, bathed in the soft glow of the computer screen, was a constant in her peripheral vision. The longing for human connection had been suppressed but now resurfaced with an aching intensity. To have him be her companion meant the world. She wished that they'd never lost contact with each other. She closed her eyes, long-ago memories flooding. When she looked back, it seemed ridiculous that they had both walked away after having been so close.

Overwhelmed, she stood abruptly, her chair scraping against the wooden floor. Needing a break, she hastened down the stairs and walked to the kitchen area. Her low-stocked shelves were a stark reality of her situation. With a resigned sigh, she reached for a can of spaghetti sauce, admitting its unappetizing contents would suffice for their dinner. With another pan of boiling water, she added the noodles. As the water boiled and the noodles softened, a flicker of hope ignited within her. Perhaps she would no longer be here when the next supply drop arrived. Freedom with Jeb was within reach. With renewed enthusiasm, she added the cooked noodles to the pot of sauce and stirred.

She looked over her shoulder as Jeb came down the stairs. He glanced at her and turned to pick up the table and placed it close to the bed. When he glanced back her way, she lifted a brow in question.

"This way, we can both sit at the table at the same time."

She nodded, then turned back to her stirring. What he'd done was a small thing, but after having eaten alone for so many months, she reveled in the idea of sharing a meal sitting across from someone. Not just anyone, though. Someone who once meant the world to her. Someone who stayed with her. Someone she once loved.

She popped the bread into the toaster oven and spread butter over the top when it was toasted. "Dinner is ready," she called out. As she set the plates on the table, she sighed. "I'm afraid it's not gourmet. Hell, it's probably barely edible. But it's food."

She sat on the bed, and he sat in the chair. They began to eat, neither complaining about the fare. The silence was comfortable, but she welcomed the chance for conversation when he spoke.

"Do you remember the camping trip we had in the backyard of the Bakers' house?" he asked.

She laughed, then lifted her hand to cover her mouth as she continued to chew, swallow, and giggle at the same time. Nodding, she exclaimed, "I had forgotten about that."

"We wanted to see what camping would be like, but the Bakers didn't have a tent, so we made our own. A couple of the little kids didn't want to be in the backyard overnight, so it was just us and two of the other kids, I think."

"You're right," Skylar agreed. "David and Yessenia."

Jeb's eyes widened with a mixture of awe and disbelief. "Yeah! I can't believe you can remember their names."

"I remember the names of all the Baker foster kids we met over the years." Her response was tinged with a hint of nostalgia. The words were a bridge to their shared past.

He held her gaze, the initial shock in his eyes melting into a soft, reflective smile. "I didn't realize it at the time, but I think I just saw them all as very temporary people passing through my life. Nothing permanent." His words trailed off, and a distant look filled his eyes. He glanced down at his plate and added, "Except for you."

Skylar felt a whirlpool of emotions churn inside her. There was so much she wanted to question. So much she wanted to rail against, considering the years that had stretched out between the last time they saw each other and now. Her mouth opened, the *why* question teetering on the tip of her tongue, but a safer inquiry emerged. "Tell me about the Navy." It wasn't a question but a command. She wanted to know what had filled his life so much that she became an afterthought.

Jeb paused, his gaze locking with hers as if deciphering the layers of her question. He didn't indicate if he'd discerned her reasons but simply nodded and leaned back in his chair, the wood creaking under his weight. "I wasn't sure what I expected. Looking back, I'm not even sure what I wanted. Some people join the military because they think it's the only job they can get. Other people join because they're searching for some kind of adventure or something different in their lives. Maybe you remember that by the time I was a senior in high school, I wanted to understand my dad more. He'd been in the Navy when he met my mom and when I was really little. He got out to be home more often for us."

She nodded, not telling him that she remembered everything about their conversations. "I remember you talking about joining as a way to forge a connection with your dad. Did that work out for you?"

His shoulders hefted in a shrug as he sighed. "I can't say that it did, but it gave me purpose."

She smiled at his raw and unvarnished honesty. It was always a trait she admired about him. A wave of pain washed over her, remembering the last time he'd been honest with her, and his words had stung. At the time, the pain of his honesty had pierced her heart, but looking back, she could understand his emotions.

As he continued, his expression now more at ease. "I suddenly had a different kind of family. I'd had my birth family. And then I had a family with the Bakers." He paused as his voice grew rougher. "And I had you."

He swallowed deeply and cleared his throat. "And then, I found myself in a different kind of family. That's what boot camp does. It breaks down all your barriers and, in many ways, your past. We all come in as equals. And we're trained to care for our fellow sailors. We form a camaraderie. It's drilled into us that these are the people we'll live with and fight for."

A wave of emotions crashed through Skylar. Even though it made her vulnerable, she wouldn't hide from him. "I'm envious of that family you found in the Navy," she admitted, holding his gaze. "Although I'm glad you had those people on your side. I never found that." She almost added that she'd never found that type of camaraderie outside of anyone but him but managed to bite back those few added words. "Please, tell me more."

"I spent time on the East Coast and had a four-month tour on a naval aircraft carrier to Europe. It was during that time that I started working on my online courses. Once back in the States, I began learning everything I could about becoming a SEAL. I transferred to the West Coast and then had a six-month tour in Asia. By the time that tour was over, I had put in my application for BUDs. I was stunned when I got accepted on the first try. I knew that to get through that training, it would take everything I had and more."

"And you made it." A mix of pride and a pang of regret filled her words. She was filled with remorse that she hadn't been part of his life during that time but was so proud of him. He'd had a chance to reconnect with the idea of what his dad's life had been like at one time. He'd served his country. And then he completed the training in what she knew was arguably one of the hardest jobs in the world. "I'm really proud of you. Mrs. Baker would tell me what you were doing, but I'm sorry I wasn't around to cheer you on."

The silence that fell between them was thick, laden with years of unsaid words and unshared experiences. It was a curtain that had been formed the day he left for boot camp. The veil was so dense and impenetrable that neither had tried to tear it down. Now, years later, she wanted to rip it into shreds, toss it to the side, and cast it away forever.

"I want to show you something."

He jerked slightly, then nodded. "Okay."

She stood and said, "Leave the dishes. We can clean later." Without giving him a chance to change his mind, she walked to the stairs. "It's up there." Once she was on the second floor, hearing his footsteps behind her, she walked to the old ladder that extended upward. Placing her foot on the bottom rung, she glanced over her shoulder. "Trust me?"

His gaze found and held hers. "Absolutely."

With a nod, she climbed upward, lifting her hand above her when her head reached the trapdoor leading to the third floor. Pushing it up and over, she continued the climb. Once there, she scooted over and looked down, seeing Jeb following.

He popped his head through the opening and looked around in surprise. "I thought this space was unusable."

"It is… as a lighthouse." As he continued to climb upward, she added, "You can see some of the glass is broken, although a lantern could be placed up here, I suppose." She stepped carefully on the floor before sitting. He quickly followed and sat next to her. It was already dark, but they could see the silhouette of the trees and hear the waves crashing on the rocks in the background. "I knew I had to check the space out. And once I determined that there was a safe place for me to just sit for a while, I've come up here every day, weather permitting."

They were silent again, and she watched as his gaze moved over the horizon. Taking a cleansing breath, she let it out. It was time—time to cast away her fears and find out all she could to erase the past thirteen years. "Tell me more. Tell me about traveling the world. Tell me about the women you loved in every port. Tell me about your friends. Tell me why you got out. Tell me about Lighthouse—"

A deep chuckle erupted, and his eyes lit. "You don't ask for much, do you?"

She shrugged, feeling more exposed than she would have liked. "I haven't seen you in almost thirteen years. There's a lot of catching up to do."

They stared at each other for a moment, and it was as though the old Jeb was back, and she could tell exactly what he was thinking. She saw regret in his eyes and knew he wondered about the thirteen-year chasm.

Finally, he nodded. "I can't tell you about the missions I had as a SEAL, but as hard as the training was, it was worth it when I made it through. And the men at my side became brothers. As far as the ports, we weren't always welcome, so much of my time was spent on the ship." His shoulders hefted in a shrug. "Plus, I was determined to get my degree, so most of my free time was taken up in studying." Grinning, he added, "And the idea of women in every port, at least, for me, would be greatly exaggerated. To be honest, the bars and brothels that lined the streets near where ships docked held no appeal to me."

A ribbon of pleasure curled through her. Knowing he was not living a wild life made her feel better. It was a ridiculous notion to be jealous of the years they spent apart, but she would at least be honest enough with herself to admit it. Dragging herself back to the conversations, she prodded, "And the reason you left the SEALs?"

At this question, the lines in his forehead deepened,

and the air left his lungs in a deep, heavy sigh. It flashed through her mind that perhaps the reasons were too painful, and she shouldn't have asked. But before she could pull back the words, he dangled his forearms on his bent knees, and held her gaze.

"There was no one particular reason," he began. "The first time I stood on a ship, I told myself I was looking out at a horizon my dad had looked at once. Yet I can't say I felt any closer to him or found any peace. I stayed in the Navy because I didn't have another career plan. But I wanted to push myself and become the best that I could be. And for me, that was SEALs. I loved the brotherhood. I loved the adrenaline rush from our missions and training. But after about ten years in the Navy, with the last seven of those as a SEAL, I knew there was a limited lifespan in that career. And I wanted to be master of my own fate instead of having an injury dictate what I could do. Or hell, an early death."

"I understand." Her simple words caused his gaze to snap to her face again, but she meant them and wouldn't take them back. "Obviously, our experiences were different. But until a few months ago, I had taken, and taken, and taken from what everybody wanted to dump on me. I went from being the poor little foster kid that nobody wanted to the college student who no one really wanted to befriend. Then I got a job where I was finally valued, not because of me, but because of what I could do for them. But craving attention so badly, I took everything they wanted to throw me and look where I ended up. Literally imprisoned on an uninhabited island in a building that no one should live in. All because I was too good at my job. Too good that they can't get rid of me, yet so good that I found out things I shouldn't have." She shook her head as she winced. "I'm sorry, this conversation wasn't supposed to be about me. But all I meant was that I understand your desire to take charge of your life."

Now, hating that she had hijacked his time to tell her about his life, she quickly rushed, "Please, continue. Tell me how you ended up at the security firm."

Once again, he held her gaze, and she knew there was little she could hide from him. After all these years, she felt he could still read her like a book. But thankfully, he didn't put her on the spot.

Finally, unclasping his hands, he lifted his palms up slightly. "I knew I wanted to continue in the same career genre. I wanted to be able to use all of my skills—computer programs, cybersecurity, and active rescues, if possible. I spent some time researching a number of security businesses. I wanted to live on the West Coast, so I concentrated on seeing what was here. Some security businesses mostly specialize in bodyguards, especially in LA, which didn't interest me. But it was another SEAL—actually Poole, one of the men you met—who told me about Lighthouse Security Investigations. I dug deeper and interviewed with Carson, and I knew it was everything I wanted it to be."

"Why are you known as Keepers?" A little snort escaped, and she shook her head. "Obviously, it's a play on lighthouse keepers, but whenever you talk about Keepers, there is such pride in your voice."

"Keepers are the true guardians, guiding people to

safety—unsung heroes. The original LSI is in Maine, and the creator firmly believed in the ideal of the old lighthouse keepers. And you're exactly right… it is a point of pride."

Now, a wistful sigh escaped her lips. She reached across the space and placed her hand on the wooden deck. It only took a moment for him to place his palm over hers. The feel of his skin touching hers sent shivers through her whole body. The connection was so new and so familiar. She blinked back the tears that threatened to fall. Swallowing past the lump in her throat, she said, "I've never experienced that level of pride. I might be proud of the work I've done in the past, but the last few months have obliterated that particular emotion."

"Don't let Alistair Montague rob you of anything else, Skylar. You've given your best, and that's your sense of pride. And now, you're still doing that, only to right the wrongs that you've discovered. Again, that's where your sense of pride is. Don't let anyone take that from you."

They were quiet for several minutes, the connection of their hands holding across the wooden flooring exemplified by the connection of their hearts. Suddenly, he said, "I never forgot about you. I know you think I did, but I didn't."

She waited, uncertain what he meant since he'd already told her he'd attempted to visit her during her first year in college.

"I admit that after I made the aborted attempt to talk to you when you went to college, I threw myself into my life in the Navy and then as a SEAL, but I occasionally checked your social media for any news or updates. And when I got my annual Christmas card from Mrs. Baker, she always included information and updates about you."

Skylar jolted slightly, pressing her lips together, choking down the desire to snap and ask why he never tried to contact her. Instead, she stumbled over her words. "I didn't really do social media."

Nodding his head slowly, he said, "Yeah, I noticed. Mrs. Baker let me know you graduated with your advanced degrees. By then, I was a SEAL and focused on what I needed to do. But I had enough computer skills to do some digging and saw the name of the company you worked for. It must've been listed as one of Montague's subsidiaries because I didn't recognize it. I… I made assumptions. I assumed you were living a life that was what you hoped it would be. It never dawned on me that your life might be different than I thought."

After a moment of silence, he said, "Your birthday was two months ago."

Startled at his strange pronouncement, she remained silent as a hot feeling snaked through her.

"Every year, I always thought of you on your birthday." He winced, then rushed, "That's not the only time I thought of you, but I guess I'm just saying that I especially thought of you on your birthday. This year, I knew you would've just turned thirty. Maybe because that's such a milestone birthday, I did some more digging and came across some online photographs of you out with friends. In fact, there was even one of you sitting next to a guy, and the next picture showed your hand with a sparkly ring."

At his words, she gasped, her fingers twitching in his. "Those fuckers!"

He blinked, and she continued. "Those pictures weren't of me. I wasn't dating anyone, and I sure as hell wasn't engaged. Whoever's hand you saw was not mine."

His expression was one of surprise, but it quickly morphed into anger. "Those photographs were planted."

"Yeah." She snorted. "Showing me having a life when I was stuck here was a way of keeping anyone from wondering where I was." Another sigh escaped her lungs. She tried to pull her hand away from his, but he held tight. She dropped her forehead to her bent knees instead.

"I'm so fucking sorry, Skylar. Not just about this, but everything. Including the way I fucked up our goodbye."

Twisting her neck, she looked to the side, easily reading regret in his eyes. But right now, she had no desire to go down that road. Lifting her head, she blew out a breath that puffed her cheeks. "Don't be, Jeb. Regrets don't do either of us any good. Anyway, it's all water under the bridge. All that matters now is getting out of here. Your people are hacking into the systems I built and checking to make sure they work. If all goes well, we can get out of here in the next day or two."

Jeb remained next to her, his presence steady in the dark. But fatigue clung to Skylar like a heavy cloak, draping her in emotional and physical weariness. He stood and gently pulled her to her feet. "Let's go back down. I can see you're exhausted."

He moved through the trapdoor first, and once he was down, grasped her around her waist and guided her to the second floor after she secured the door. They walked downstairs, and she headed into the bathroom, quickly moving through her nightly routine. She pulled on her flannel pajamas, taking comfort in the embrace of the worn and faded material. Glancing down at the jar of face cream, she was thankful that personal items were included in the food deliveries. Finally, staring into the mirror, she noted the dark circles under her eyes.

Walking back into the main room, she spied that Jeb had moved the table back toward the kitchen corner. He had even washed the dishes. Her bed now beckoned invitingly for her to climb under the covers. With no more words to say or emotions to reveal, she slipped beneath the sheet, pulling the blanket up to ward off the nighttime chill.

As he stood in the middle of the room, his gaze upon her, she could sense the unspoken words in the air between them, but her bone-weary fatigue was real, so she closed her eyes.

In the quiet that enveloped the room, she heard, rather than saw, his movements as he retreated into the bathroom. She was barely aware of when he came back out. Opening her eyes in the dark, she could see his faint shadow standing nearby, looking down at her. But mercifully, he remained quiet, respecting the sanctuary of her exhaustion.

He placed the blankets on the floor, creating his makeshift bed. As he settled underneath his covers, she felt a fleeting sense of connection in the quiet of the night. Finally, allowing the embrace of sleep to pull her under, the worries of the day were put to rest.

15

THIRTEEN YEARS AGO

Jeb's gaze lingered on the calendar pinned to the wall of his modest room. Today's date was circled in red with the words "Leave for boot camp" written in the middle of the square. Underneath, in smaller print, was the reminder that he had to be at the bus station by five this evening. Mr. and Mrs. Baker kindly offered to drive him, but the last thing he wanted to do was have public goodbyes. He'd already arranged for a taxi to pick him up.

His gaze drifted to the backpack at the foot of his bed, a sparse collection of possessions he'd take with him. Once at boot camp, he knew he'd be provided everything from his underwear, socks, clothes, and outerwear. He rolled up two pairs of jeans and a few T-shirts, as well as a pair of running shoes, just to have if they ever had any free time to go into town. Toiletries and his wallet completed what he planned on taking. Opening his wallet, he pulled out the picture of Skylar and him taken last year on her birthday. Grinning, he pushed it back in carefully, then shoved it in the back pocket of his jeans.

Mrs. Baker had already prepared a small bag of food for the trip since the bus ride would last several hours. Excitement and dread warred within him. Ever since the tragic news of his parents' deaths, his life had been a ship adrift, tossed by the whims of fate. The Bakers' home had provided a safe harbor but never truly his own.

Graduating from high school the week before had been another milestone overshadowed by it not being able to be witnessed by his parents. Same for today—his father would have been filled with pride at Jeb's decision to join the Navy like he had so many years before. His mother would have cried at his impending departure. Jeb had learned that his parents' death would always cast a shadow over his life's accomplishments.

But today, he wouldn't be completely alone. Glancing at the clock on the dresser, he knew that Skylar would soon be home from the last exam of her junior year. When he received the notice about when to arrive at the processing station for boot camp, he hated the unfortunate timing that had it fall on her last school day. But then, maybe that was better. It would be a while before he could see her again, and saying goodbye to his best friend and the girl who held his heart would be hard enough.

Skylar. The girl who holds my heart.

There was no doubt about it. To the outside world, they were nothing more than two orphaned kids sharing a foster home. And that was the extent of their relationship. But she was truly his best friend, and he also held that honored position with her. But over the past year, it had been hard not to look at her as more. Skylar was beautiful with her long, thick, glossy hair. She was still petite but had developed curves that he knew caught more eyes than just his. And her eyes. Those gorgeous light blue eyes with the violet ring.

And he could tell there were times when she looked at him, and her gaze dropped to his mouth. It took all his willpower not to lean closer and kiss her. But he refused to go there. Not until he'd made something of himself. She deserved more than just a young man with empty pockets and unfulfilled dreams.

He hoped it wouldn't be too far in the future before he could come to her, having a career, making money, and being his own man. He wanted to offer her the world. Plus, for now, she had her eye on college and a career, and he didn't want to stand in her way.

But at least this afternoon, on their last day together before he left, he would tell her how he felt. He'd hinted over the past few weeks, and each time, her cheeks had pinkened with blush, and her beautiful blue eyes would shine. He was certain she felt the same about him. Declaring his feelings before he left for the Navy was what he'd been waiting for.

His thoughts were interrupted as a car drove up, and he recognized one of the social workers from the county. His bed would be empty today, ready for the Bakers to care for another foster kid. Looking down at his neatly made bed, his musings were touched with a hint of sadness.

With a small shake of his head to dislodge those thoughts, he turned his attention to his backpack, ensuring everything was ready. The front door opening was heard, and Skylar greeted Mrs. Baker. Grinning, he knew she'd run upstairs to see him.

A moment later, he heard raised voices. With multiple kids at the Bakers' house, a cacophony of voices was often heard, but this was different. One of the voices he could hear sounded like Skylar. Darting out the door, he was at the top of the stairs when he heard her harsh words.

"I don't care. I don't want to see my parents! They mean nothing to me and haven't for years. I walked away from them, and I'm better for it. I don't need them in my life!"

"Now, Skylar, I understand how you feel," the social worker said. "But your father is petitioning the court to at least have supervised visits with you. It's been years since you've been with them, and I think it would be good for you to talk to them."

"Absolutely not! As far as I'm concerned, they're dead to me. I'll be eighteen soon, and no judge can force me to talk to them if I don't want to."

Jeb's feet were rooted to the floor as the revelation stunned him. *Skylar has parents who are alive?* His belief that her past was parallel to his own orphaned existence crumbled instantly.

Before he could move, his gaze landed on Skylar racing up the stairs. Her feet skidded to a halt when she saw him at the top. Her eyes were wide, the blue now stormy. Her hair was messy as though she'd ran her hand through the tresses in her anger. Her chest heaved as she sucked in air as though there wasn't enough oxygen.

"Jeb," she whispered, anguish on her face, as she reached her hand up toward him.

He also found it hard to breathe as he stared numbly. Her words still resonated, bouncing off the walls of his mind, creating an instant chasm. *"My parents mean nothing to me. Haven't for years. I walked away from them. I don't need them in my life. They're dead to me."*

Instead of pulling her in for a hug or asking how he could help, all he could focus on was how she was not who he thought. Her mouth opened, but he spoke first. "You have parents? They're alive?"

Her mouth snapped shut and twisted in a grimace. "Yes," she bit out.

He gasped. "You lied to me all these years?"

Pain slashed across her face. "No, I never lied. You once asked me about my parents, and I said they were gone. That was the truth."

"I remember that day, Skylar. I had just told you my parents died, and when you said yours were gone, too, what was I to think?"

Her arms lifted to the side. "You were to think that I was telling you the truth. My parents were gone from my life."

"Because you walked away." Heartache and betrayal clouded his vision. He dragged his hand through his hair, tugging at the strands he knew would soon be shorn off. "Jesus, you ran away? Is that why you ended up here? Because you kept running from your parents? Christ… how could you deceive me all these years?"

"I didn't! I had to leave!"

"That's not what you just said. You said you walked away. You *have* parents, and you left them! Christ, Skylar, I would've given anything… no, everything, to have had one more day… hell, one more minute to tell my parents how much I loved them. I thought you were like me. I thought you understood that loss. But no. I had no family. You still had yours, and you walked away. Then you fucking lied to me."

Tears ran down her face, but they were unheeded by him. He felt gutted as the knife of truth plunged in and then twisted. He'd wondered why she never talked about her parents but assumed their loss was too painful. Now, all he could see was someone with what he desperately wanted, and she threw it away. At that moment, grief over his parents roared back in a way he hadn't felt in years. In an instant, he felt a shift deep inside. What he felt for her was tarnished. What he'd thought was between them had changed.

He turned and stormed back into his bedroom, now glad that he'd finalized his packing. He grabbed the backpack and his jacket, slinging them over his shoulders. Stomping back into the hall, he saw Skylar still standing there, with a mouth open, wide-eyed, shocked expression on her face.

"Wait, you're leaving now?" she asked, desperation clinging to her voice.

"I have nothing else to say other than goodbye."

She reared back as though slapped. "You still have a

little time. Give me a chance to explain. Hear *my* side of the story."

He hesitated, seeing the heart-wrenching expression on her face. But emotions pummeled him like he was trying to fight an entire battle all by himself. Grief, fear, disbelief, uncertainty, and even dread managed to get a hit in on him. He was surprised he didn't keel over with the pain.

As he stared at Skylar, even more emotions managed to get in their punches. Closing his eyes for a few seconds, he pulled up the last image of his parents that he kept stored in his memory. His chest ached as the years fell away. He was a little boy again, being told that his parents had been killed.

And Skylar had led him to believe that she understood when, in fact, she still had parents.

Throwing open his eyes, he brushed past her, his heart in turmoil, and stomped down the stairs. Mrs. Baker met him at the bottom, and he offered her a quick hug, whispering thanks for all she and her husband had done, then said goodbye.

When he drew back from her embrace, he could see the anguish on her face and knew she'd heard the argument he'd just had with Skylar.

"Jeb, honey, I really think you should give her—"

"I have to go, Mrs. Baker. Forget the taxi. I'll walk to the bus stop." He halted, hearing soft footsteps on the stairs, and turned to see Skylar standing near the bottom. Her fingers clung to the banister as if it was her lifeline. Lifting her hand toward him, she dropped to the step when her legs wouldn't hold her up without the support. He had no idea at the moment that her image would haunt him for the rest of his life.

Clinging to righteous anger, he managed to offer her a chin lift as his only goodbye. It wasn't how he planned to say goodbye to her, but at that moment, he had no more words left to say. Turning, he bolted out the door.

He made it a block down the street when he could feel the back of his neck tingle. Turning, he glanced over his shoulder toward the Baker house, and his eyes drew upward. There, on the ledge outside the attic window, sat Skylar. Her legs were drawn up, and her arms wrapped around her shins. It was the position she used when she felt vulnerable.

The urge to run back filled him. He should give her a chance to explain. But once again, the image of his parents came to mind, and his heart squeezed so tightly in his chest that he wondered if he'd even live to make it to boot camp. *I made a promise to myself, Dad, that I'd join the Navy just like you.* At that moment, nothing else mattered. Turning away from the Bakers' house, he continued down the street toward the bus stop.

The last glimpse of Skylar, vulnerable and alone, lingered in his mind as he headed toward a future stormy with regret and unresolved feelings.

16

PRESENT DAY

Jeb's eyelids snapped open, a surge of adrenaline jolting him awake. His heart hammered against his rib cage. A sheen of sweat clung to his back, chilling him as he sat up abruptly. He steadied his breathing as he took immediate stock of his surroundings. *Still in the old lighthouse. Still on the makeshift bed on the floor.* Skylar's steady breathing was a soft, rhythmic sound in the silence, punctuated by a tiny snore that brought a smile to his lips. She always denied her snoring, a little quirk he found endearing. *Like so much about her.*

He looked at the watch on his wrist. *4:00 a.m.* He rubbed his hand over his face, waiting for his heartbeat to slow as he remembered his dream. Or rather it was the remnants of a nightmare filled with images of the past he'd rather forget. Walking away from Skylar, his best friend, without saying goodbye or telling her how he felt about her. And mostly, not giving her a chance to tell the full story. He'd judged her before he knew all the facts. All these years later, it still haunted him.

Hell, who am I to judge anyone? As a SEAL, he had blood on his hands. Always for a good reason… or on an order. *But that hardly makes me a better person.*

He'd been so naive when he was first taken into the foster system. His parents had died, and he assumed the other kids were orphans unless they talked about their backgrounds, giving a different view. The Bakers certainly didn't make it known why each child was there. It was only as an adult that he came to understand the myriad of reasons a child might be in foster care. And with that knowledge, he wondered about Skylar and the kind of life she'd endured as a small child to be taken from her home. But by the time he was old enough to understand the possibilities, it was too late to find out.

Recrimination sat like a heavy stone in his gut. His hand moved to his stomach, pressing inward to ease the sharp pain. *No, it's not too fucking late… I have a second chance.*

Kicking off the blanket, he rose swiftly to his feet, stretching his frame to ease the stiffness from sleeping on the hard floor. While it was true he'd slept in many worse places, age tended to make everyone long for a good mattress instead of a hard, wooden floor for a bed.

It only took two steps to be at Skylar's bed, and as he loomed over her sleeping form, hesitation washed over him. This was his chance to learn her story and seek the forgiveness he desperately desired. Fearing that it was too late for her to extend the grace he sought, he continued to stand over her bed, taking her in once his gaze adjusted to the dim light. She was as beautiful in sleep as she was with her eyes open and her smile beaming. *Will I ever see her beam her light on me again?*

Uncertain of what to do, he allowed the slight illumination from his watch to cast its glow over Skylar's face. Her skin was pale, and her long lashes lay like crescents on the tops of her cheeks. With her eyes closed, the mesmerizing blue was hidden.

Suddenly, her eyes bolted open, and she gasped as he jumped. "What?" she cried out. Sitting up, she bumped her head on his chin. "What's wrong?"

"Nothing," he rushed to assure her, rubbing his sore chin. "I was just… checking on you."

Her hand was now clutched to her heaving chest as she breathed rapidly. "Jesus, Jeb! You scared me to death!" After another few seconds of silence, where the only sound was her breathing, she looked up. "Why were you checking on me?"

"I…" Unable to think of what to say, he scrubbed his hand over his head, then plopped down on the edge of her mattress. She scooted over toward the wall, giving him more room. Licking his bottom lip, he whispered, "Tell me about your parents… please."

She was visibly startled as her whole body jerked. "What? My… my parents?"

Wincing, he pressed on. "Yes. Your parents. I want to know about them."

The request hung in the air as the silence stretched between them, a chasm that he prayed could be breached.

Her shoulders slumped. "As I said last night, Jeb, it's all water under the bridge."

"Not to me."

At that, her fingers clutched the quilt a little tighter as her eyes searched his in the faint light still coming from his watch. Her hard expression gave evidence that she was going to argue or refuse. He acknowledged that it would have been her right to do so after the way he walked out all those years ago without hearing her side. He held his breath, waiting.

Finally, after a long moment, she sighed heavily, and her fingers eased their grip. "Why?" She tilted her head slightly to the side as her eyes searched his face. "Why now? What does it matter? What can it change?"

Uncharacteristically terrified, he wanted to give her the right words but feared saying the wrong thing. Staring at her guileless face, he went with what was in his heart. "Years ago, when I was young and stupid, I made an assumption. And when I was a little older but still young and stupid, I discovered that assumption was wrong. I reacted poorly and walked away from the best friend I'd ever had. I regretted it, but still wasn't man enough to figure out how to fix it. By the time I acknowledged how much I missed you, I thought your life had moved on, and guilt had me stay away." He dropped his chin to his chest, shook his head, and snorted. "I was a shit friend. And not a man I'm proud of." Lifting his eyes to her, he pinned her with a sincere stare. "Maybe it won't change anything for us. Maybe it won't make a difference. Thirteen years may be way too late. But I'm asking you to share your childhood before I got to know you. Something I should've done a long time ago."

She twisted her head and stared out over the tiny room, and he remained quiet, hoping she was gathering her thoughts of what to say to him and not to shut him down.

Turning her face back toward him, she heaved a sigh of resignation. "My parents are dead. Now. They weren't when I was at the Bakers. But as far as I was concerned, even at the young age I was put into the system, they were dead to me."

By this time in his life, he understood the horrors that parents could inflict on their children. Suddenly, he wasn't sure he was ready to hear what they had done to her. *But I'm the one who forced the issue, so I'm the one who needs to see it through.*

She sucked in a breath through her nose and then let it out slowly. "I don't know if they ever cared for each other, but they let me know every day that I was a surprise they hadn't counted on and weren't happy about. My father drank excessively and could barely hold down a job. My parents were substance abusers. Alcohol and drugs. Most of their money went to support their habit. Feeding and clothing a child wasn't high on their list of things to do, and that's even if they remembered they had a child they should take care of. When I was an adult, I read my file from the social worker to see what some of the reports were before I was old enough to remember. I don't know why… maybe just a morbid curiosity."

"What did you discover?"

She pressed her lips together and breathed deeply through her nose. "A neighbor who was kind enough to come over to check on me found me in the bathtub, almost drowned when I was only a year old. It was reported, but my mother gave some excuse for why she left the room. This same neighbor reported another time that she saw bruises on me when I was only two. Again, my mother gave the excuse that I was a very uncoordinated toddler and fell a lot."

"Jesus, Skylar," he whispered, his voice shakily leaving his lungs.

"I remember always being hungry, but it wasn't until I was in school that a teacher noticed how small I was. Shorter and much skinnier than any of the other children my age. Social services went in and discovered there was virtually no food in the house, but my parents had another excuse of having to wait for the next paycheck to come in."

Skylar's fingers danced nervously over the quilt in a pattern as she avoided his gaze. When she finally spoke, her voice was a quiet echo of a haunted past. "My parents started selling drugs to have the money to buy drugs. I remember being afraid of the people coming in. By the time I was six years old, I would hide in my room with the door locked and sit in the back of my closet, hoping no one would come looking for me. I tried to stay out of my parents' way because if they were stoned, drunk, high… hell, it didn't matter…. they were pissed off all the time. I was slapped, hit, knocked down—"

This time, the sound coming from Jeb was a growl. His heart clenched at her words, his fists balling unconsciously. The image of her as a frightened little girl cowering in a dark closet struck him with a visceral pain.

"I would hear noises... arguments... Mom yelling that Dad was selling her for drug money." Skylar's body shook as her mind fell back to her childhood. "He told her it was only until I got older."

Jeb gasped, but she continued. "I didn't know what that meant. I just knew that when others came to the apartment, I would hide in my closet."

Silence settled as Jeb's body vibrated and his fists clenched. "If they weren't already dead, I'd—"

She looked up, holding his gaze, shaking her head. "Mostly, I was just neglected."

Throughout her commentary, her expression hadn't changed. He'd wanted to look away, feeling the pain of the small little girl who just wanted to be loved but wasn't even fed enough to grow. The pain inside his chest felt like his heart was going to explode.

His hand slid over the quilt, wrapping his fingers around hers, hoping she'd accept the small gesture and not jerk away. Her fingers twitched underneath his, and he held his breath. But finally, they relaxed, allowing him that simple touch that he hoped conveyed all the emotions swirling inside.

"That day... the day you were leaving for boot camp... when I said I walked away, I meant that. I was eight years old when I first ran away from them. I walked down the street and into a convenience store. I'd never been in one before, and I was stunned to see rows of candy, goodies, things I'd seen other kids have in their lunchboxes that I've never even tasted. I didn't understand that I needed money to pay for them, so I simply pulled things off the shelf to eat."

"Oh Christ, Skylar." His lungs ached, and he was uncertain if there was enough oxygen in the air to keep him breathing. "I'm so sorry."

"The police were called, and I was taken back home. Social services were called in once again." She snorted. "I have no idea what my parents said at that time. I just know I was slapped hard enough when everyone left to know it wasn't safe to tell anyone."

"How did you finally get out?"

Blowing out a long breath, she dropped her gaze to where his hand wrapped around her fingers. She remained perfectly still for a long moment before she lifted her head.

"I finally had a teacher that saw bruises on my body. She and the school counselor questioned me, and even though I was afraid, they were so nice. So I told them what it was like at home. Several other adults came into the room, and I remembered one was the principal. Then a policeman came in, and I was terrified. But the counselor held my hand, and I kept talking. At the end of the day, I didn't go home but was taken to someone else's house. They called it a foster house, but I didn't know what that meant. A nice lady let me sit at a big table in her kitchen, and she fixed me dinner. I'd never had anyone fix me dinner before. And when food was in the house, we never sat at the table together."

A wistful smile crossed her face, and she closed her eyes. "I can still remember what I ate. There was mac and cheese, which I'd never had. And fried chicken that was so crispy, I kept taking bites even though it was too hot. There were green beans, which I thought might taste funny but were delicious. And a fluffy roll dripping with butter. I had a big glass of milk, and there was even dessert. A chocolate brownie." Her eyes opened and held his gaze captive. "I was nine years old, and it was the first true home-cooked meal I'd ever had in my life. Over the next few weeks, I was moved into a few other houses before I landed with the Bakers. I asked about my parents and was told that the state had now taken control of me, and I would be placed in homes where I would be cared for and fed."

He wanted to speak, but the words came haltingly. He wished for the ease of speaking that some of his more articulate friends possessed. Instead, he reached over and covered both of her hands with his, feeling as though just holding one wasn't enough anymore. "I've never been as glad for the Bakers as I am right now. And I've never been more sorry for how I took them for granted. And I've never been so ashamed for not understanding all the different reasons someone might need to be there."

Skylar scoffed. "Jeb, there's no reason to beat yourself up. You were young, dealing with your own grief, and no one could expect you to take on that level of understanding."

"But by the time I was eighteen years old and walking out the door, my actions were abominable."

She closed her eyes and sighed heavily, remaining quiet for a moment. Finally, she lifted her chin while shaking her head. "That day was doomed to be miserable, no matter what. I dreaded that day. I'd spent all day in school, taking exams, when my mind was on you leaving. The idea of saying goodbye to you was already ripping out my heart. Stepping into the house, just wanting to see you, and having to hear that my father, who supposedly had gotten clean and was divorcing my mom, suddenly wanted to see me. Seriously? I was going to be an adult soon, and he'd literally been absent my entire life. I'll never understand why the social worker thought I might want to see him. But that news I could have dealt with. It was the timing that was shitty. Coming right when you were almost ready to leave… Jesus, could it have been more fucked up?"

"The day may have been doomed, but that was not the goodbye I wanted us to have," he said, his voice heavy.

She swallowed and blinked rapidly. "I was glad to leave my parents, but when you left, I felt as though the best of me also walked out the door. I've never experienced such pain."

Her words hit him in the gut, and he was desperate to make things right. "I have no excuse, Skylar. I was ripped up about saying goodbye and had spent a lot of the day thinking about my parents and wondering if they'd be proud of me joining the Navy. Maybe that's why I reacted like an ass. Finding out that your parents were alive and mine weren't… I fell into a black hole and said things I never should've said."

Skylar's voice softened. "I never talked about my parents after I was finally taken away. Counselors and social workers sometimes told me that it would be better if I talked out my feelings, but I didn't believe that. Talking about my parents only returned my mind to the closet where I used to hide."

She swiped her hand over her cheeks, and he realized a tear had escaped. He hated that he was the cause of her tears and clenched her hand tighter.

She looked down at their intertwined hands. "When you assumed that my parents were also dead, I didn't tell you the truth. It wasn't that I lied to you, but I didn't want you to know I didn't have the wonderful parents you had."

The silence that followed was heavy, filled with unspoken apologies and regrets. Not being a man who came up with words easily, he used his actions. Sliding around on the mattress so that he was next to her, he leaned his back against the wall, wrapped his arm around her shoulders, and pulled her gently against his chest. A wave of relief washed over him as she came willingly, wrapping one of her arms around his abdomen. They sat, each offering physical comfort in lieu of words.

Finally, he let out a rough sigh filled with regret. "There is nothing I can say that would make the life you were forced to live with your parents any better. And to say that I admire your honesty and resilience, while true, doesn't change the fact that you had to be resilient."

"Jeb, I wasn't the only one who was resilient. You lost your loving parents and had to deal with grief at such an early age. Looking back, how can I even begin to expect you to feel anything else?"

"Still... on the day I left, I wasn't a kid anymore. I should've known better. I should've acted better—"

Another scoff erupted, and Skylar shook her head, twisting slightly to look up at him while staying tucked in closely. "I hardly think that just because you'd turned eighteen, you suddenly had the wisdom of the world filling you. Let's face it, Jeb. We were lucky to be brought up in a loving foster home. We were both still young and naive. We may have faced things other kids didn't have to face, but that didn't mean we suddenly had the maturity to handle all the emotions coming at us. You were dealing with another type of grief, having to say goodbye. So was I. Because saying goodbye to you was going to gut me."

His arms tightened around her, and he blurted, "I was going to ask you to wait for me."

He felt her body jerk as she shifted again to face him more fully. "Wait for you?"

"I didn't want to hold you back. I knew you had to finish your senior year, and you had college plans. I was going to be in the Navy and didn't know when we might meet up again. I was going to tell you how I felt about you beyond just being best friends. And I was going to ask you to wait for me so we could be together again. I didn't want our friendship and our time at the Bakers' house to be all we had." His voice was a raw whisper. "But I let my inability to handle my churning emotions get in the way. And that I regret more than anything else in my life."

17

Skylar's mind was a tempest. Her thoughts and emotions swirled chaotically, colliding like Ping-Pong balls within her chest. She grappled with an ache that oscillated between her head and her heart, each vying for dominance.

Yet nestled in Jeb's embrace, she allowed his words to flow over her, calming her rattled soul.

In her heart, she'd long since forgiven him for the way he walked out of her life. She understood the complexity of their past, the tangled web of unspoken truths and unshared pains. Some would say she blamed herself for not telling him the truth about her parents earlier. Others might say that she hadn't really forgiven him but just decided to push him to the far corners of her mind.

But the truth was, she had clung to her cherished childhood memories of him. He was the only true friend she had growing up. He was the beacon in the rough seas of her life. And she had quietly fallen in love with him by the time he was ready to leave for the Navy. Whether he reciprocated those feelings was irrelevant. Loving someone meant forgiving them. Now, hearing that he had planned to ask her to wait for him, warmth traveled through her veins, settling in her heart.

She raised herself slightly, eager to lock eyes with him after he explained his intentions from long ago. "None of this really matters, Jeb." Her soft voice was a mixture of reassurance and melancholy. Catching a flash of hurt move through his eyes, she hurried to explain her words. "We can't go back and change things. When I said it was all water under the bridge, that's true. Even if you had asked me to wait for you back then, who knows what paths we would have taken? You've admitted how young and naive we were. I'm not sure we would have had the maturity to turn our budding feelings into something permanently successful."

She wasn't dismissing their past but accepting their journey. It was a recognition that their roads had shaped them into the people they were now. At this moment, quietly surrounded by Jeb's strength, she resolved to face whatever future lay ahead, unburdened by the shadows of what could have been.

Seeing the slight curve of his lips, she kept going. "I've reconciled my past with my parents. In my own way, I've grieved my childhood, which was not good. You've grieved your parents' passing and a childhood that was not what you would've enjoyed if they had lived. We became friends at a time when we both needed each other. And while our goodbye was marred, we've now grown, matured, and lived enough life to know what's important."

He lifted a hand to cover her cheek. "And what's that, Skylar?"

"That *now* is all that matters. Not the past. Just now... and the future."

His voice was raw. "I'm sorry for the way we had to meet again, but I'm not sorry that you reached out or that I came."

Their gazes devoured each other, but she could feel him holding back. Tired of denying what she wanted, she swung her leg around to straddle his thighs. Clutching his cheeks, she held him and leaned in for a kiss. Even if it was a soft, once-in-a-lifetime, never-to-be-repeated kiss... she wanted to take charge for once and not just let life happen.

As soon as her lips met his, warmth infused her body, and she melted into him. He never gave her a chance to second-guess her decision. His lips were pliant under hers, moving gently as they tenderly explored.

Then she pulled back, her chest heaving, and stared into his eyes. They were black, the pupils blown so that all she could see were dark, intense orbs. His hands gripped her hips before he slid them up her body to her cheeks. He held her in place for a long moment. A slow smile curved his lips, and her mouth mirrored his expression. Without further preamble, they crashed together.

Lips melded and moved. Tongues tangled and tasted, danced and devoured, each trying to vie for dominance.

Their bodies were held tightly together for what seemed forever, but they spoke only with their mouths. Slowly, their hands began the new exploration. His fingers glided along her sides, his fingertips barely skimming the sides of her breasts, and she hoped he wasn't disappointed in her lithe curves. Her fingers roamed over the hard planes of his chest and feathered lightly along the ridges of his abdomen. All while their mouths continued to meld together.

His hands gripped her waist, and his fingers slipped underneath the hem of her flannel pajama shirt. Then he stopped and pushed her back slightly. As they separated, her eyes flew open, disappointment already shining. "Wha..." she moaned.

He chuckled, the deep sound rumbling from his chest. "Just wanted to make sure. I don't want to get carried away and become another one of your regrets."

Her tongue dragged along her top lip, feeling the tingling from their kisses. "There was never anything about you that was a regret. We just needed to mature before we could handle who we really are."

"So you want this... whatever is happening between us?"

She lifted her hand and cupped his gorgeous face. "Jeb, the truth that I no longer want to hide is that I not only loved you all those years ago, but I fell in love with you along the way. Maybe thirteen years have passed to hone us into who we are now, but my feelings haven't changed."

His dark eyes morphed into warm chocolate but lost none of their intensity. Leaning closer, he met her lips again and pulled her closer. She felt his erection press against her core and wished the layers of material weren't between them. Rocking slightly, she swallowed the groan he emitted, feeling the sound through his chest against hers.

His fingers slipped back under the hem of her shirt, and the tingles she had felt on her lips now moved to her stomach as she anxiously awaited his exploration. The rough pads of his fingers danced along her ribs, eliciting a giggle against his lips. The material of her shirt pulled upward with the movement of his hands.

He palmed her breasts, and she sucked in a gasp as the ache in her nipples only grew in intensity as he rolled the taut flesh between his thumbs and forefingers. Trying to focus on one area, she wiggled again but was overwhelmed with feelings. Her core ached against his erection, her breasts tingled under his palms, and her lips welcomed his mouth. Arching her back, she pressed forward, and if he found her slight frame lacking, the moans coming from his mouth didn't give that impression. Instead, his ministrations made her feel all woman.

Suddenly, his mouth left hers, and before she could protest, he jerked her shirt over her head and tossed it to the end of the bed. Now, naked from the waist up and with nothing to hide his face from her, she watched as his brown eyes darkened even more as he stared. The urge to cover herself was strong, but the appreciation in his expression had her remain still.

"Christ, you're beautiful, Skylar," he breathed, his voice low and reverent.

"It took me a long time to become comfortable in my own skin," she admitted.

His gaze jumped to hers, and his brows lowered in question.

Rolling her lips inward, she shrugged. "When you're tiny in a world of women with luscious curves, it can be a little intimidating."

His gaze snapped back up to her eyes, an incredulous expression in his lower brows and tight jaw. "You should never be intimidated by anyone for any reason. You are utterly beautiful."

She not only heard his words but felt them to her core. He bent forward, his mouth encircling a nipple, sucking it in deeply. She held his shoulders, her fingers digging into the muscles. He moved between her breasts, giving each attention as though they had all the time in the world. But the nerves that connected her breasts with her core fired with sparks that had her rocking over his erection even more.

He only wore boxer briefs, and dropping her chin, she stared down, surprised he wasn't bursting through the stretched material.

"You keep rocking those hips and staring like that, and I'm not gonna last."

"That's fine because I don't want you to last. Or at least, maybe last only enough until we're truly together."

He lifted his head and locked gazes with her again. "Is this what you want? The last thing I want to do is take advantage of you, Skylar. You've been trapped in a bizarre situation and alone for months. I don't want to misread what's happening—"

She clutched his cheeks once again, bringing her face close. "Let me make this perfectly clear. It's true my situation is bizarre. I've been alone here for months. And beyond that, even when I was living my life and working my job, I felt very alone. I had no idea if you would even respond to the cyber crumbs I left, leading you to me. I certainly had no idea you'd show up here, recognize me, and volunteer to stay. But you are not taking advantage of me. This is me standing on my own decisions. I'm taking down Alistair Montague and Colonel Spelling. I've decided to get out of this toxic environment. I'm taking part in my own rescue. And you're the only man I've ever truly loved even though it's been thirteen years since we've seen each other. So yeah… I know exactly what I'm doing. If we stop now, I'd be happy but a little unfulfilled. And if we keep going, I want to take this all the way."

He hesitated a second before his lips curved into a wide grin, and he rested his forehead against her. "I thought you might give me a yes or no answer, but you gave me a whole lot of words. But by God, you're right. You know your own mind, and thank God, you want me."

She thought he was going to kiss her again, but instead, he moved so fast that before she knew it, she was on her back, and he was covering her body with his own. Her legs fell open, and his hips fit between her thighs, with his erection now pressing close to her core. His bare chest skimmed hers as he kept his full weight lifted with his forearms pressed into the thin mattress on either side of her shoulders.

He lowered his head slowly, dragging his nose along hers, nuzzling her ear, and then nipping at her pulse point at the bottom of her neck, finding erogenous zones she didn't even know she had. If she thought her nerves were firing earlier, it was nothing compared to the fireworks sending sparks throughout her body.

He shifted upward, and his brow lowered once again. "Skylar, I don't have a condom."

"Jeb, I haven't been with anybody in years, but I have an IUD."

While he rested his ass on his heels, he reached forward and snagged the waistband of her pajama bottoms and dragged them down her legs, hooking her panties as well. She didn't even see where he tossed them, not caring where they fell. Shifting again, he was soon rid of his boxers.

Her gaze dropped to focus on his cock, and she almost laughed aloud. He was so much larger than any man she'd ever slept with. Although casting her mind back, she'd only been with three. Her first in college was a complete disaster with a minuteman who had no idea that he should take the time to help a woman orgasm. The other two were men she had dated for a few months years ago, but neither had been memorable… in or out of bed.

But doing nothing more than staring at Jeb's cock, she knew he was truly memorable.

Her gaze now dragged upward over his abs and chest, staring at the sun tattoo and noticing the one on his shoulder of a lighthouse. She'd never wanted to get a tattoo. Not because she was against them but because she had never thought of a design she wanted permanently embedded in her skin. But just seeing the two that he had, she suddenly thought that maybe smaller images of those would be perfect.

She continued her perusal up to his face, finding his dark eyes on hers, his lips quirking slightly on one side. "You're the most beautiful man I've ever seen in my life," she admitted.

"Well, considering you're the most beautiful woman, I'd say we make a good team."

She lifted her hands, smoothing them along his arms as he lowered himself toward her with his cock at her center. "I don't want to wait, Jeb. Believe me, I'm ready."

He reached down and slid the end of his cock through her slick folds. Lining up to her sex, he thrust forward, impaling her in one long, smooth movement. She gasped at the fullness, then held on tight for the ride. She lifted her hips to meet him as his movements increased. He bent slightly, taking a nipple in his mouth, sucking deeply as he continued to thrust.

Once again, the fireworks flashed throughout her body and had her closing her eyes for only a few seconds before she opened them again, determined not to miss one moment of their time together.

No more thoughts came to mind as she gave herself over to the physical sensations of fullness and friction as their bodies moved together. With each thrust, she felt as though he were touching her soul, and every time his cock dragged back out, all she wanted to do was clutch him closer. She wrapped her legs around his waist, hooking her heels against his ass. Every inch of him was muscular, and instead of feeling just tiny, she felt protected.

Deep inside, a coil tightened, and her fingers dug into his shoulders harder. He shifted enough to slide his hand between them, his thumb circling and then pressing against the nerves that had her crying out as electricity shot through her entire body. As her release rushed over her, she closed her eyes, letting the sensations collide with her emotions, and carry her away as her body slowly eased.

Jeb continued to thrust, and she slowly opened her eyes to see his taut neck and flushed face as he threw his head back with a grimace, crying out his own release.

She continued to cling to him as they rode out the final twinges, and then he slowly pulled out and rolled them to where they faced each other, side by side.

Neither spoke as their bodies cooled. A sliver of doubt moved through her, but Jeb kept his eyes on hers and reached up to cup her face, gently rubbing his thumb over her cheek. The simple movement was calming, and she felt that she was the center of his world at that moment.

They both smiled. "That was really…" She stopped when no other words came to mind that could describe what she'd experienced.

"Better than I could've ever imagined," he said. After another moment of peaceful afterglow, he shifted off the bed. "I need to clean up. Stay right here, and I'll be back."

He disappeared into the bathroom and soon returned with a warm, wet washcloth. It appeared he'd already wiped himself off, but he leaned over and gently cleaned her thighs and between her legs. Once he'd returned the washcloth to the bathroom, he walked directly to her, then hesitated. She lifted her arms and scooted toward the wall.

"The bed is small, but I'd rather share it with you than be separated." Shrugging, she added, "But only if you'd be comfortable with that."

A wide grin crossed his face, and he slipped in next to her. The twin-size bed barely held both of them, but he wrapped her in his arms, and she rested her head on his chest.

She felt sure she wouldn't go back to sleep. She'd just had sex with a man she never thought she'd see again even though she'd fallen in love with him as a teenager. It was the stuff of dreams or maybe even a cheesy movie. Certainly, it could end up as the plot in a romance novel. But in real life? Her real life? She couldn't believe her dream had come true in the middle of her nightmare.

And she fell asleep with Jeb's protective embrace encircling her.

18

Jeb's watch vibrated against his wrist, and he shifted away from Skylar to answer the call.

"You need to hide." Leo barked the order.

"What the fuck is going on?" he asked, pulling on his briefs and black cargo pants.

"Natalie has just spotted a boat that has landed at the southern tip of the island. There's too much interference to see what's happening, but it looks as if two men have disembarked."

"No fucking way that's a coincidence," Jeb said, considering that in the six months Skylar had been stuck on the island, she said she'd never had a visitor. "ETA?"

"On foot, about ten minutes."

Disconnecting, he whirled to see Skylar sitting up in bed, pushing her messy hair from her face with her hand as she blinked. He pulled on his long-sleeved T-shirt.

"What's going on?" she asked, her voice rough with sleep.

"You've got visitors." He threw her pajamas at her. "Get dressed."

Her eyes widened, and she leaped from the bed, immediately jamming her feet into her pajama bottoms. "What do I need to do?"

"We don't have time to escape before they get here. I'm stepping outside to get out of their sight, but I'll be right with you. If they're just coming to check on you or bring supplies, fine. Otherwise, I'll handle them."

"But..."

"You trust me?"

She didn't hesitate as she jerked her head up and down in a nod. "You're the only person in the world I could think of contacting, Jeb. Of course, I trust you."

He leaned over, snagged the pillow and blanket off the floor, and tossed them onto the bed. His gaze took her in, from her messy hair to her socked feet.

"I'm slipping out, and you get back in bed. They're coming at a time when they would expect you to be asleep, so play along."

"Is there anything I should say? Or not say?"

He placed his hands on her shoulders and leaned down so his face was directly in front of hers. "Pretend everything is just as you were before I came. Pissed off that you're stuck here. Wondering when this is going to be over. Getting tired of not seeing progress. All of that. Act completely normal, as you would have if they had shown up before I arrived."

Nodding in haste, she agreed. He hated walking out

but knew it was the best way to hear what was happening. Planting the small listening device in the room, he raced up the stairs and planted one there. Heading back down, he stopped long enough to give her a quick kiss, hard and fast, then said, "Lock the door behind me."

He slipped out, heard her push the bolt, and then darted out of sight into the edge of the woods. It only took a few more minutes before he heard a noise crashing through the underbrush and shook his head. Their inability to be more discreet let him know they weren't professionals and certainly not military trained. Refusing to be overconfident, he didn't relax his stance.

As the intruders stumbled along the narrow path, Jeb recognized that with a little difficulty, he'd be able to overtake them when needed.

Skylar climbed back into bed, thinking that would be the best place to be in case the men just forced their way inside. Glad that the room was dark, she hoped she'd be able to hide her nervousness. A few minutes later, she could hear the unmistakable sound of boot steps approaching. The noise was so loud she was surprised they were not more like Jeb and his fellow Keepers, who had approached with such stealth.

Even though she was prepared, the knock on the door still caused her to jump. Heart pounding, she started to call out, then remembered what Jeb had said. *Act as though I wasn't expecting anyone to come.* Another knock sounded, and she got out of bed and walked to the door. Since she had no way to see out, she called, "Who's there?"

"We're here to bring you supplies," a man's voice said.

That surprised her since the only supplies she'd ever received had come by helicopter drop.

"How do I know that? I didn't receive any notification that someone was coming."

"Mr. Butler sent us. He's the one who sends you the supplies."

It flashed through her mind that if Jeb weren't here, she would have been all alone and completely vulnerable with these intruders. While grateful he was close, her hand shook as she threw open the bolt and cracked the door open, peering out to see two men standing on the stone slab just outside the door. Their features were barely visible in the predawn sky. They were dressed warmly in large coats and hats. Refusing to back up, she said, "I wasn't expecting supplies today. And I've never had them brought this way."

"Let us in."

"No" was barely out of her mouth before the two men moved forward, pushing her back into the small space. They stepped over the threshold and closed the door. Crossing her arms in front of her, she said, "What are you doing?"

The taller man looked around the small living space, and she tried to ascertain whether his gaze was searching for something or he was just curious.

"You said you came here to bring supplies, but I don't see anything with you."

"We've got supplies in the boat. We wanted to make sure of what you needed before we hauled everything in."

"I don't know who gave you your instructions, but I was never supposed to be here this long. While I would be grateful for whatever supplies you brought, they shouldn't even be necessary."

It appeared the taller man was in charge since his gaze swept over her and the space, plus he was the one answering her questions. The other man pulled his hat off to expose his red hair. He didn't appear overly curious, letting the other man do all the talking.

The taller man lifted his hands and shook his head. "You're complaining to the wrong person, lady. We've got nothing to do with who's here, how long you're here, or anything. We were just told to bring supplies."

"Fine. Bring them in and leave."

He took a few steps toward the bed, dropped his gaze to the messy covers, and then looked over at the kitchen, his gaze continuing to search the area. She glanced at the red-headed man standing in one place, then turned to the other. "What are you looking for? As you can see, this place is hardly big enough to turn around, so I can't imagine you think I'm hiding extra supplies here."

He looked down at her, his eyes cold. Nerves slithered down her back, and she had no hope of hiding her fear, but Jeb said to act naturally. *Well, being terrified is natural!*

The inquisitive man turned to the other and said,

"I'm going upstairs. You go get the supplies from the boat."

The red-headed man grumbled and sent a glare toward his partner before sliding it over toward her. Standing her ground, she refused to look away. He finally turned and stomped out the door, closing it firmly.

Her instinct was to call out, but she knew she had nothing to hide from the second floor. "Go ahead, but I'm coming up too. There are expensive computer equipment and programs up there that I can't duplicate. I'm not going to let you mess things up." Without giving him a chance to deny her, she started up the stairs directly behind him.

Once there, she watched as his head swiveled slowly over the space. She nervously looked to ensure there was nothing of Jeb's up there but knew he would have taken care of it before heading out the door. Still, she couldn't seem to stop her galloping heartbeat.

The man appeared diligent, but she couldn't imagine what he was searching for. *Did something tip them off that another person was here? Was there a bug she didn't know about that the Keepers missed?* Summoning up more bravery than she felt, she asked, "What are you looking for?"

He didn't reply but turned quickly, staring down at her. She was used to people being taller than her and realized that in the past, she would often step back, maintaining her own personal space. But now, she wanted to see what he was doing. Strangely, the lighthouse felt like her place, and he was the intruder. His glare made her insides quiver, but she kept her expression steady.

He finally mumbled, "I just wanted to see what was up here," before turning to walk back downstairs.

"I'm going to call my contact," she said. "I want to know why the protocol for delivering supplies has been changed, and I wasn't told. Especially, considering you came while it's still dark outside, demanding entrance."

The man stopped at the bottom of the stairs and twisted around to glare. "There won't be any need for that. Everything looks in order here, and we'll soon have your supplies." He moved to the kitchen area and grabbed the kitchen chair. Plopping it in the middle of the floor, he sat on it backward, resting his forearms on the back.

The only other place for her to sit would've been the bed, and she refused to sit there while he was still in her space. She felt vulnerable enough without adding to the awkwardness. Remaining standing, she clasped her hands together. "You still haven't told me who you are, who sent you, and your real purpose."

"Who we are, doesn't matter. Who sent us also doesn't matter. Someone knows you're here and that someone wants supplies delivered. Our purpose was to—"

"I want to know your real purpose," she emphasized. "I hardly think that delivering food means you need to search this place and look upstairs. I'm pretty sure a deliveryman can't understand computer code."

A flash of anger moved through his face, and her insides quivered again. She was trying to be brave, but it was hard when she was so nervous. She reminded herself that Jeb was just outside, listening.

"You talk big for someone who's stuck out here."

She couldn't think of a quip, considering he was right. She was stuck out here. *But if they have a boat–*

The sound of boots stomping on the stone just outside the door met her ears.

"Jesus, Mac, do you have to make so much noise?" the man barked as he stood and walked toward the door. "I'm coming—"

Suddenly, the door burst open, swinging inward and cracking the man on the forehead. He cried out as he stumbled back, and when his jacket flew open, she spied a gun holster.

Seeing Jeb rush in, she cried out, "He's got a gun!"

Jeb had deftly knocked the man unconscious and rolled him over, tying his hands behind him with zip ties. Pulling the man's gun out of its holster, he searched for more weapons.

Her heart raced, but she couldn't believe how easily Jeb had manhandled the man to the floor, rendering him unconscious and disarming him. "The other one is coming back," she rushed.

"Already got him," Jeb reported.

Her eyes widened. "Oh…" she mumbled, realizing Jeb would have everything under control. "He wasn't bringing supplies, was he?"

Jeb held her gaze and slowly shook his head. "No."

"So… they were here for…?"

His jaw tightened, and for a second, she was distracted by how the dangerous glint in his eyes only made him more attractive. And it didn't escape her notice that he offered no answer to her question.

"Right," she muttered, letting out a long, shaky breath.

"How much more coding do you need to do for us to get out of here?"

"I was going to finish this morning. It's not too much—"

"Do it. Do it now. I'll take care of the trash."

Without question, she nodded, then turned and ran up the stairs without glancing back at the man on the floor.

19

"Are you about finished?" Jeb hovered over the top of Skylar as she sat at the bank of computers, her fingers flying over the keyboard.

"Yes, but I'll do better if you get off my back! Give me ten more minutes."

He grumbled but stepped back. She was still in her flannel pajamas, but he'd brought up her thick socks, not wanting her feet to get cold. When he'd kneeled to slide them onto her feet, she'd looked down at him with a surprised expression and smiled. She reached over to cup his face as she uttered her thanks.

He turned away to answer his phone, seeing it was Carson. "We'll be done in about fifteen minutes. Ten to finish coding and five for her to get dressed." As soon as the words left his lips, he realized how they sounded. Not one to get flustered, he stumbled as he quickly added, "Um... she's in pajamas..." Closing his eyes, he was grateful his boss didn't get flustered.

Carson said, "New plan. Several boats are hovering

on the south end. May be comrades of the two you subdued. Need to get you out some other way."

"What's the plan?"

"Natalie and Abbie have been watching the satellites. Hop is in Seattle, ready to fly to you. Bennett and Dolby are with him."

"I'm almost finished downloading the program," Skylar called out.

"Get that finished, get changed, and be ready to leave at any moment." Turning his attention back to Carson, he said, "What's the new plan?"

"By land. You'll go northeast. You'll come to a beach on the island's east side in about three miles. There, we can pick you up."

"And the boats hovering around?"

"Natalie reports some of them are foreign fishing boats which shouldn't be this close to the mainland. Maybe they are pushing their luck, or maybe they are suspect. We'll stay on top of everything."

"Right. I'll contact you as soon as we leave." Disconnecting, he turned to shout up the stairway again when her socked feet popped into view, quickly followed by the rest of her as she dashed down the steps.

"I'm ready," she said as she rushed into the living level. "At least as ready as I'll ever be. I've used artificial intelligence to set up the system to act like I'm here." She continued to talk even as she jerked her pajama top off.

Jeb's gaze shot to her naked breasts, and he had difficulty focusing on all the words coming out of her mouth.

She shoved the top into a small bag. Pulling on a bra and then a long-sleeved T-shirt and sweater, she continued. "Each computer is set to respond to basic demands or prompts. My phone will alert me to anything requiring more coding, which I can do remotely. The other programs will continue to run as though I'm here."

She shoved her pajama bottoms off, stuffed them into the bag, and pulled on her jeans. Sitting on the edge of the bed, she jammed her socked feet into shoes and tied them while still rattling off what she had set up on the computers.

Bolting off the bed, she raced into the bathroom and closed the door. A minute later, the door opened, and she kept talking about her computer programming while she brushed her hair and braided it into a long tail down her back.

Stepping out, she looked up at him and finally stopped talking, focusing now on his face. Chuckling, he stepped closer. "I wondered when you might come up for air."

She blinked, then grinned. "Sorry. I don't usually chatter nonstop. I guess I'm just trying to reassure you that I got the programs coded correctly."

Stepping closer, he leaned down and nuzzled her nose before kissing her. "It's all good, Skylar. I know you got it taken care of."

She pressed her lips together when he stepped back and nodded. "So… what do I need to do now?"

"Grab the rest of your things and your coat. We'll be hiking for a bit."

She thrust her arms into her coat. "We're not taking the boat the two men came in?"

"The area is compromised. Some others are around, and we're unsure if they're just fishermen or interested in what's happening here."

"Shit," she mumbled as she zipped her coat. "I wish I'd known I was going to be here for so long. I would have brought a heavier coat." Looking at him, she gasped. "You don't even have a heavy coat."

He stared as though seeing what she was putting on had just struck him. "Don't worry about me, but why don't you put on another sweater before putting your coat on."

She looked as though she might argue, then shrugged off her coat, grabbed another sweater, and pulled it over her other shirts. "I take it that you think we're going to be outside for a while?"

"According to my boss, we have about three miles to get to a beach where we can be picked up."

"Three miles?" She blinked, trying to think of the last time she'd walked very far. Coming up blank, she offered a nose-crinkled wince. "Oh, I hope we're not going to have to run. I do a little yoga, but that's about it. I'm not very athletic."

He lifted his knuckle under her chin until he held her gaze. "You're perfect the way you are, Skylar. Although, I'd like to see you eat healthier because I think some of the supplies they gave you were shit. But don't worry about today. You weigh about what one of my rucksacks did when I was training the SEALs. If necessary, I can carry you anywhere we need to go."

Her lips curved, and she laughed. "Let's hope it doesn't come to that." She looked around, then turned her attention back to him. "I'm not sorry to leave this place, but does it sound weird to say that it's strange? I've lived in this tiny building for months. Alone. Well, alone until you came."

"It's okay. I understand what you're saying. I've had a few places that I served while in the military, and even if I was only there for a few weeks or a few months, a part of me knew that I'd always remember it. "

"It's like wherever you lived, you leave a little part of yourself there."

"And maybe you take a little part of it with you when you leave," he said.

"I like that idea better." With a last look around, she looked up and said, "Okay, I'm ready."

They slung their small bags onto their backs and slipped out the front door. He radioed LSIWC to let them know they were leaving and to get updated directions. Carson confirmed that the boats near the southern tip were still suspicious even though no one had tried to dock along the rocky coast.

Twisting around to look down at Skylar, he ordered, "Stay right with me and let me know if you have any problems. Don't be afraid to tell me how you're doing. We'll start at a fast clip, but we can slow down when needed."

She nodded and followed him as they started through the dense woods. There was no path, considering the entire island was uninhabited, except for the few small dwellings on the very most northern tip, but that was thirteen miles away.

Around them, the thick forests of Western Hemlock and majestic Western Redcedar towered, their branches interlocking in a canopy overhead. Below, the earth was blanketed with lush moss carpets covering the roots and fallen trees. The dense foliage diffused the morning light, casting a scattered pattern on the forest floor, making it difficult to traverse.

It didn't take long for Skylar's breathing to become labored, and her pace slowed. Jeb, sensing her struggle, adjusted his pace. Despite the absence of immediate danger, he didn't want to take a chance on someone discovering that she was no longer at the lighthouse and start looking before they had a chance to get away.

Her voice, slightly breathless, broke the silence. "Jeb," she called.

He stopped and looked over his shoulder. Her face was flush, and she begged, "I'm so sorry, but can we sit for a moment?"

"Absolutely," he agreed, his eyes scanning the area. His attention snagged on a fallen tree, its trunk giving them a perfect seat. When they sat down, he reached into his pack and pulled out a canteen, passing it to her. "I filled it full of some of the filtered rainwater."

"Thank you! You were so smart to think of this." She took the canteen from him, then added, "I guess this is all second nature to you, isn't it?"

He surveyed the thick forest teeming with birds and mammals, not to mention the sea life offshore. He'd traveled to many places as a SEAL and even as a Keeper, always loving the chase to discover a new place. Looking over at her, he replied, "The dedication to a mission or rescue is second nature. But as much as I love traveling to new places, I admit that seeing a place where so few humans have been is one of my favorites."

"I did some research when I was first brought here," she said, her eyes sparkling with enthusiasm. "There are ten mammals on these islands, and six of them are found nowhere else on earth!"

Brows lifted, he shook his head. "I had no idea."

"I remember one is a kind of black bear." Suddenly, eyes wide, she blurted, "Um… that's one I hope we don't meet!" She paused, biting her lip thoughtfully. "There are a couple of bats, a shrew, a type of otter, and a few others that I can't remember. A particular caribou used to roam these islands, but they're now extinct. That seems sad, doesn't it?"

"Yeah, it does. A friend of mine… a fellow Keeper, is dating a woman who's a scientist who studies how global warming affects plants. I'm sure some of that affects the animals that are this far north."

"That's interesting! I've never met anyone in that line of academia."

"You'll get to meet her."

She hesitated, then asked, "Will I?"

"Sure." He twisted on the log to face her more fully. "You'll get to meet all the Keepers and their wives and girlfriends."

"Oh." She pressed her lips together, rubbing them back and forth, now silent.

"Unless… well, I guess you don't have to if you don't

want to. But… I just thought…" His voice trailed off, uncertain of her reaction.

"I just didn't know if I'd see you again after all this." Her voice was tinged with a vulnerability that hung heavily in the air between them. Her hand gestured vaguely as she finished. "You know… the rescue."

He was silent for a moment, painfully conscious of the pressing need to continue moving to the rendezvous point. He yearned for a moment to talk about what they meant to each other. Even though they'd had sex, they were interrupted before having the opportunity to settle anything. Part of him feared she might not want more after their escape.

The timing was shit… something that had occurred to them many years ago. Clearing his throat, he reminded, "We'll be working together as we figure out how to help the feds bring down the black-market tank parts scheme."

Her cheeks flushed a light pink. "Oh, right. Yes, of course. I… um… yeah…" She turned up the canteen and took a healthy sip. Wiping her mouth with the back of her hand, she handed the canteen back to him. "I hope I didn't drink too much. I know we'll need more later."

He immediately felt a pang of regret. He'd just fucked up by not taking time to talk about their reconnection. Not just a reunion of old friends but a rekindling of long-buried emotions that had surged like a storm. His fingers lingered on hers as they passed the canteen, and the electricity between them only solidified his knowledge that what they had was real.

"I can go on now," she announced, breaking into his inner turmoil.

There was so much he wanted—no, needed to say, but now was not the time. He stood and offered her a hand as she slipped off the large tree trunk seat. He loved the feel of her hand in his but needed to clear away some of the underbrush as they walked. Reluctantly letting go of her fingers, he forged ahead while using his watch as a compass and radio to his coworkers.

"If all goes as planned, we'll get picked up from the beach. First, we have to make it past the cliffs."

"Cliffs?" she repeated, her eyes reflecting a flicker of concern.

"No worries. We'll bypass them. We should have a good view of the shoreline and maybe some seals—the wildlife variety."

Her laughter filled the air. "So you weren't the *wildlife* kind of SEAL?"

He chuckled, shaking his head. "I was probably a tame SEAL compared to a few of my single team members. A few of them would shut down a bar and then go home with someone they'd met. Me? I was more likely to leave early, alone, and spend time reading a book."

A gentle smile curved her lips. "I can see that," she said softly.

"Yeah?"

"Yes. I know people can change, but what you described was much like the Jeb I knew growing up. It's easy to see you being less… um… wild."

Continuing onward, he checked his phone. With maps and satellite images sent to him, he looked over his shoulder again. "We don't have much farther."

The gratitude on Skylar's face was palpable, and he slowed his steps, reaching his hand out toward her. She stared for just a few seconds and then slipped her hand against his palm. He closed his fingers around hers and filled with resolve. The first chance he could, they would continue their conversation about who they were now and what they meant to each other.

Turning to look ahead at the path now flooded with more light as the trees became sparse, they came to a grass-covered area that led to tall cliffs overlooking the ocean. The water crashed upon the rocks below.

"Oh my goodness!" she exclaimed. "It's beautiful and scary!"

"We'll stay at the line of trees and not get too close to the edge of the cliffs." He lifted his hand and pointed ahead. "Look, there are seals on the rocks."

She gasped and leaned forward. "Oh, I wish I could take a picture!"

He pulled out his phone and snapped a few downward where the seals lounged in the morning sun on the rocks. Selfies weren't his thing, but he wanted to capture this moment. Tugging on her hand, he held the phone in the other hand and snapped several pictures of them together with the ocean in the background. The smile on her face was worth the moment it took out of their journey. Skirting the cliffs again, he said, "You can see the beach where we're heading."

Skylar nodded and looked up at him. "It's still a ways off, but I have this."

He could have made the trip much quicker and easier if he had been alone. But he knew this was not easy for her. But he couldn't be more proud of her hiking along the rough terrain, keeping a smile on her face.

"You're right, Skylar. We've got this."

20

Skylar's legs ached, and her lungs hurt with the exertion, but the beautiful vista seemed to give her energy. That, plus the fact that she could see the beach in the distance, gave her the extra push to keep going. "I swear, when we get out of this mess, I'm going to start exercising."

Jeb chuckled and squeezed her hand. "You're perfect just the way you are."

"That's a sweet sentiment, but if I was athletic and in shape, you'd have an easier time."

"You're doing great. We should only have a few minutes to go—"

Just then, the sound of a helicopter caught her attention, and she lifted her free hand to shade her eyes but was unable to find it. She was also unable to keep the fear from her voice. "Do you think that's someone looking for us?"

"No, that's our transportation out of here."

Twisting her head toward him, she smiled. "Really? How can you tell?"

"I know the sound of different helicopters. That's Hop."

"What's a Hop?"

Jeb laughed. "Hop is Frank Hopkins. Former Air Force pilot and Special Operations. And a Keeper."

Relief flooded her mind. "Thank God!"

The helicopter circled the area and landed on the sandy beach they were approaching. With renewed vigor, her pace increased, matched by Jeb's.

The last part of their escape journey didn't seem as tiring as they hurried down the hill leading from the sides of the cliff to where the sandy and rocky beach awaited. A large man, well over six feet, stood outside the helicopter with a wide smile as they approached.

As friendly as he appeared, she was grateful for Jeb's presence at her side. The helicopter was large, and considering she'd never flown in one before, butterflies flitted in her stomach at the prospect of flying in the helicopter.

It crossed her mind to ask if it was safe or if Hop was a good pilot. But she clamped her mouth shut, knowing Jeb would never put her in danger. And the last thing she wanted to do was insult one of the people coming to save her.

"Don't be nervous," Jeb said.

She glanced up, eyes wide. "You are joking, right?" When he didn't reply, she continued, "I have a feeling you spent a lot of time as a SEAL in all kinds of aircraft."

He chuckled. "Yeah, I guess you could say I've been in my share of birds."

"Well, this is my first helicopter ride. I can't stop the nerves!"

She remained quiet as they approached, and Jeb let go of her hand. She'd been surprised he hadn't dropped their connection before allowing his coworker to see them, but he'd held tight. Now, the two men greeted each other with grins and backslaps.

Jeb turned and reached over for her again. "Skylar, this is Hop. A good friend and a fuckin' great pilot."

Her hand was engulfed by Hop's much larger hand, but his grip was gentle, and she smiled up at him. "It's nice to meet you, Hop."

"Heard great things about you, Skylar. Good to get you off this island and back to civilization."

Her mind momentarily reeled at his words. The months spent on the island had isolated her from civilization. The idea of re-entering society both excited and terrified her. Jeb's arm wrapped around her shoulders. "It'll be fine. I'll be right with you."

Her brow furrowed, unsure of the full meaning of his statement. Focusing on the task at hand, she accepted his assistance into the helicopter. She knew little about helicopters but was glad that it wasn't tiny. There were three rows of seats. Hop was in the front, and she assumed the one next to him would be for a co-pilot. When Jeb climbed into the second row with her, she pressed her lips together. As glad as she was to have him near, it exemplified there was no co-pilot.

Before she had a chance to think more about what

was happening, the blades began whirring overhead, and she looked at her lap as Jeb leaned over to buckle her in. He then placed headphones over her ears.

"Ready?" he asked, his eyes moving over her face.

She knew he was trying to ascertain how frightened she was. Determined to be as brave as possible, she nodded. "Ready!" She hated that her voice resembled a squeak.

"All right! Let's get 'er goin'!" Hop called out, his voice enthusiastic.

The helicopter lifted off the rocky shore, banking sharply as it ascended. She blinked as her stomach lurched, but hearing Hop's whoop of joy, she laughed. Gripping tightly to the armrests, she avoided the window and looked at Jeb instead. His hand covered hers, and she now offered him a true smile. Turning to look out the window while her stomach continued to somersault, she was fascinated by the scenery below.

"The island is gorgeous from up here." Suddenly, emotions threatened to overwhelm her. "It's weird…" Her voice faded out.

"What's weird, Skylar?" he inquired.

She gazed out at the lush expanse of the island, her voice soft and reflective. "For months, I've been stuck in one place just thinking how much I wanted to get back to my life. So you'd think I'd look at this island as nothing more than a prison. I'd researched all about it during my time there, but now, it seems weird to think how absolutely beautiful it is."

He gave her hand a reassuring squeeze and leaned

closer. “It’s not weird to experience conflicting emotions about a place.”

His voice was filled with such understanding that she turned to look at him. “Did you serve in places that seemed awful and beautiful all at the same time?”

“Absolutely. I had missions in places that I couldn’t wait to get out of. Some real hellholes where I couldn’t imagine anybody living, yet people would eke out their existence and call it home. And then I would find some kind of beauty there.”

“I discovered that years ago when I first learned to fly,” Hop said.

Skylar turned her attention toward the front, curious to see what else Hop had to say.

“My uncle taught me to fly. I grew up in the mountains of Tennessee, and while I thought they were beautiful from the ground, I’d never seen anything so majestic as when we were in the air, and I could look down and see them from above. I guess I’ve always felt that way. And what Jeb just said is true. When I was running special ops in the Air Force, I sometimes served in places that seemed ugly as fuck on the ground, and then, flying above them, you could see beauty looking down at the landscape as a whole.”

She nodded slowly, understanding what they were saying. Looking out the window again, she watched the ocean waves crash against the rocky shore and the thick, green forests covering the island. She spied several boats in the water as they passed the southern tip.

“Those are the ones Natalie was watching,” Jeb said.

"She identified them as fishing boats, but some were foreign and not where they were supposed to be if they're legitimate."

Her chest depressed as the air left her lungs. "This is all so crazy." A hysterical giggle slipped out. "And that's coming from a woman who's been living in a dilapidated lighthouse in the middle of an uninhabited island for six months!"

A smile slipped over his lips in response. "It'll be fine. Natalie will make sure no one is after us. She'll stay on it."

"She sounds tenacious," Skylar said.

"Like a dog with a bone," Hop called out from the front. "She keeps Leo on his feet!"

"Leo?"

Jeb grinned. "Leo and Natalie are married. Both Keepers are fucking amazing at their jobs. They worked as Army Deltas together for years as friends, but once they got out, they finally got together, and now both work for us."

She turned back to the window as a wistful smile crossed her face.

"You should rest," he encouraged.

"I'm not sure I can." A quiet descended on the three, and she finally leaned her head back and closed her eyes. Exhaustion moved over her, and she soon drifted off.

21

Jeb emerged from the SUV and then turned to offer Skylar a hand. She had slept for most of the flight to California, only waking when they started to land. She rubbed her hand over her eyes, and a grin spread over his face. Though the years had passed, her mannerisms remained endearingly familiar. It was like staring at the young Skylar once again.

Her eyes darted around, seeming to absorb her new surroundings with a keen intensity. They were at the LSIWC headquarters, making their way from the parking area to the walled patio bordering the bluffs leading down to the shoreline. The water crashed in the background, much like it had on the island, but he hoped it would bring her a sense of peace instead.

The sun was setting, shooting colors throughout the sky. She paused, her gaze transfixed on the sunset. She sighed, and he hoped it was in relief, but she was so quiet that he couldn't get a read on her thoughts.

Hop had disappeared inside the compound, leaving

them to approach the building alone. Jeb knew that Carson would be waiting to meet with Skylar in the conference room just inside the building. But since Skylar seemed entranced with the sunset over the water, he stepped closer and put his hands on her shoulders. Bending so that his lips were close to her ear, he whispered, "Are you okay?"

She twisted around to look at him, her face a bare whisper from his. "Yes. I'm just…" Her gaze dropped to his lips and then shot back to his eyes. "Sorry. I'm just a bit overwhelmed." With a self-deprecating snort, she admitted, "And a little scared."

"Scared?" Incredulity filled his single-word response.

"Yeah—"

The door behind them opened, and approaching footsteps interrupted them. Jeb turned and offered a chin lift, draping his arm softly around Skylar's shoulders. "Carson, thanks for everything. And yes, this is Skylar White."

"Jeb, good to see you. Ms. White? I'm Carson Dyer. Good to meet you in person."

Skylar straightened her spine, all semblance of nerves hiding as she thrust out her hand to accept Carson's. "Please, call me Skylar." She inclined her head to the side. "I was just admiring your view." Her gaze swept up to the lighthouse, and a chuckle slipped out. "This is much bigger and in much better shape than where I've been staying."

Carson regarded her and then smiled. "Thank you. And I'm sure Jeb can take you to the top for an even more amazing view if you're interested. If you're too tired today to climb the steps, you're welcome back anytime."

"Thank you," she enthused. "I'll take you up on that offer… at a later date."

Carson nodded, then stepped back and extended his arm toward the door. "If you'll allow Jeb to show you to our visitor's conference room, we'll get started."

"Of course," she agreed.

Jeb noticed her lips trembling slightly and dropped his arm from her shoulders. Taking her hand, he guided her inside. He was so used to the LSIWC compound but immediately tried to see it through Skylar's eyes. Professional entryway with a large desk overlooking the space. He smiled at the familiar face sitting behind the desk.

Rachel Moore stood and walked toward them with a welcoming smile. "Jeb, good to see you back."

"Rachel, this is Skylar White."

"Of course it is. Welcome to Lighthouse Security Investigation West Coast, Skylar. I know you must be tired. Let me show you to a place you can freshen up for a few minutes before heading into the conference room."

"Oh, I think Mr. Dyer expects me to—"

Rachel leaned in toward Skylar with the air of sharing a secret. Her voice was hushed yet playful. "Don't worry about Carson. He'll wait." She winked at Jeb. "Go on in. I'll bring Skylar in a few minutes." Without giving him a chance to object, Rachel looped her arm through Skylar's, guiding her to a door just behind Rachel's desk.

Jeb watched the back of Skylar disappear through the door. Just that simple separation caused his heart to beat a little faster.

"She'll be okay. Rachel will take good care of her."

At the clap on his shoulder, he turned to see Teddy Bearski. The former sniper was their equipment and weapons manager.

"Rachel knows what she's doing," Teddy assured. "She'll give her a chance to meet a couple of the women in their locker room. Make her more comfortable."

Jeb knew Teddy had special feelings for Rachel. Considering Rachel was an exceptional person, Jeb breathed a little easier.

"You coming?"

He followed Adam into the large conference room, seeing most of the Keepers gathered. Their usual meetings took place deeper inside the secure area of the compound where their large workroom was located. And while he trusted Skylar, since she was not an employee—or like Landon, a trusted FBI agent—they would meet in the non-descript but highly secure and functional room.

Exchanging greetings with the others, he offered his thanks, knowing it wasn't needed or expected but giving it all the same. He looked over at Carson and said, "Rachel snagged Skylar. They'll be here in just a few minutes."

Carson chuckled while nodding. "It's all good. They'll be in soon."

The murmured conversations around the table came to an abrupt halt as the door opened. Not only did Rachel escort Skylar into the room, but Natalie, Abbie, and Tricia followed them. And they were all smiling. Skylar looked over at him with a little smile on her face.

Brows raised, Jeb took to his feet, his heart light to see a smile on Skylar's face. Jeb did the introductions. She handled the crowded room perfectly, but Jeb could see the slight tremor of her hands as she settled into the chair next to him. Once they were seated, he placed his hand over hers, catching her quick glance and the soft curve of her lips.

Carson quickly set the tone for the meeting after introducing Landon.

"Skylar, you have a great deal of information that we would like you to share with us. Landon obviously represents the FBI as an agent who has been involved ever since you first let us know what was going on at Montague Industries."

She nodded as she glanced at Jeb, hopefully accepting the smile of encouragement he gave her, and then turned to the other Keepers at the table. "I naively assumed that trying to be the best and do the best I could for my employer would result in job security. I wasn't looking for employee of the month accolades, but… I wanted acceptance. Acknowledgment. And I blithely welcomed the idea that they recognized my worth and would compensate me accordingly." She shook her head and scoffed. "I was so wrong."

"Skylar," Carson called out, his voice low.

She lifted her head, turning toward him.

"No one here blames you for anything to do with Montague Industries. We understand you started out as an employee, only seeing what they wanted you to see. Only working on what they wanted you to work on. It wasn't until they understood the…" he hesitated, then continued, "Program coding brilliance you possessed that they realized that if you were completely isolated, they could make you do what worked for them." He offered her a wry grin. "That was their mistake—thinking they could control you."

She held his gaze, then finally nodded, her lips curving slightly.

"What can you tell us?" Landon prodded. "How did you get involved with the inner workings of Alistair Montague?"

She pressed her lips together, then with perfect poise, she said, "I was hired right out of my master's program, but the company was a subsidiary of Montague Industries. There were many programmers tasked to maintain security. That was my job at first. A large room filled with tables and computers. Then I was moved to the *higher-level* cubicle section." She laughed. "I remember thinking how cool it was to be moved to my own cubicle after only one year of employment. I was told that no one else had been promoted that quickly.

"At that time, I was given more direct tasks of *hacking* into certain government and military sites. I was told this was used to show the government and military where they needed to beef up their online presence and security. I also worked on what I later called the side hustles of Alistair… his websites used for political involvement. Still thinking it was all above board, I was showing where the weaknesses in their sites were. I was moved into an office after only another year. Again, that was unheard of at the company, where many people spend their entire careers in the cubicle city. I was only twenty-six years old and had an office."

"When you landed in an office, did your workload change?" Carson asked.

Skylar nodded, her shoulders relaxing slightly as she appeared more comfortable telling her story. "Yes. At first, it was just more in-depth work, similar to what I had been doing. That was when I met Gerald Butler, my new direct supervisor. Finding out he was Alistair's head of Montague Industries' Cybersecurity Division. And that was when I realized who I really worked for. Slowly, my job duties changed. I was writing more and more code, digging into the dark web, and everything was encrypted. I was an expert at it, and after two more years, Gerald came to me with another *promotion*. He said my skills could be better used but that the requirements would involve me being more isolated from the others who wouldn't understand what I was working on. By then, I was suspicious of Alistair's hand in politics and with politicians, but it was an amazing paycheck, and I finally had the financial freedom I craved. Looking back, he knew of my background and played on my insecurities and social isolation."

"Where did they place you then?" Abbie asked.

"I was taken to one of the smaller office buildings

that was part of Montague Industries and was given access to a secure basement office. It was… strange."

"Strange?" several Keepers asked all at once.

Skylar nodded. "Strange in that it should have seemed bleak but was actually nice. The office was large, well-lit, and had all the security and computer access necessary. There was a kitchenette with a fully stocked refrigerator. There was a comfortable sofa for me to work on, away from the desk, or to sleep on if I wanted. I no longer had anyone else around, but Gerald checked on me. Strangely, working by myself didn't bother me. But what I was discovering made me need to figure out how to extricate myself from the Montague spiderweb."

"But it wasn't easy, was it?" Jeb's voice sliced through the weighty silence the others gave her as she gathered her thoughts. His chest tightened as he reflected on Skylar's journey—from the abused and neglected child to earning a master's degree in computer programming and cybersecurity. She was compensated for her talent and knowledge. Valued. Needed. Everything she craved as a child.

The revelation that his path had mirrored hers struck him with the force of a physical blow. He might have been born into a loving family that nurtured him, but when they were ripped away, he was left adrift with nothing. At least until the Bakers' house became a safe harbor and he found a kindred spirit. *Skylar.*

When he joined the Navy, he wanted to excel and become a SEAL. Be the best. Prove that he had what it took to belong to the elite—a foster kid who made it to the top. And even when he felt the Navy was no longer in his future, his ambition didn't wane. Landing a job at LSIWC was a personal triumph. It must have been like her finally having her own space— the ultimate knowledge that the foster kid without a family had made it.

Even at LSIWC, he spent most of his downtime at the compound, wanting to provide support for any mission, day or night, any day of the week. In fact, some of the other Keepers expressed concern and were worried that he spent too much time at work. Worried that he didn't have enough of a life outside of being a Keeper. But now, understanding the extremes that Skylar underwent to settle the inner longing to be needed, he realized they were not so very different from adults. The simple longings of their childhoods now haunted their lives.

Inwardly scoffing, he knew he'd recognized their similarities long ago when they were kids seeking each other's company. But when he faced the tumultuous emotions of leaving for boot camp, he allowed his fear to blind him to their shared experiences. Once again, shame filled him that he'd walked away, knowing it took a desperate act on her part to bring him back into her world.

Now, as he gazed at Skylar, her outward composure belied the internal turmoil he knew she had experienced. Sitting at a table, surrounded by strangers, she was a portrait of quiet strength and vulnerability. He was awed by her courage, just as resolute as she was years ago, perched on the attic window ledge.

Skylar took a deep breath and let it out slowly

before continuing. "By then, they didn't trust anyone except me to encrypt their most secure communication systems. Working alone and being alone, I was able to ensure that Alistair Montague and his highest-highest-level cronies had a way to correspond with politicians, military personnel, multibillionaires, and oligarchs. To be honest, I found most of the correspondence to be boring. I might've come from poverty, but I didn't find the wheeling and dealings of the uber-rich to be very fascinating. But as I became more aware of what all he had his hands in, I realized he was not just a rich businessman with a lot of money to throw around. Seeing that he backed certain politicians with massive donations wasn't surprising. What shocked me was discovering how the dissemination of everything from conspiracy theories to absolute untruths affected how people voted. It didn't surprise me that he corresponded with military leaders. Then I discovered that he was not only perpetrating the theft of some of our military equipment, he was also selling it on the black market to some of the people who our military would be fighting against."

"And the island?" Carson asked.

Skylar dropped her chin and shook her head at that simple three-word question.

And Jeb's heart ached for her.

22

Exhaustion cloaked Skylar even though she'd slept in the helicopter. She felt sure the other Keepers and the FBI agent probably cared little about her life with Montague Industries. Yet they'd given her the grace to explain how she got to where she was and why. The elusive and complex reasons that were hard to define mattered deeply to her. It wasn't just about distancing herself from the villainous exploits of Alistair Montague. She wanted to be seen as what she truly was —someone who had striven for excellence only to be ensnared in a web of deceit. By the time she understood how deeply she had uncovered the descent into illegal activities, it wasn't safe to crawl back up to the light.

And now, Carson had asked about the island. She closed her eyes for a moment, trying to decide how to explain where she'd landed. It had been easier to explain the bizarre situation to Jeb. Here, she was ensconced in a sea of unfamiliar faces. They were friends and coworkers of Jeb's, but only Natalie, Abbie, and Tricia were fleeting acquaintances she met when Rachel took her to a women's locker room to freshen up. They'd shared a few moments explaining that they knew what it was like to sit with a testosterone group and be outnumbered. Tricia had offered a hug, whispering, "You'll be fine. You can hold your own with all of them."

But those words of encouragement were put to the test when she'd walked into the room and observed it was filled with a collection of men who, at first glance, could all be male models. Tall and broad, some with friendly smiles, but she knew they could react with deadly force if needed. Others had a harder look, a glint in their eye, or a tight jaw that gave evidence that they'd seen their share of battles fought and won.

As Skylar's gaze flitted around the table, a quiet sense of fortune settled inside her. None of the Keepers held a hostile expression. While not all overtly warm, their faces were devoid of animosity.

A hand on her shoulder startled her, and she glanced to the side to see Jeb calmly offering his support. She let out a long breath, and her lips curved slightly at the encouraging feel of his hand on her. An anchor in a tempest sea. Nodding, she continued.

"It isn't surprising to imagine that I was also being monitored. So what I was finding out about Montague Industries, and particularly Alastair Montague, wasn't a secret. They still wanted me to continue doing my job, but I suppose I was a loose end for them. There was no family for them to threaten to keep me in line. I had no social life or good friends either. For that matter, I didn't even have a pet. Saying that now sounds rather pathetic, but that was how my life had become. I suppose my freedom was the only thing they could truly hold over me."

She snorted and shook her head. "Well, that and my life. Anyway, they told me they were moving me again. Only the accommodations would be much nicer this time than in a basement office. I would go to an outdoor resort, living in a reclaimed lighthouse on a beautiful island with lush forests and beaches. All my needs would be taken care of. And they would need me to do this for a couple of months as they were working on a particularly *sensitive* business deal. I wasn't afraid when Gerald explained this, but I also didn't want to go. Of course, he appealed to the one important thing I should be embarrassed about. Money. Growing up without it, he knew it was hard for me to turn down what they were offering. I would receive a full year's salary for just the two months at the *resort location*. So I decided to do this for them, and then I would resign. I had already signed an NDA and a non-compete, but I could live for a while just on my savings."

"And when you got there?" Natalie asked. "Surely you protested."

A bark of rueful laughter sounded out. "The *refurbished* lighthouse was both true and an exaggeration. As I'm sure the others told you, it was a somewhat crumbling building, the bathroom was rudimentary, at best, and the beautiful island with beaches could not be enjoyed. I had all the necessary computer equipment and generators to keep everything running. I was taken by boat and shown that the place had all the food and basic requirements. I protested, but they told me to at least check out the second-floor computer equipment."

She hung her head and blinked back tears. "While I was there, the two men who dropped me off left in a hurry. Why didn't I run after them and jump back on the boat? I tried, but the boat was already in the water when I followed them. A storm was coming, and I barely made it back to the lighthouse before it hit. I got ahold of Gerald, and he acted shocked that the place wasn't as he described. He promised that it would only be for a short while and he'd get me out. I was too shocked even to be able to respond normally."

Landon spoke again. "What did they have you working on when you got there?"

"This is where we get to the crux of what you need to know. I appreciate you allowing me to explain how I got here because otherwise, I'm sure you would consider me quite unstable."

The other Keepers quickly shook their heads. "Life kicks us in the ass more times than most of us like to remember," one of the Keepers said. He grinned. "I'm Dolby."

She smiled her acknowledgment, and then another more grim Keeper said, "Sometimes life just keeps kicking in the ass. You can't feel bad about that. You figured out a way to get out of there, and that's all that counts. Well, and the fact that you're willing to take down an asshole like Alistair Montague. And by the way, I'm Bennett."

She also smiled, acknowledging him and understanding his tight-jaw expression. "As I was writing code for the encryption Gerald required, I was also writing code for my own encryption. It was blended so they had no idea what I was doing. But essentially, it allowed me to monitor their communications in a way that I could record and save them. I had no idea if anyone would care, but it felt like something I should do. At the end of one month, I was sent a message saying a helicopter would deliver supplies. I wondered where he might land but was shocked when a helicopter hovered overhead and lowered a basket. I scrambled outside to take everything out of it, and then the helicopter left. I thought, at least I only have to live this way one more month. But at the end of that month, the helicopter came again. And again. And again. I emailed, called, and begged Gerald to get me out of there. But he kept saying that it was important I stayed a little longer. When I finally worked up enough nerve to threaten to stop working, I was told that I wouldn't receive supplies."

"Goddamn fuckers," Jeb growled next to her. The curses of the others around the table almost drowned out his voice.

"Did you ever threaten to expose him?" Landon asked.

A hysterical bark of laughter bubbled up from deep inside her chest. "I might be naive, but I assure you I have watched enough TV to know never to tell the bad guy what you know or what you might do with the information you have. In movies and TV, that's always the person who gets killed. Believe me, as much as they wanted me to work for them, my life would be worthless if I threatened to expose them. I played along."

Hop grinned. "But you played him, didn't you? You played them all."

A small grin slipped out in return, and she nodded. "I had determined that they didn't deem it necessary to bug the lighthouse. No audio or video. Why they didn't, I can't imagine because that would seem like security 101." She shrugged. "I suppose they assumed no one was on the island. Therefore, there was no way they had to worry about that. Of course, they monitored my computers. That was the only thing they assumed I would use to reach out to someone. And while that *was* what I used, they underestimated that if I had the skill to keep all of their correspondence secure, I would be able to do the same for me."

"We understand there is a past relationship between you and Jeb. I assume that's how you decided to... *involve* us."

Carson's question was well-meaning, but she winced nonetheless. "Sorry about the problems I caused with some of your programs. But you're right. It was the only thing I could think to do. While Jeb and I had not seen each other in many years, I knew he'd left the Navy and worked for a security company." She felt her cheeks heat, and while she appreciated Jeb's hand on hers under the table, she forced her gaze to stay on Carson as she continued.

"Since part of what I was working on was hacking, I was able to get into some of your systems while building a screen so that no one else would know what I was doing. I allowed trails from your end to lead to the island location and was able to hide everything from Gerald. I wasn't sure anyone would come looking for me, but it was the best I could do."

"It was fuckin' brilliant, that's what it was!" Leo said, gaining several "hell yeah," and "damn straight," from the others.

She shrugged off the compliments, wanting to move on to what she was sure the FBI agent wanted to know. "Anyway, while the hate group, disinformation, conspiracy theories, political maneuvering, and all of that was alarming, it was the discovery of what was happening with the military equipment that most bothered me. The code name that was used was Alphabet. But it didn't take long for me to realize that for all his correspondence about Alphabet, it was actually Colonel Spelling, the Army's liaison with the tank manufacturer. He requisitions more than he needs. Part of my job was to write code to change numbers for contracts. Not being told why, I did what I was asked. Once I was on the island and determined to find out why I was being held prisoner and away from everyone else, I made the connection. My program was being used to change numbers so that more tank parts and other munitions were being ordered. Once they were loaded for transport, Colonel Spelling used more programs I had written to send some to legitimate places, and others were sold on the black market."

"And you have proof of this?" Landon asked. His gaze never wavered, and she could feel the intensity boring into her.

"I have everything." She turned to Jeb. "I need a secure computer."

Jeb dropped her hand and jumped up from his chair. He stalked out of the room, and Skylar pressed her lips together while he was gone, uncertain what she should say or do.

Abbie leaned across the chair space left by Jeb. "Are you doing okay? I know this is a lot."

During the few minutes she'd had with Abbie, Natalie, Tricia, and Rachel, she quickly realized they understood the situation, and no one seemed to judge her for who she'd worked for.

Offering a tremulous nod, she said, "It is a lot, but it's good. I'll just be glad when I can turn all this over to you."

Right on cue, Jeb walked in with a special laptop. She had no doubt it contained the ultimate security program they had. *And I can make it even more so.* Thanking him, she took the computer and ran through programs, adding her own coding. Glancing up, she noted, not for the first time, that every eye was on her. "Um…" she mumbled. "Sorry, but I'm adding my own security."

Carson chuckled. "No worries. We want our system to be as safe as it can be, and it seems you're the best."

After a few minutes, she looked up. "Okay. I've sent you what I managed to uncover on the tie between Montague Industries and Colonel Spelling. I've also sent you the black market operation run by Colonel Spelling for Montague."

"Can you keep monitoring the situation?" Landon asked. "Tell when the next shipment will be diverted?"

Pressing her lips together, she nodded. "Yes. It will be next week."

Hours later, after reviewing the information over and over, Skylar was almost at her exhaustion limit. Rachel ordered food for everyone, and the others worked just as hard as Skylar. The other Keepers were moving in and out of the room, and Jeb had explained that they were working in their area of the compound. She had nodded, unoffended that she was on the outside. Working with Montague Industries in various locations had taught her the importance of ensuring that employers knew who was privy to particular information.

Carson walked back into the conference room. "Okay, Skylar. I think we have passed everything we can to Landon right now. Our people are working with them, but whatever is happening is up to Landon and the FBI. What happens next is their call. What we're concerned with are your comfort and safety."

It didn't escape her notice that a look passed between Carson and Jeb. Unable to understand the meaning, she glanced toward Jeb. "My safety?"

Jeb leaned closer, placing his hand over hers again. "You have to know you're in danger."

"Under normal circumstances, my absence from the island shouldn't be detected for a while." She thought back to the two men. "But you're thinking about the men who came, aren't you? Or the fishing boats that might not have been fishing boats that were hovering around the southern part of the island?"

Natalie returned to the room. "I've been following the satellite images for the past couple of hours, Skylar. We don't know what tipped anyone off, and we jammed the security around the island before Jeb and the others arrived."

She turned the information over in her mind, coming up with only one conclusion. "They were already after me, weren't they? I've been kept there long beyond what they originally said, but they must've known that there was only so long I would put up with their lies. Those men were sent to kill me. If it hadn't been for Jeb, I'd be dead."

"You had the foresight to contact us, even surreptitiously. You had as much to do with your rescue as we did," Jeb insisted.

"What happens now?" she asked, trying to keep the tremor from her voice.

Carson spoke first. "We have a safe house that you can use."

"I don't want to put anyone here in danger."

Carson waved away her concerns. "We live with danger every day. It's part of the job."

Jeb leaned over and whispered, "I want you with me."

She swung her head around, wanting nothing more than to accept his offer, but she hesitated. Seeing a look of uncertainty move through his eyes, she whispered, "I can't stand the thought of something happening to you because of me."

Understanding now moved through his features, and he shook his head slowly. "Nothing will happen to me. I'll honor your wishes, but I want you with me."

"That's where I want to be, too."

"Then it settled." Jeb looked over at Carson, and the two men offered chin lifts. Skylar hadn't been around many alpha men in her life but was already recognizing a chin lift as a way of offering greetings, agreements, or even respect. *It was also hot as hell.* She pressed her lips together to quell the grin threatening to slip over her face.

"Your security will be our first priority," Carson said.

"What will you do about the black market?"

"Not our call," Jeb answered, drawing her attention with a brow-lowered expression of confusion.

"But—"

"Keepers might be the ones who dig up the intelligence—or rather, in this case, you did the digging. But we turn cases like this over to the proper authorities. They work it from there in a way that can result in prosecution," Carson explained.

Jeb squeezed her hand. "We don't do this job for the glory. It's all about just getting the job done. However we have to make that happen." Standing, he gently pulled her to her feet. "Now, let's head home."

As they said goodbye to Carson and made their way to the reception area, a group of women walked in and greeted Rachel before turning to Skylar.

Skylar stood stiffly, uncertain of what was happening. Abbie stepped forward, waved at the approaching women, and then turned to Skylar. "I took the liberty of calling some of the others to gather a few items to make your stay more enjoyable."

"Hi! I'm Jeannie, Carson's wife. Abbie explained what was happening." She waved her arm to the others around her. "These are some of the other Keepers' wives. We know you've arrived with none of your possessions and wanted to make sure we took care of you."

Skylar's gaze dropped to the shopping bags in the women's hands, and had a flashback that she hadn't experienced in over twenty years… standing at her first foster home with a social worker who held a shopping bag out to her saying, "I wanted to make sure you were taken care of."

Jeb's arm around her shoulders tightened slightly, and she blinked back into the present, focusing on the scene in front of her and the generous offering being presented. "Oh my, this is too much."

"Nonsense," Natalie said, waving away her protestations. "Me? I don't like to shop, and God knows I spent too many years in fatigues to know what's fashionable, so I just told them that you were my size and to go have fun." She laughed and inclined her head to one of the pretty blondes in paint-splattered overalls. "Stella is an artist, and I knew she had flair."

Stella rolled her eyes. "It's true that I love color, but I did tone it down for you since I wasn't sure about your choices. We have jeans, T-shirts, sweaters, intimates, pajamas… just all the basics. By the way, I'm with Chris. He met you on the island."

"Oh, yes. I remember," Skylar said, pushing past her nervousness and smiling.

"And we didn't forget about the toiletries," another woman interjected. "I'm Marcia. I'm with Dolby."

"Nice to meet all of you. This really is too much. Truly, I'm overwhelmed."

"We'll let you get settled, and then we'll get together," Jeannie said, offering a warm hug.

Skylar thanked them again, then turned to Jeb.

"You ready?"

Laughing, she replied, "As ready as I'll ever be."

23

The drive to Jeb's house was cloaked in silence. He glanced over often, but she sat still, her silhouette etched against the light filtering through the windshield. Her hands were clasped together, resting in her lap. Her intelligent gaze seemed to take in every detail of the passing landscape.

His mind wandered to the homes of the other Keepers. Several of them had splurged on houses that overlooked the ocean or offered a majestic view of the mountains in the background. When he'd embarked on his search for a permanent place to live, it would be the first house he'd ever owned. The idea of spending a substantial amount for a down payment and then being in debt for years was hard for him to wrap his mind around.

While in the Navy, he often lived in base housing, saving on rent. Now with a respectable nest egg, he certainly had enough money for a down payment. But he'd learned as a child how quickly life could change. Sinking all of his money into a down payment on an expensive house was a frightening prospect, considering that he might need the money for something else if there was an emergency.

So his house hunt was meticulous and unhurried. He scoured online listings and visited numerous properties for sale. Move-in ready and at least three bedrooms with two full bathrooms were necessary. Even with no family to visit, he was tired of cramped living spaces. Other than that, he wasn't sure what he wanted. He sure as hell didn't have a *style,* but he was sure he'd know it once he saw the right place.

Finally, he toured a house that called to him. It had the requirements he desired and something special that let him know he'd found a place to call home. Now, glancing to the side once more as he pulled into the driveway and parked in front of the garage, vulnerability filled him as he wondered what Skylar's impressions were. He lived in a neighborhood, but the lots were large, even if the houses weren't. It gave everyone a sense of space, and being at the end of a wooded cul-de-sac afforded additional privacy.

Skylar leaned forward and looked out the windshield, then turned to him with a soft smile on her face. "Is this it? Is this your house?" The soft curiosity in her voice made his heart skip a beat.

"Yeah," he muttered. As they climbed from his SUV, he said, "I'll give you a tour of the place, then come back for the bags."

She nodded and glanced at his outstretched hand before quickly linking fingers. They walked to the front door, and after disarming the security, he led her inside. "As you can see, it's not very big. The former owners knocked down a couple of walls, so it's open."

"Oh…" Her voice was full of wonder. "I love how the living room opens into the dining room and the kitchen," she enthused. "It feels like a house you can breathe in."

He hadn't thought of it that way, but she was right. After living in her tiny lighthouse, his place would seem large. He gave her a tour of the downstairs and showed her the half bath, laundry room, kitchen, and pantry. He wasn't surprised when he opened the refrigerator and saw fresh milk, some vegetables, a rotisserie chicken, and a loaf of bread. It appeared one of the Keepers had made a quick grocery run when they knew he was coming back.

Turning, he waved her toward the back door from the kitchen, which led to a patio surrounded by green grass and ending with the woods at the back. "This leads to the back. I don't use it much when it gets cold, but I have hosted a few cookouts for friends." He turned to see her staring into the backyard, but her thoughts were still hidden.

"Come on. I'll show you upstairs."

At the top of the stairs, he opened a door to the right, showing her a bedroom containing a desk, computer equipment, and a treadmill on the other side. The next door opened to a full bathroom. Another bedroom offered a queen-size bed, dresser, and chair beside a bookcase.

"And the owner's bedroom is across the hall," he said. Stepping in, he felt some of the cares of the past several days fade away now that he was back in his own space. And having Skylar here only made it better. The room held a king-size bed, a matching chest of drawers and dresser, and an upholstered rocking chair. He inclined his head toward the large owner's bathroom, which had a double sink and a separate shower and tub.

"I really like your home," Skylar said, smiling at him.

He noted she referred to his place as a home and not just a house. Relief filled him, and he grinned widely. "It took me months of touring dozens of houses before I decided on this one."

Tilting her head to the side, she said, "Really? Was it hard to find what you were looking for?"

"It wasn't that I was terribly picky. It was just that nothing felt right. Until this place."

Her inquisitive gaze stayed on him. "What made this place right?"

With a spark of excitement in his eyes, he inclined his head toward the back wall. "You'll understand when you see this." He walked to the other side of his bedroom and threw open the curtains, exposing a sliding glass door. Turning, he lifted his arm toward her and wiggled his fingers. She easily acquiesced, and linking fingers with him again, she looked outside and gasped.

Outside the bedroom was a deck. It wasn't huge, but

it was big enough for two comfortable chairs with a small table between them.

"Come on," he encouraged. He opened the door, and they stepped outside.

She stood at the railing for a moment, looked around at the trees, and lifted her gaze to the mountains in the distance. She barely seemed to be breathing, and he felt nervous, waiting for her reaction. The moment hung in the air, charged with emotion. Finally, she turned to look at him, blinking rapidly to hold the tears at bay. "I get it. This is perfect."

"Like you, I never realized how much I needed a place to sit and look out over the world. The downstairs patio is great, but I find myself out here most evenings. It's not a big deck, but it's just enough that I can sit and think. Mostly, I remembered."

She took a step toward him and placed her palm on his chest. Looking into his eyes, she whispered, "What did you remember?"

"I remembered a girl who invited me to share her magical space. I remembered that girl becoming my best friend and the hours we'd spend sitting and looking out over the neighborhood. I remembered the girl I always wanted to protect from anything that could harm her. And realizing by the time I was getting ready to leave for the Navy, I'd fallen for her."

She blinked again, but this time, a single tear rolled down her cheek before she quickly swiped it away. "You remembered, too?"

"I never forgot about you, Skylar. Ever. I never thought I'd see you again. And I sure as hell never thought I'd have a chance to be with you again. But when I toured this house and saw the small deck, it reminded me of some of my favorite times in my life." He sighed. "It also reminded me of the biggest fuckup I ever made."

She placed her other palm on his chest, and his arms wrapped around her waist. They stood gazing at each other as the setting sun sent streaks of pink and orange to meld with the blue. He knew that soon, the sky would turn indigo, and the stars would shine down on them. He'd sat out here enough times to know exactly how nightfall would appear. But he never imagined that he'd be able to experience it with her after having received her forgiveness.

She lifted on her toes and kissed the underside of his jaw. He felt the warmth of her lips ever so softly. "Jeb, I don't know if things happen in life for a reason. Many people do. All I know is that I have to take life as it comes. The good and the bad. The happy and the sad. The ecstasy as well as the agony. Even though we'll never forget our past and don't want to, we can't live back there. We have the here and now. We're now the smarter, more mature versions of us. And being here with you now is exactly what I want."

A weight lifted off his chest as he stared into the pale blue eyes of the woman he was getting to know again, remembering the girl she'd been. And she was right. He would never forget their past, and they needed to live now, cherishing the journey they had embarked on. "I know you're exhausted, so I'll go down and grab the bags out of the SUV. We can fix a quick dinner and then crash early."

She stepped back and nodded. "You can drop the bags across the hall, and I'll deal with everything. It was nice of you to offer to let me stay here."

He snorted and shook his head. "Nice has nothing to do with it, Skylar. Now that we've reconnected, I don't want us apart. And as far as the bags go, that's totally your call. The room across the hall is all yours, including the bathroom. But I wouldn't mind you sharing this space, either."

Her eyes opened wide as she glanced around the large owner's bedroom. A crinkle formed between her brows. "As amazing as that sounds, Jeb, I don't want to do anything that would make you regret me being here."

"I want you here with me. Of course, I want you safe. But mostly, I want you with me so we can continue to find out if what I think is growing between us is really there."

She nibbled on her bottom lip, then said. "Tell you what. We'll stick the bags in the other bedroom. Where we sleep can be wherever we feel is right for us." She hefted her shoulders in a little shrug. "And then we'll take it from there."

Bending, he kissed her mouth, his body finally relaxing for the first time after leaving the island. "Sounds good to me. Easy. Uncomplicated. And everything just focused on us."

They had a simple dinner of heated chicken and sautéed vegetables with thick slices of buttered bread. By the time they'd eaten, Jeb looked over, and the dark shadows underneath Skylar's eyes had him standing quickly. Taking her by the hand, he led her to the bottom of the stairs. He gave her a little nudge when she turned her pale-eyed gaze to him. "Go take a long, hot bath while I put the dishes in the dishwasher. I'll be up soon, but take your time."

The relief on her face was palpable. "Thank you! I haven't had a hot bath in months." She lifted on her toes to kiss his cheek before heading up the stairs. He heard the bathwater running in the hall bathroom. The idea of having her in the larger owner's bathtub where he could join her ran through his mind, and then he quickly squashed that notion. *This time is for her.* Adjusting his crotch, he walked back to the kitchen, where he took care of the leftovers and the dirty dishes.

Once finished, he walked upstairs, not hearing any noise from the bathroom. Knocking lightly, he called out, "Just checking on you, Skylar. Do you have everything you need?"

A splash sounded out. "Yes. Sorry! I almost fell asleep in the tub. I'll be right out."

"No worries. Take your time. Run more hot water if you want."

Laughter met his ears. "I'm a prune already."

"I'm heading in to take a shower. I'll be out in a few."

It didn't take long for him to shower and dress in low-slung sweatpants and a long-sleeved T-shirt. He walked out of the bathroom, and his gaze immediately flew to the vision outside on the deck.

Skylar sat on one of the chairs, her knees drawn up and her arms around her shins. His feet skidded to a halt as the sight took his breath away. A sight he remembered well from so many years ago. A sight he thought he'd never see again. And a sight that struck him right in the chest. Lifting his hand, he massaged over his heart. Not to erase the ache but to hold the warmth in.

24

Skylar indulged in a hot bath, luxuriating in the warm water and the bath oil provided by the women. She stood to wash her hair in the shower before leaving the warm haven. The new panties and pajamas were a perfect fit, but she shivered with a chill when stepping into the hall. Wondering if Jeb had a robe she could borrow, she tiptoed into his bedroom while he was taking a shower.

There was no robe to be found, but she discovered one of his sweatshirts in the closet. Hoping he wouldn't mind her borrowing it, she pulled it over her head, grinning to see that it hung down her thighs.

She turned to leave his room when her gaze was drawn to the view from the deck. As though her feet were on their own mission, she walked to the sliding glass door and snatched a blanket lying on the end of his bed. Pulling the door open, she slipped outside. The cool night air brushed her cheeks as she wrapped the blanket around her shoulders.

She contemplated sitting on the deck floor but opted for one of the thick, cushioned chairs. Drawing up her legs, she wrapped her arms around her shins and rested her chin on her knees. She sucked in a deep breath, filling her lungs with fresh air as she gazed over the trees. In the distance was another neighborhood, and she could see a few houses. In the background were the mountains.

A breeze sent a chill through her, and she pulled up the hoodie of the sweatshirt, not wanting to retreat indoors too soon. She wanted to savor the newfound freedom, letting it permeate every cell of her body.

Her mind drifted back to her first daring climb out of the attic window at the Bakers' house. Back then, the wide ledge offered a fearless perch for a young girl desperate for liberation. Now, as an adult, it seemed foolish and risky. Back then, it gave her a sanctuary to be alone with her thoughts. And now, as an adult who'd just come out of another situation where her choices had been taken away, she finally felt a sense of freedom once again.

She sensed Jeb's presence before she heard the soft whoosh of the sliding glass open and she smiled. Enthralled with the view, she remained steadfast, her gaze facing forward.

He settled into the chair beside her, and they sat without speaking for several minutes. She didn't attempt to guess his thoughts. She believed in the sanctity of private thoughts, understanding that not every silence needed to be filled with conversation.

Finally, he asked, "Are you warm enough?"

She twisted her head to see him staring at her and smiled. "I have your sweatshirt and blanket. I'm in good shape, but I should be asking you that question. Do you want to share my blanket?"

Neither spoke for a moment, and she felt sure he remembered when she offered to share a blanket when they sat on the window ledge.

He grinned and nodded. Standing, he stepped to her chair, and she allowed him to pull her to a stand. He sat down, then gently tugged on her hand to guide her to sit in his lap. She ensured the blanket was now wrapped around both of them.

It was a position of comfort. But the fact that her core was pressed against his crotch also made it a position of intimacy. They sat in silence for a few minutes before she said, "I can see why this was the reason you bought the house. It's a lovely home on its own, but this view is so perfect for letting your mind wander."

"I've sat out here so often, letting my mind do just that. Sometimes I think of work. Sometimes the past. Sometimes my parents. Sometimes I wonder about the future."

"That's why we were such good friends, Jeb. Even when I was younger, I could just sit and think. I wouldn't have to try to solve all my problems, but I allowed myself the opportunity just to let thoughts drift through my mind."

The sun had finally set, leaving darkness and the stars to share their view. An unbidden yawn slipped out, one she couldn't have held in if she tried. His arms tightened around her, and she tucked her head against his shoulder, her forehead pressed just under his chin. She was relaxed, and the idea of falling asleep in his arms called to her. Uncertain whether she would spend the night in his bed or the guest room, she decided to let it be his call. After another wide yawn from her, he chuckled, and she felt the rumble of his chest against her shoulder.

"I think it's bedtime, Skylar."

She wanted to sit longer on the deck but knew he was right. She nodded, the top of her head moving underneath his chin. "I can barely hold my eyes open," she confessed.

Without speaking again, he stood, and she expected her feet to land on the deck floor. Instead, he lifted her easily in his arms and managed to open the door, barely jiggling her. Once the door was closed behind them, he walked to his king-size bed and set her on the side.

Kneeling in front of her, with his palms on her thighs, he said, "You are more than welcome to sleep across the hall in the guest room if that's what you prefer. I want you to be comfortable, but I'd love for you to sleep here with me. We're both exhausted, but I think I'd sleep better if I knew you were safe."

Her lips curved, and she nodded. "I'd like that too."

"Good." He pulled the blanket from around her and spread it over the foot of the bed. She pulled off his sweatshirt, and he draped it on the chair next to the bed. Instead of walking down to the other side, he crawled over her and settled in at her back, tucking her in tight.

She twisted her head and, seeing his face so close, couldn't resist a light kiss. "Good night," she whispered against his lips.

"Good night, Skylar. Catch you on the other side."

With those words resounding in her ears, she closed her eyes and fell into a deep sleep.

Swimming from the depths of a deep, restful sleep, Skylar luxuriated in the warm cocoon enveloping her. As she slowly became aware of her surroundings, she first noticed the early sunlight flooding through the sliding glass doors where the curtains had not been closed. She then realized the heaviness she felt was an arm securely wrapped around her middle and a thick thigh pressed between hers.

And if she wasn't mistaken, Jeb's erection was snuggled against her ass. She immediately wanted to press her legs together as she felt the flood of need fill her core. But considering his leg was between hers, she used what was available and rubbed herself on his thigh.

"Christ, woman. Did you wake up and start dry-humping me?"

She grinned at his sleep-rough voice. "Did you wake up and press your hard-on against my ass?" she quipped in return.

He chuckled and pulled her tighter against him, his erection proving her point. His hand slipped up to cup her breast, his fingers rolling her nipple. The chuckle died in his throat as he groaned, "You feel so good. You are the best way to wake up."

She increased her movements on his thigh, but that only served to increase the need for more friction. Not willing to wait, she shoved her thumbs into the waistband of her pajama bottoms and slid them down, barely managing to untangle her legs, the sheets, and the pajamas. Finally kicking them off, she grabbed the bottom of her top.

His hands left her breasts as he took over, and she shifted as he wriggled her shirt off. She started to roll toward him, but his hands on her waist stopped her movements. "I want to keep going where we left off," he mumbled, his teeth lightly nibbling on her earlobe. With his hands encircling her and her back to his chest, he cupped both breasts, gently rolling and tugging on her nipples. Vibrating need moved through her body, and she could have easily traced the path of nerves between her breast and core.

His leg was no longer between hers, so dry humping his thigh wasn't a possibility. Desperate, she slid her hand over her mound, fingering the bundle of nerves that created a mind-numbing need that overtook all other thoughts. Sliding her finger through her slick folds, she was barely aware of his grunt in her ear as one of his hands continued to tease a breast while the other hand slid down her tummy, nudging her hand out of the way.

"I have you, Skylar," he murmured.

His words were growled from deep inside his chest,

and they reverberated throughout her body before settling in her mind. *I've got you.* Before any other cognizant thought hit her, he slid one finger inside her channel and crooked it in just the right way and just the right angle to cause a full-body shiver. Since her hand was no longer occupied with herself, she reached back to force her hand between their bodies, wrapping her fingers around his cock.

The nibbles on her earlobe turned to small bites as he worked his way from her ear to her shoulder, trailing biting kisses all along her neck. Between his mouth, his fingers tugging her nipple, and now his thumb pressed against the nerves as his fingers delved inside her sex, the coil that had tightened inside suddenly sprung loose.

If she thought she had full-body shivers earlier, it was nothing to what she felt now. It was as though her body had exploded from the inside, shattering into a million pieces before being quickly put back together again. If she'd looked in the mirror, she wouldn't have observed the same Skylar she had always seen. This new composition created an image of herself that she'd never known. She easily acknowledged her intelligence and what she considered to be a passable appearance. But now, lying boneless in his arms, she felt desired and cared for.

She wanted to roll over and face him, but her body was like liquid. All she managed was to twist her head around to kiss him somewhat awkwardly. He didn't seem to mind as he swept his tongue inside her willing mouth.

As his hand slid from her sex, he lifted her leg and placed the engorged head of his cock at her entrance from behind. Instinctively, she arched her back, shifting her hips toward him. He took advantage of the change of angle and thrust his cock fully into her sex.

She thought she'd lie in pleasant relaxation as he found his own release, but the change in position created such a new feeling that her body immediately electrified again. His cock thrust deep inside from behind as his hands moved between her breasts and still circled the bundle of nerves. His mouth nipped where her neck met her shoulder, and she was overwhelmed with sensations.

All her cares fell away. Everything that had pressed on her for months, even years disappeared from her mind.

"Are you close, sweet girl?"

The vibrations of his words were felt against her back as they left his lungs. The whisper of breath was felt along her shoulder. Unable to speak, she nodded.

He shifted his hands, changing the angle once more, and his thrust felt deeper, reaching a part of her she never knew existed. She broke again, the millions of pieces flying everywhere. But this time, his entire body tightened behind her, his muscles tensed, and he roared a primal sound as he fell apart with her.

His grip on her slowly eased as her shivers slowed, but his warmth remained. As his cock slid from her body, she took the opportunity to shift around to face him fully. His dark brown eyes held her captive. She remembered thinking he was so cute when she first saw him at the Bakers' house. And as he became a teenager, she appreciated the tanned skin, dark hair, and stubble along his jaw.

But now, as an adult, she couldn't believe this gorgeous man lay next to her. Smooth skin over defined muscles. Luscious lips that made her want to trace them with her finger and taste him with her tongue. The stubble was now a trimmed beard, and the dark hair was shorn close to his head. His body was a work of art, but she knew a sculptor could never capture the dark-eyed gaze she felt to her very marrow.

"If you keep staring at me like that, round two may come quicker than you think."

She smiled, choking back a giggle. "You're the most beautiful man I've ever seen, Jeb. I can't help but stare at you."

"I'm beautiful? Sweetheart, nothing is as breath-taking as you. From the first moment you opened the door when you were ten years old, I was captured by your eyes. So pale and so intense. And now, as a woman, no one holds a candle to you. You are all I can imagine ever wanting or having."

"Wow," she whispered, giving in to the urge to trace his lips with her forefinger. "If you keep talking like that, I'll be ready for round two."

His sensuous lips curved into a slow grin, and he took her mouth in a deep kiss. Their bodies were now pressed tightly together, her breasts against his chest, and their legs tangled. Their hands explored slowly, but their lips remained sealed together.

It was a while before they made their way downstairs for breakfast. But for her, it had been the greatest way to wake up. Glancing over her shoulder as he walked into the kitchen behind her, she took one look at his face, and it let her know that he also enjoyed their wake-up sex.

She knew they were living in a bubble but was determined to enjoy it before shit hit the fan.

25

ONE WEEK LATER

Jeb climbed from the vehicle parked in the scrub brush off a lonely road outside Missoula, Montana. Moving with several other Keepers, they stationed themselves near a hill overlooking an intersection, tasked with keeping a watch on the arrivals of trucks.

During the past week, Skylar had worked with the Keepers and FBI as she turned over all the incriminating evidence and information she had gained. She'd expressed her frustration that some of her information would not be usable. Landon and his superiors went through everything she had gathered. Emails, texts, and even encrypted messages proved that Colonel Spelling was organizing the black market sale of munitions and equipment parts.

According to Landon, not all her evidence would be admissible in court, but he assured her that the FBI had spent years with their eye on Alistair Montague, and she wasn't the only source of their evidence trail. While other employees were mentioned, Landon explained that Alastair Montague's lawyers could claim he had no idea the people working directly under him were masterminding a black market munitions operation.

Deciding that it was better to stop them, even if they could not get everyone, the FBI was ready to take down the next shipment.

While this was the FBI's show, LSIWC had been asked to provide continued intelligence and support. The support was easy. Jeb, Leo, Dolby, Bennett, and Adam provided surveillance and backup on the ground while the FBI covered the munitions plant. The agents also had boots on the ground, and the Keepers were in the area where the shipment would be diverted.

Skylar and Natalie were in a van not too far away. Both were monitoring the situation. Natalie watched the satellite images so she could give the investigators directions. Skylar monitored Colonel Spelling's encrypted messages.

Jeb hated for Skylar to be involved outside the compound, wishing she was safe at home. He trusted Natalie to take care of her, but the FBI agent driving the van made him nervous. Too much of a rookie. He would have preferred a Keeper to be with them, but Landon's supervisor insisted that Natalie and Skylar's involvement needed to be monitored by an agent to ensure everything was by the book.

Now, with everyone in place, they waited. The wind whistled along the flat plains covered in grasses, scrub brush, and low trees. In the dark, he could only make out the silhouette of the mountains in the distance.

Normally, Hop would be with them, giving air support, but he was unable to get to them. Without a Keeper in the air nearby, Jeb had to trust that the FBI had everything under control.

"You okay, man?"

He turned to see Adam nearby.

"Yeah. Just have a feeling… not a good one."

"Got anything to go on?" Bennett asked.

He shook his head. "Hate that Skylar's still involved. Hate that we don't have our own air support. I don't know," he growled, also hating to show a vulnerability. "Just hate feeling like this simple takedown could go so fuckin' fubar."

Leo approached with a solemn nod. "It fucks with your mind when the woman you love is caught up in it all. The normal ass-kicking energy that we usually go into an assignment with slips through our fingers as we worry about them."

Jeb locked eyes with Leo, his chest deflating as the air left his lungs, with Leo's words echoing in his head. *Woman you love... woman you love.* The truth was undeniable, but he hadn't admitted it to Skylar. *Hell, we only reconnected about ten days ago.* But the years they'd known each other at the Bakers' house had woven a deep bond. He and Skylar shared the same childhood meals, schools, holidays, and experiences. While their adult lives were separate, their past relationship interlaced with the newness of their reunion.

With a heavy nod, he turned his gaze back to the expansive plains and the highway lying before them, bathed in the eerie green glow of his night vision goggles. His eyes methodically swept the area, seeing nothing to report. His attempt to push Skylar back from his thoughts didn't work. His thoughts drifted to the past week, witnessing Skylar each day at LSIWC as she worked in the conference room, proving how valuable she was in cybersecurity and using her skills to investigate. He could learn much from her and hoped she would stay when the mission was over. *But stay where?*

She had slept in his bed each night after they made love, their bodies intertwined. They'd shared meals in his kitchen, watched TV in his living room, and sat on the small deck talking for a while each evening. Yet he had been too uncertain to ask her what her plans were. The only thing she'd mentioned was that she wouldn't go into witness protection. Landon had said Alistair would have no reason to send someone after her once everything was exposed. Since she had no firsthand information on him other than what she'd managed to pull from the computers to share with the investigators, she wouldn't be a witness.

Jeb was in the dark as to her exact plans after the black market scheme had been taken down. And it was that uncertainty that filled his mind now.

"Trucks have just left the munitions plant." Jeb startled at the unknown agent's radioed voice.

"I can track them," Natalie responded.

"I confirm that the first two trucks are the ones contracted to the Army base in Kansas. The third truck is contracted to the Army base in Texas." Skylar said. "The last two in the convoy are the ones being sold separately. They should turn off from the highway to meet up with the alternate drivers."

Hearing Skylar's voice through the comm-link at the height of a mission sent a grin across Jeb's face. It was a sound that he adored but had never imagined hearing while on assignment. Her input was invaluable. She was smart, but seeing her delve into the investigative side of cybersecurity made him long for her to stay with them. And, more selfishly, him.

She had assured him that they might not have come together as a couple, even if he hadn't walked out in youthful anger many years ago. Or if they had become a couple, they might not still be together. *"Jeb, that time apart is what truly made us who we are today."*

While he recognized the truth in her words, he often found himself wandering down the path of what their lives would have looked like if he'd handled things differently. He probably wouldn't have become a SEAL. And then wouldn't have his career with LSIWC. Just the other evening, she had chided him to stop the what-ifs.

But unable to change the past, he was learning to adopt the Skylar way of thinking. *Take life as it comes, learn from our mistakes, move on, and live.* He smiled and shook his head in quiet admiration.

Natalie's voice cut through his once again wandering thoughts. "You should be able to see the trucks coming along Highway 93."

"I see them coming," Bennett radioed.

Jeb saw the distant procession of headlights as they approached. The tank hulls transported from the manufacturer's plant were carried on large flatbed trucks and shrouded by tarps to hide the contents.

The convoy of trucks lumbered toward the intersection, engines growling in the otherwise stillness of the night. The first three trucks veered toward the highway. FBI agents would tail them until they reached their destination at military bases.

The last two trucks diverted in a different direction, continuing to roll down the small Montana road, drawing closer to where Jeb, the other Keepers, and the agents waited.

Keeping vigil, they watched as the two trucks finally pulled to a stop on the side of the road. They sat still with the drivers ensconced within the truck cabs. After almost twenty minutes, smaller headlights came down the road, belonging to a solitary pickup truck from the opposite direction, stopping in front of the first truck.

Two men alighted from the pickup, their movements deliberate as they walked to the first rig. The driver from that flatbed tractor-trailer climbed down to meet the men. Jeb watched as the second rig driver also threw open his door and climbed down from his cab. The four men talked for just a moment and then made the transfer. The two rig drivers walked to the pickup truck, started it, and continued down the road.

Jeb followed the exchange. The two men who'd arrived in the pickup truck now each climbed into a rig and continued along the small road.

He and the others waited to hear Natalie radio the trucks' directions and locations since she was monitoring the satellite images. He also wondered if there had been any communication between the drivers who made the switch that Skylar would have picked up. After a moment, a trickle of fear began moving through his mind. Turning to the others, he spied Leo's tense jaw. *He feels it, too.*

"Something's not right," Jeb rumbled, turning toward their vehicle, his steps hastening to a jog. He didn't need to look behind him to know the Keepers were following.

Just as they reached their SUV, Leo was already radioing, "Keeper one, come in. Come in, Keeper one. Do you read me?"

"I'm driving," Adam said, sliding behind the steering wheel. "You keep trying to get ahold of Natalie and Skylar."

"Keeper one, are you there?" Sharing a look with Leo, he clenched his gut as his heart pounded. He knew there was the possibility that Skylar, being unused to active missions, might not respond. But there was no fucking way that Natalie would not have responded to Leo's call out. And with both of them silent? *Something is fucking wrong!*

Bennett and Dolby immediately reported to Landon and Carson. "Natalie and Skylar are not responding to calls. Does anyone have eyes on their van?"

Landon cursed. "Dammit! I can't get the agent to respond either. I'm heading to their location. Meet me there."

Jeb opened his mouth to give directions to Adam, but he was already flying down the road and called out, "Got it. Heading to them now."

It only took a few minutes to get to the dirt road the FBI van had driven down. He turned and looked behind him, seeing headlights as Landon radioed, "I'm just behind you. Take a right at the next intersection. They were parked half a mile down that dirt road."

Another minute passed, but there was no van. Jeb gasped. "Goddammit! They're gone!"

"Shit! There's something over there in the grass!" Dolby called out, his voice shaking.

Adam had barely stopped the vehicle when Jeb and Leo leaped out, racing forward with Landon on their heels. "Shit!" Landon cried out to the side, leaning over a body lying on the ground. Shining their lights around, there was no sign of Natalie or Skylar.

Landon looked up. "It's the agent who was with them. He's been shot, but he's not dead." He radioed for medical assistance while other agents swarmed the area, some immediately starting medical assistance.

Jeb stood, his gaze swinging around the area, his mind racing wildly, which never happened on a mission. Barely aware that Adam was already on the line to Carson, he felt Bennett grab his shoulder and say, "Stay cool. We work this like we work everything else."

Leo was furious, but Jeb knew his fellow Keeper was just as blown away as he was. Everything had been turned over to the FBI. "Why the fuck would someone go after Skylar and Natalie now?" he growled, gaining Leo's attention.

"I have no idea." Leo shook his head. "Montague taking them in the middle of an FBI raid would be stupid. They can't possibly get away with anything and would have to know that all the evidence Skylar had was already turned over."

Adam turned toward them. "Carson has got Abbie and Rick on this. They're looking at satellite, but Natalie's lighthouse tattoo is also tracking."

"We need a bird—" Jeb began.

"Carson's on it. He's got a contact in Northern Montana that he's calling," Adam reported.

Before Jeb could rage about a random contact they didn't know, he watched Leo nod as though the information was good for him.

Leo looked at Jeb and explained, "This is the former Special Forces teammate Carson and Mace are talking to about starting a new Lighthouse Security Investigation. He's a pilot. He's also been running some of the early rescue missions by himself."

"Do you trust him?" Jeb bit out.

"Logan is as trustworthy as they come."

His heart rate didn't slow, but he knew Leo wouldn't trust just anybody to help find Natalie.

Carson radioed, "Logan Bishop is on his way to you. ETA is thirty minutes, but you can cut that down by driving north on the highway. We'll keep track of both of you and let you know where you intersect. In the meantime, we're tracking Natalie's tattoo and Skylar's necklace. We'll stay on top of this and get you to them. We'll get both of them back."

Jeb heard the surety in Carson's voice, but he'd known since he was eleven years old that nothing in life is certain. Not even the safety of the ones you love.

Bennett grabbed his shoulder again and, with a little shove, pointed him in the direction of their SUV. Shaking out of his thoughts, he refocused on the task at hand.

I'm on my way, Skylar.

26

LSIWC COMPOUND

Carson's gaze lingered on his boots as he waited for Logan Bishop to answer his phone. He noted the creases etched into the leather, a testament to the assignments he'd worked on. Restless, he held the phone to his ear, hoping his call would be answered.

Mace had served with Jack Bryant in the Army Special Forces years earlier. Jack now ran Saints Protection and Investigation out of his compound in Virginia. And through that alliance, Mace had met Logan, formerly a SEAL. Mace's new brainchild to expand Lighthouse Security Investigations with Logan was already in the works but was kept under wraps at this time.

In the SEALs, Logan Bishop was known by his call sign of Preacher, but now he just went by Logan, eschewing his former identity and embracing civilian life. He flew his helicopter for private tours of the rugged mountains of Montana and for mountain rescues of hikers. But Logan's story was layered, only known to very few people. He also orchestrated covert rescues at the behest of the government.

Mace began the process of convincing Logan that he should become the leader of another branch of LSI. Logan agreed, but it took several years to build up a business like what Mace and Carson had.

Carson knew many people he could call for assistance, but Logan was the only one he knew in Montana who could get to his people quickly.

A growly voice answered the call. "Bishop."

"Logan, it's Carson Dyer. I need your bird in the air as soon as possible."

He could hear movement in the background and had no doubt that Logan was already throwing the covers off his bed. "What's happening?"

"An FBI raid in Montana gone wrong. Two of my people who were in an FBI van monitoring the situation have been kidnapped. The agent with them was shot. While I have people on the ground, my pilot's little boy just went into the hospital for minor surgery."

"Where do I need to be?"

Relief flooded Carson. He knew Logan would help, but it was hard to hold back how his breath flowed easier when Logan's immediate affirmation sounded like a beacon in the dark sky.

He gave the location, then added, "My people that were taken are women. You'll rendezvous with some of my men and head to where we're tracking them."

"Do you have trackers on them?"

"You know we do. One is only wearing a tracker in her necklace, but the other one already has the tattoo.

Granted, if they're separated, we might not trust the necklace, but now we can track that both are together."

"Send me all the information, and I'll get my bird ready. I can be in the air in ten minutes."

Another sigh of relief left Carson's lungs. "You've got my gratitude."

Logan barked out a grunt to hide his grin. "This won't be the last time we work together."

"Then we're both lucky as fuck."

Thanking Logan, Carson disconnected the call. Inside the compound, he looked around. With Keepers working the mission in the compound and out in the field, as well as supporting Jeb and Leo, he knew he had the best team of people.

He looked at Abbie and said, "Send the coordinates to Logan Bishop. He'll be flying to meet our team and take them wherever they need to go to get Natalie and Skylar back."

Calling Landon, he said, "Have your people track both sets of trucks that have left and keep monitoring to see if other trucks are leaving the plant. The first five trucks may have been decoys only. Someone knew what the fuck was going down to take my people. Your mission is now yours, Landon. Mine is getting my people back."

"Already on it," Landon promised, his words tight. "Agent Tidwell, the one who was shot, was able to say that the man who came to the van had FBI insignia on his jacket." He let out another curse. "Carson… fuck, man. Shit… as far as I'm concerned, this mission is being run by my superior, anyway. Whatever you need from me, you got it."

"Appreciate it. I'll be in touch."

He disconnected, then looked around at the hardened faces of the men and women working for him, their expressions lined with concern and determination. He knew they were pissed about Natalie and Skylar. It was more than just dedication to a job. It was camaraderie, a bond forged in a shared purpose. It was a commitment to friendship. It was loyalty. Being a Keeper, giving their all until everyone was guided home.

Not for the first time, he tossed up a heartfelt prayer of thanks to Mace Hanover, who started the first LSI, and then brought Carson on board for the West Coast office. Now, that Logan had agreed, they'd have another set of Keepers to work with... and rely on when needed.

Abbie looked up, her face pinched with worry. "I've sent a message to Logan Bishop. It's taken care of."

Nodding in her direction, he said, "Okay, everyone, keep working the problem. Let's bring our people home."

27

Skylar sat on the cold, hard floor of the van, her heart pounding as she grappled with the quicksilver turn of events.

While immersed in her work next to Natalie at the bank of computers inside the van, she barely paid attention to Marty Tidwell, the FBI agent assigned to drive the bureau's van and accompany them as she and Natalie worked. With his youthful appearance and overeagerness, she often ignored him, preferring to focus on work. The hum of computers and the subtle clicks of keystrokes were all she heard between the radio messages from the agents and Keepers.

She barely registered that he noted another agent was approaching. The sudden opening of the back van door had been a jarring intrusion into their cocoon of concentration. The response from the agent sitting close to her caused her hands to halt over the keyboard.

"Who the fuck are you?" the agent called out.

It was at that second that her and Natalie's heads

swung around in unison to see the newcomer. A man, clad in an FBI jacket, had entered holding a gun in his hand. The moment stretched before erupting into violence. Their agent assigned lunged forward, but the intruder fired. The gunshot cracked in the confined space and sent the agent reeling back as blood blossomed over his chest.

Skylar's raw scream filled the van, and her hands flew up instinctively as she ducked. Natalie leaped from her chair, but the intruder was prepared and swung his gun hand around, hitting her on the side of the head. The impact sent Natalie crashing to the floor, a trickle of blood already running down the side of her face.

With their agent shot and Natalie unconscious on the floor, Skylar was paralyzed by fear. She stared at the interloper, her eyes wide as her heart galloped in her chest. Her breaths were pants as she struggled to suck in air. Her mind screamed for her to move, but her body refused to obey. Frozen, she stared, not daring to move.

Moving in a blur, the man grabbed her arm and twisted it behind her back. Her struggles were feeble against his strength. He secured her wrists behind her with zip ties, then shoved her to the floor of the van, doing the same with her ankles, securing them quickly even though she continued to fight.

Turning his attention to Natalie, who was still lying on the van floor, he secured her in the same way. Skylar's mind raced with panic and disbelief swirling together. She watched in horror as he walked to the back of the van, opened the door, and dragged the wounded agent out the back. Then he stomped back through the van and settled into the driver's seat. The van began bouncing over the rough ground of the plains before making its way onto a road.

Skylar glanced at the clock on the nearest computer and noted with incredulity their lives had changed in only three minutes. Terrified the agent was dead, she closed her eyes, wishing she'd paid more attention to him.

Desperate to check on Natalie, she scooted closer, her movements hindered by her bindings. Natalie's face was ghostly pale, and a knot was forming on the side of her head. She reached over as close as she could so that her words would be next to Natalie's ear. "Natalie, Natalie. Can you hear me? Please, wake up."

Skylar was uncertain how badly Natalie was hurt but feared the longer she was knocked out, the harder it would be for her to regain consciousness. Skylar nudged Natalie several times, but the bumping of the van was already rocking both of their bodies, and Skylar thought that the physical toll on both of them was enough stimulation to wake Natalie if she was going to. Her heartbeat raced as more panic set in.

Her mind whirred with frantic thoughts. She glanced up at the computer table height and wondered how she could get a message off to Jeb. For that matter, how to get a message off to anyone without the driver noticing. With her hands bound, she couldn't type. When Natalie was hit, her headset was knocked from her head, and when he zip-tied Skylar, he grabbed the headset from her and tossed it to the side. *Along with a few strands of my hair!*

She cursed the kidnapper for his thoroughness even as she lamented her own shock-induced inattention to the route he was driving. Now, she had no idea where they were in relation to the maps and geography that Natalie had been keeping track of.

Feeling a crushing sense of helplessness, she grappled with the enormity of the situation. This was no random attack. It was a calculated abduction executed with chilling precision. Their captor or whoever sent him had inside knowledge of where the FBI van was located and who was inside. Alistair Montague's influence filled her mind, sending a shiver down her spine.

She trusted the Keepers explicitly, and they trusted Landon. However, for a mission this extensive, numerous FBI agents of all ranks and levels were privy to the takedown of the black market scheme. Knowing the reach of Alistair Montague, she had no doubt that anyone along the line could've infiltrated the mission.

Is the kidnapping part of a larger scheme? A diversion to facilitate getting the tank hulls to the black market buyer? Or a targeted strike against the Keepers?

Her attention was suddenly drawn back to Natalie as she began to rouse and moan softly, blinking her eyes open.

Leaning down again, she whispered, "Natalie, Natalie. Come on, keep your eyes open. It's me, Skylar." Much to Skylar's relief, Natalie's eyes stayed open.

Natalie breathed deeply several times, then her brow furrowed, and a wince crossed her face. "What the fuck?"

"I don't know, but the man who shot Agent Tidwell

and hit you is driving right now."

Those words seemed to sink in as Natalie's gaze jumped toward the front, and her body wiggled around slightly. "Help me sit up."

The best that Skylar could do was to lean her back against one of the attached computer tables on the side of the van. Using her legs for leverage, she pushed against Natalie's shoulder, helping to shove her into a seated position. It wasn't pretty and probably caused Natalie pain, but it was effective. "Sorry," she muttered.

"No worries," Natalie replied.

"Stop moving around back there!" the driver yelled. He twisted his head, and seeing both women sitting up, he warned, "Don't try anything. You may have some value, but my orders are to get the computer analyst. Nothing says you have to be in one piece."

Natalie's gaze jumped over to Skylar, who could only shrug and shake her head. "I have no idea what he's talking about," she whispered.

"I guess that someone wants you, and seeing me at a computer also must've made him think he was getting a two-for-one."

"Or he didn't know which of us was me," Skylar surmised.

Natalie nodded. "You're right." Looking around, she asked, "Do you have any idea where we are or where we're going?"

Skylar's face heated as she shook her head. "It all happened so fast that I was just scared. Then when my brain started trying to figure out what happened, I realized I had no idea which way he'd driven."

Barely whispering, Natalie said, "As soon as we've gone silent, Carson will be on this. He'll have someone follow and track us."

Suddenly, Skylar remembered what Jeb said about all the Keepers having a tracker in their tattoo and remembered the necklace that he had placed around her neck. "I have a necklace."

"Yep," Natalie mouthed.

The road had smoothed out, and with fewer bumps to jar them as they sat on the floor, she tried to imagine what highway they might be on. The van slowed as the driver flipped on the blinker. She pressed her legs against the table to give her leverage as the van turned onto another smooth road. Soon, they traveled through a well-lit parking lot, light shining through their windshield. Now, their faces were not just illuminated by the computer screen, and she was able to see Natalie's head more clearly. Skylar breathed easier as she observed that the bleeding had stopped. After several more twists and turns, the van came to a halt. The driver left the vehicle, called out a greeting, and someone threw open the back door. Blinking at the bright lights now shining in, she could see they were in a metal building but had no idea where they were.

Looking to the side, Natalie cursed. "Oh fuck. This is the inside of an airplane hangar."

A gasp slipped through Skylar's lips. "They're taking us somewhere by plane?"

Another man appeared and stared at the two women in the back of the van. He leaned forward, and with a rough hand on Skylar's arm and leg, he pulled her forward and then hefted her out of the van. His hand gripped tightly as he stood her upright, her feet touching the ground.

Uncertain of what she should do and afraid to move too much, she stayed still as he repeated the movements on Natalie. Natalie, of course, managed to curse his intelligence, his lineage, and even his dick size. If Skylar hadn't been so scared, she would have laughed aloud. As it was, she just pressed her lips together, terrified the man might hit Natalie. Or worse. *Oh God, don't let him kill her!*

"Shut up, bitch."

He walked away, and Skylar breathed easier. She wanted Natalie with her, not knocked out again.

"Not a plane. A bird," Natalie said, having turned around and looked toward the open door of the hangar. Skylar twisted around at Natalie's words and saw that just outside was a helicopter. Hop had piloted the only other helicopter she'd ever ridden in. He'd done everything he could to make the ride smooth, and she'd eventually relaxed so much that she fell asleep. Looking at the smaller aircraft and the man who appeared to be their pilot, she felt her comfort was the last thing he cared about.

"Will the Keepers still be able to track us?" she whispered. She had no idea how Jeb would find her and was sure he'd try. She just didn't know if he would be able to.

Natalie nodded. "Yes. Believe me, my Leo will go to the ends of the earth for me. And I know that Jeb would do the same for you."

She wanted to reach over and hug Natalie for her words of comfort, but with their hands behind their backs, all she could do was nod and offer a weak smile.

Another man came around from the side of the hangar, glanced at the girls, and looked over to the man who'd driven them there. "I thought there was just one I was taking."

The kidnapper shrugged. "When I got there, two women were working the computers. I didn't have time to figure out who was who and which one I needed. The one with attitude written all over her face got clipped when she didn't like me shooting the agent with them. The other one hasn't been a problem."

Hasn't been a problem. Those words resounded in Skylar's head. She glanced at Natalie and wished she had the Keeper's strength. *I never learned to fight and barely learned to speak back to anyone. Not my parents. Not the kids at school. And not my supervisors, who kept moving me and then dumping me in shitty places.* And now, kidnapped, she was still being accommodating. Angry but having no idea what to do, she once more stayed quiet and waited for direction from Natalie.

"Two or one—it doesn't matter to me," the man said. "Let's get 'em on board."

With their ankles zip-tied and their wrists behind their back, there was a little movement that Skylar could accomplish. She watched Natalie get manhandled, and it didn't seem like there was much either of them could change about their situation. One of the men picked up Natalie and shoved her into one of the back seats in the helicopter while the driver maneuvered

Skylar next to the aircraft. She witnessed Natalie's glare flaming toward the man, but he just laughed.

"You keep being a bitch, and I'll take out your little friend. I don't know which of you is so important, or maybe he wants both of you. But you better check that attitude and not be a problem in this helicopter, or I swear to God, I'll shoot your friend."

Natalie quieted at the threat toward Skylar.

Skylar's heart pounded with a mixture of fear and resignation as her captors hoisted her into the aircraft. Her shoulders screamed in protest, as the unnatural position of her hands bound behind her back sent sharp jolts of pain radiating through her body. The rush of blood returning to her numbed hands was like a thousand needles pecking her skin. She wiggled her fingers, wincing at the raw, stinging sensation where the ties had cut into her flesh.

Her momentary relief was short-lived. She gasped as the men swiftly restrained her again, this time securing her arms to the chair. The position was less torturous, but escape was impossible. Glancing toward Natalie, she noted they restrained her the same way. A sense of gratitude moved through her that Natalie would be more comfortable on the flight. They were right next to each other, their fingers able to touch.

Still wondering if the driver had been an actual FBI agent or just wearing one of their jackets, she looked out the helicopter window to see him leave the van with his agent jacket still on and climb into another vehicle before driving away.

The pilot settled into his seat, buckled in, then put

on his headphones. He glanced behind him and grinned. "Hang on tight, girlies. I'll get you where you're supposed to be and then collect a fat paycheck for my trouble. Not a bad way to earn a living." He chuckled as though he'd made the funniest joke, then turned back to the front.

She glanced to the side to see Natalie's assessing gaze on her. It dawned on her that Natalie would naturally try to protect her, and while Skylar was thankful not to be alone, she didn't want Natalie to worry. *I'm strong. I'm tough. I can take care of myself. Or at least try.* Skylar mouthed, "I'm okay."

Natalie nodded, her lips quirking slightly. Soon, the blades began to whirl, the motor vibrated, and the helicopter lifted off. Once again, Skylar's stomach felt left behind.

As the aircraft ascended, the world below vanished into the inky blackness of the night. Unable to tell which direction they were going, she realized her fate was now in the hands of someone who kidnapped and transported humans against their will. Her veins filled with ice. She twisted around to look at Natalie, who'd also been looking out the window but had now turned toward her.

Natalie mouthed, "The others will find us."

Skylar nodded, praying that Natalie was right while terrified that she might be wrong.

Natalie then added, "Our men will find us."

Our men. My man. The words were a lifeline, bringing Jeb's face to her mind. *Is he my man?* Jeb had once meant everything to her, and now was a constant in her thoughts. Memories from the past week flooded her mind. The way she woke up each morning with his arms around hers, her cheek resting on his chest, and their legs tangled. They made love every night that she'd been in his house, in his bedroom, in his bed.

She'd had every intention of moving into his guest room when he made the offer that she could stay at his house. In the safety of his home, they had become reacquainted, bridging the gap of years spent apart. They reconnected in a way that felt both new and familiar.

Journeying down memory lane, they shared stories of their pasts and dreams for the future. He talked about his years in the Navy and his desire to be an asset to the Keepers. She opened up more about her childhood, sharing stories about life with her dysfunctional parents before she came to the Bakers. They sat out on his little deck, and the years and the distance fell away, and they were two souls continuing on the same path.

Each night, as she chose his bed over the guest room, she saw in his smile a reflection of her own growing feelings.

And every night, they made love, exploring each other's bodies. She knew she was falling harder and harder every day. She had no idea what would make him *her man*, but she had an idea that he was just that.

She sucked in a deep breath and let it out slowly, calming her frazzled nerves and steadying her racing heartbeat. Natalie was right. Jeb was her man. Her anchor. Her hope. And he would come for her.

28

The ride didn't last long before the helicopter began to descend. The dawn was just breaking over the horizon, giving a hint of the landscape below. A modest-size city in the distance. A river just below. And a group of warehouses that appeared unoccupied if the lack of humans or traffic was any indication.

Natalie touched Skylar's hand, and she looked over. "Touch my watch," Natalie mouthed. "Tap it twice."

Brows lowering, she didn't question the strange request but stretched her fingers over to barely reach the black-faced watch on Natalie's wrist. Tapping it twice, she saw no change in its appearance.

"With the sun just peeking, it looks like civilization in the distance," Natalie said aloud.

Skylar twisted her head, her gaze dragging from the window to the Keeper sitting next to her. She pressed her lips together, saying nothing.

"A river snaking along. That's pretty," Natalie continued.

"Shut up!" came the order from the pilot.

"Just enjoying the view," Natalie quipped. "At least with the sun rising over the city in the background, it's nice to have something to look at other than dark."

"Yeah, well, I don't give a shit about your constant comments," he groused. "So shut the fuck up."

Natalie made wide eyes at Skylar and dipped her head to indicate the window.

Uncertain of what was expected of her, she was sure she needed to say something. "Um… those warehouses next to the river look big…" Her eyes were wide, but Natalie's little smile and nod let Skylar know she must have said the right thing. Her gaze moved over Natalie, then landed on the watch on the Keeper's wrist and remembered Jeb using his as a radio. Lifting her brows, she watched as Natalie gave an imperceptible nod.

"Jesus, not you, too," the pilot groused. "Shut the fuck up, both of you, or when we land, I'll shut you up in a way that you won't like."

Skylar's chest depressed in fear, but Natalie's lips simply quirked upward. Both women fell silent, and Skylar prayed that what they'd said aloud would give whoever was listening to Natalie's radio more information to help guide them in case the trackers weren't working.

The helicopter landed with a thump. Skylar had wanted to be out of the air, but now, seeing the desolate building rise in front of them, she wasn't sure this was better. It looked very much like a good place to dump a body. She shivered and swung her head over to the pilot exiting the helicopter.

With the morning light providing more illumination, she was able to see a door open on the side of the warehouse. Two men walked out, one in a uniform with a rifle slung over his shoulder. "Shit, Natalie, do you see—"

"Yeah," Natalie groused.

Completely out of her element, she blurted, "I have no idea what to do."

"Do whatever they say," Natalie advised. "We want to stay alive long enough to be rescued. And believe me, the Keepers are on their way."

"What were we telling someone earlier?"

"They'll have the time coordinated with me saying it was a city in the distance with a river to the west. Knowing there were warehouses nearby helps, as well."

"I thought our tracers would do the job," Skylar said. Fear now ran through her, and she knew it would be harder than she had hoped for the Keepers to find them.

"They will have me since mine is a tattoo. But there's always the problem of wondering where you are in case someone took away your necklace. This way, they could hear both voices, know we are together, and not just that perhaps someone jerked off the necklace and had it in the helicopter with me."

"Jesus, that's complicated and so incredibly simple."

Natalie snorted ruefully. "Remember, even when we have the best intelligence at our fingertips and all the technological bells and whistles, sometimes it's the simple things that keep us safe."

The two women remained quiet as they watched the pilot greet the other men who came from the warehouse. They didn't have to wait long before the three men walked back toward the helicopter.

"Would you think less of me if I told you I was scared?" Skylar, her heart threatening to beat out of her chest.

"I'd think you were crazy if you weren't scared," Natalie replied.

"What if they try to separate us?"

"Then make sure you stay compliant and stay alive."

She understood Natalie's words but was so out of her element that she had no idea what to do. *Stay compliant.* She almost laughed aloud. *If there's one thing I can do, it's be a follower!* She couldn't decide if that thought made her want to laugh, cry, feel confident, or be angry.

The door to the helicopter opened, and she had no more time to give in to musings.

The pilot stepped in, pulling a knife from his pocket. She gasped and held her breath as he slid the blade close to her wrist. With a flick, he sliced the zip tie, and it wasn't until he stepped back and sliced the zip tie between her ankles that she realized she was unfettered. He grabbed her by the arm and jerked her from her seat. He lifted her onto the ground, growling, "Try to get away, and you'll find a bullet in your back."

Even if she wasn't compliant, she could barely get her legs to propel her forward and wasn't about to leave Natalie behind. Plus, looking at the man standing a few feet away with a rifle slung over his shoulder, she knew trying to escape at the moment would be ludicrous.

She watched the pilot as he walked around to the other side and repeated the same procedure on Natalie. He kept his arm on her bicep as he walked around the front of the helicopter and shoved her next to Skylar.

"These were the two women in the van. I didn't know which one I was supposed to get."

The guard shrugged. "We'll find out inside. Stick around because you'll be taking the boss back to wherever he says." Then looking at Skylar and Natalie, he said, "Head to the door. We're right behind you. You won't get far if you try to run."

With a glance toward Natalie, the two women walked to the open door in front of them. By now, the dawn illuminated the desolate area, giving evidence that there was no activity around. Weeds sprouted through the spiderweb cracks in the asphalt parking lot. Skylar had no idea where the warehouse was located. The paint was faded on the side of the warehouse, offering no evidence of what it was used for or who it belonged to. It loomed ahead, now seeming to serve as a hideout for sinister deeds, such as hiding kidnapped computer engineers.

Following Natalie, she stepped inside the dimly lit interior and blinked as her eyes worked to focus. They entered an empty room that appeared to be a reception area with a built-in counter on one side. The man who hadn't spoken yet led the way while the guard and the pilot brought up the rear. Continuing down a hall, they moved through a metal door and emerged into the vast expanse of the main warehouse. Skylar's breath caught, and her feet stumbled at the sight of the massive room filled with wooden crates and large tarps covering unidentifiable shapes.

Her attention snapped to a figure emerging from behind a stack of crates. Recognition flooded her as Gerald Butler stepped into view, his presence making her blink, not believing her eyes. His disarmingly cordial smile belied the tension that crackled in the air. He stopped in front of them and inclined his head as he greeted them. "Skylar, it's been a while since I've seen you. You look well."

A knot of fear tightened in her stomach, but it was quickly overtaken by unsuppressed anger. "I suppose the extended *vacation* on the island *resort* did wonders for me," she retorted, her voice laced with bitter sarcasm. "After all, it was only supposed to be for about two months, but here I am, six months later."

She caught a brief hint of surprise when his eyes flickered. Though Natalie had advised compliance, Skylar bristled at the thought of being manipulated and trapped again.

He nodded without appearing angry with her words. Inclining his head slightly to the side, he said, "I'm afraid things became more complicated." His gaze moved to Natalie.

Suddenly, she was afraid that now that the kidnappers had identified who she was, they might attempt to get rid of Natalie, considering her to be extraneous. She continued without giving anyone a chance to speak, "This is another computer programmer. She was working with me."

Gerald's brow lifted, offering a sardonic grin. "Yes... an agent, I presume."

The way he sneered the word *agent* caused a trickle of unease to slide through Skylar's blood. "No, she's a private programmer who was helping me."

He stared, saying nothing, his gaze assessing. She had no idea if her words had the effect on Gerald that she wanted. She hoped that whatever she said would keep Natalie alive and with her. But for all she knew, it was just going to enrage Gerald. Her insides quivered, and she prayed he couldn't see how much she was shaking.

"A private programmer," he murmured. "Somehow, I doubt that just anyone would be in an FBI van with an agent in the middle of a mission." He glanced at Natalie's arm. Stepping closer, he held out his hand. "I'll take that very interesting watch. And don't even think about refusing. I have no problem making Skylar hurt."

Skylar was unable to halt the gasp from leaving her lips. She watched in numb silence as Natalie slid off her watch, knowing it was their only radio contact with the Keepers. Natalie gripped it tightly in her palm before handing it over. Skylar had wondered if Natalie would throw it at him, but the Keeper's face was neutral.

He dropped it to the pavement before stomping on the device, crushing it under his boot. His lips curved upward as though in a win, but Natalie simply cocked her brow with a bored expression on her face.

His smile slid into a sneer. "I have a use for both of you."

Skylar tried to mimic his expression but was fairly

certain she couldn't replicate a sardonic smile. "You're interested in my skills as a programmer for Alistair Montague. If not, you would've had your lackeys shoot both of us instead of kidnapping. Well, now you get two programmers."

Gerald threw his head back and laughed, sound echoing in the warehouse. Shaking his head as his laughter slowed, he said, "Alistair is interested in wining and dining other multibillionaires, heads of major corporations, and politicians. His sense of power comes from manipulating elections to keep the political environment conducive to his interests." He leaned closer in an exaggerated whisper. "I make sure his cybersecurity not only protects Montague Industries"—he paused for emphasis—"but also is used to further Alistair's interests."

"The feds are looking into him. Into everything his hand is in," Skylar said, glancing toward Natalie, gaining an almost imperceptible nod.

Gerald shrugged, the news obviously not surprising. "His billions protect Alistair Montague. He isn't the most intelligent man. Not nearly as smart as most people think. He surrounds himself with too many yes-men, terrified to voice an opinion that goes against what he thinks. He's afraid that someone around him might be smarter than him. He took his inheritance and managed to invest decently. At least enough to increase his money into the billionaire status. And he likes to throw the money at the politicians who will make it easier for him to do business."

"He's the puppeteer," she said, repeating what she'd said to Jeb.

"Yes. He's a master puppeteer." Gerald inclined his head. "But not for everyone."

"You're telling me that he doesn't hold your strings?"

Gerald belted out laughter again and shook his head. "I make sure to do everything Alistair asks of me. As far as he's concerned, I'm the perfect employee. For now. But I've seen enough people come and go from his orbit and his employees over the years to know he can eliminate anyone. If he ever decides to get rid of me or goes down in a federal investigation, I want to have enough money that makes working for that pompous shit worth it. I'll never have to work again."

Clarity struck, and she nodded. "The black market sales of military equipment. That's not Mr. Montague, is it? It's you. All you."

He threw his hands out to the side and then clapped slowly, the sound reverberating throughout the cavernous space. "For someone so gifted, Skylar, you have been incredibly slow reaching that conclusion."

She winced. Not at his insult, but that he'd masterminded the entire scheme. "You're the one who had me working just for you, but everything points back to Alastair Montague, doesn't it? Even though the FBI is after him, you remain hidden."

"You're exactly right. The feds can go after Alastair Montague because, thanks to you, all the trails lead to him."

Her heart plunged as more revelations dawned. *His*

revenue stream is getting ready to close now that the FBI knows about the black market. He doesn't need me. He'll kill us both. She glanced to the side, but Natalie's face held no emotion. *But she has to know the same thing!* She looked back at Gerald as Natalie stepped closer to her. "But how did you know the FBI was going to raid the thefts tonight?" She jerked. "For that matter, how did you know I was going to be there?"

"Poor FBI government workers. They make very little money, and it wasn't difficult to find one to employ."

She gasped but noticed that Natalie didn't seem surprised. "But he killed one of his own! Another agent!"

"By God, you are naive, Skylar," he said. "Haven't you realized that money will buy anything?"

Natalie moved next to her and reached over to latch onto Skylar's hand. Drawing strength from Natalie's presence, she said, "What now?"

Gerald rubbed his chin. "The mistake I made before was thinking that if I stuck you on an island with no hope of rescue, I left you unguarded. The precautions I had would keep you from alerting anyone on the outside." He lifted his head and smirked. "I should congratulate you. But I won't make that mistake again."

Her heart threatened to stop at the idea that suddenly they were going to die. Jeb flashed through her mind. *I never told him that I loved him. For me, it's always been him since I was ten years old.*

"What I've decided is that you can still be valuable to

me. And now that I think about it, there's no reason not to use your friend as well. Some of my money is in an off-shore account, out of the reach of the FBI, IRS, or Interpol. And your acceptance of my *hospitality* here will ensure I get the rest of what I'm due put in there, as well. While I get away, you'll be held hostage here."

She glanced to the side, but Natalie's face gave away nothing. She felt sure that was to keep Gerald from having any idea what was going through her mind, but Skylar desperately wished she could tell.

He turned to the man who, so far, had remained silent. "You can take the vehicle we arrived in back to our designated location. Make sure it's wiped down, then destroy it. Your money will be in your account as soon as the pilot lifts off with me safely aboard." Shooting his gaze toward the pilot, he said, "Stay here. I'll be back. Once I see the shipments safely on their way, we'll take off."

Barely glancing at Skylar or Natalie, he ordered, "Let's go."

With the guard holding his gun at their backs, Skylar and Natalie were herded across the vast concrete floor to the end of the warehouse. From this vantage point, her eyes were drawn to a metal staircase that rose three stories, connecting what looked like office rooms stacked on each other. As they continued forward, she could now see the first-floor door led to a barely furnished office with a window looking out into the warehouse. She imagined it once was a vigilant lookout for the original owner as they watched over their employees. She lifted her gaze and noted the second-floor office also had a large warehouse window. The third floor, however, presented a blank face to the warehouse.

They bypassed the first-floor room and were prodded to the metal staircase leading upward. The staircase creaked under their footsteps that echoed loudly on the metal. Skylar's heartbeat thundered in her ears as each step amplified her growing sense of dread. They continued past the second floor, and by now, Skylar clung to the railing as she wondered how they would ever escape.

They continued to the top, where Gerald stepped into a room with two walls lined with empty, rusting metal shelves and a folding table and chair on a third wall. "When I found this abandoned warehouse," Gerard began, his words echoing slightly in the barren space, "I realized how perfectly it would fit my needs, both in housing equipment waiting to be shipped out. I hadn't planned to use this storage room, but now I see its use."

Skylar reached to the side to grab Natalie's hand, afraid she might drop to her knees if she didn't have that human connection.

"So what's the plan?" Natalie asked, her voice not giving away a hint of fear.

Skylar's fingers flinched, and Natalie squeezed her hand in return. Skylar didn't know if it was out of fear or solidarity, but the small act fortified her.

"That's easy." He pulled out a laptop from his brief-case and set it on the table. "You should recognize the security, Skylar. You set it up."

"I thought it was for Montague Industries—"

"I'm not responsible for your erroneous assumptions." He laughed. "Now, sit down and transfer the money. Don't try any tricks, or your cute friend and my friend with the gun will get acquainted in a way that will end with a bullet to the brain."

Skylar felt the air rush from her lungs. She dropped into the chair and took the passwords he gave her, knowing he would change them as soon as they were finished. Her hands shook as she quickly moved through the necessary programs and coding. Several times, she battled lightheadedness as the oxygen seemed to be sucked from the air.

"What the fuck is taking so long?" he barked.

"It's not like she's poking a few numbers into an ATM machine!" Natalie bit out. "Give her a chance to work."

"Shut up!" Gerald said.

Terrified that he would hurt Natalie, her fingers flew over the keyboard. Finally, she looked up and said, "Okay, it's done."

He checked his phone, tapping quickly. A slow smile moved over his face as he let out a breath. "Good." He walked to the door, then looked over his shoulder. "The two of you will stay here until I get away. As soon as my pilot has taken me off the continent, I'll let the FBI know where to find you." He nodded toward the guard behind them with the gun, and the two women were pushed toward the back. Gerard stood in the doorframe and shrugged. "You see… I'm not quite the monster you think I am. Stay alive for a couple of days, and you'll be found."

With that, he went through the door, followed by the guard who kept the weapon pointed at them until the door slammed shut. The sound of a bolt being slid into place echoed in the room and deep inside the hollow of Skylar.

29

The barest hint of dawn cast a golden hue over the landscape as the SUV thundered down the highway. Jeb paid no attention to the surroundings as he focused on the time that had passed since Skylar had been kidnapped.

"Turn right at the next intersection." Leo barked out the instructions to Adam, whose hands were steady on the wheel.

When Carson gave the instructions to meet their pilot, Logan, Adam insisted on driving. Jeb had no problem with Adam's decision, considering his thoughts swung between rage and fear. Logan's helicopter would only hold three passengers, and the thought of being left behind was not an option for Jeb or Leo. Another SUV with Dolby and Bennett was right behind them. Landon had arranged for an FBI pilot to arrive to take them, and hopefully, they wouldn't be far behind.

Adam turned onto the smaller road, and Jeb was

glad it was paved, keeping them from having to slow down on a gravel or dirt road.

"You're almost to the rendezvous point," Abbie radioed. "Logan's ETA is two minutes."

Adam brought the SUV to a screeching halt outside an old, abandoned hangar. As they climbed from the SUV, the whirring helicopter blades could already be heard. Jeb lifted his hand to shield his eyes as he looked upward and watched as it landed. As soon as the runners touched the ground, the three men raced forward while ducking, reaching the helicopter.

Adam climbed into the seat next to Logan, shook his hand, and made the introductions as Leo and Jeb climbed into the two back seats. Logan lifted the aircraft into the air without wasting any time as the Keepers nodded to their comrades from the SUV behind them.

Ian radioed, "The FBI's helicopter ETA is fifteen minutes."

Jeb winced, wishing it was closer but thankful he and Leo didn't have to wait that extra time.

"Do you have the coordinates?" Adam asked.

"Your people have been sending me the intel," Logan replied. "We're heading to an abandoned warehouse in Oregon. It seems that both tracers are there, as well as confirmation that the two women are together and alive."

The air rushed from Jeb's lungs as he heard Leo mutter, "Thank fuck."

The two men shared a look, and while Logan would be hard-pressed to define it, he knew their mirrored expressions gave evidence of not just a mission gone fubar but with the added fear concerning the women they loved.

"Do we know who has them?"

Carson replied, "In the helicopter, Natalie hit the radio on her watch. My guess is that she was subdued before that. Skylar managed to get Gerald Butler to talk at the warehouse. Not realizing he was being recorded, we now have the evidence that he was the one orchestrating the black market thefts and Skylar's kidnapping."

"Same coordinates?" Logan asked over Carson's explanation.

"Yes," Abbie replied in haste. "The signal from the tracers has been lost, but they were at some abandoned warehouses off the Owyhee River in Oregon. Your ETA should be about forty minutes."

Jeb hated the idea of forty more minutes before he could get to her. That was more than enough time for anything to happen to Skylar. He closed his eyes at the thought of how frightened she would be. He trusted Natalie to take care of her but had no idea if they would be in a situation where she could.

He couldn't remember feeling so helpless. When some boys bullied her in elementary school, he'd put a stop to it. *"You'll have to answer me if I hear you've picked on her again." They ran away like the little punk-asses they were. After that, they left her alone.* That was only the start—anytime she needed him, he stepped up as her protector. His chest depressed as the air left his lungs. *Until I fucked up. I was just as punk-ass as those kids.*

He could still see the look on her face as they stood facing each other all those years ago. He was so full of righteous indignation and ignored the pain and regret so clearly written on her expression.

The feel of a hand on his arm had his eyelids snap open, and he swung his head to the side to see Leo's gaze heavy on him.

"Whatever you're thinking… wherever you just went… let it go."

Swallowing deeply, he said, "I once acted like a jackass and walked away from her. It was years ago when I first joined the Navy, but still… I fuckin' walked away."

"Doesn't matter," Leo growled.

Jeb opened his mouth to argue, but Leo wasn't finished.

"I wasted a lot of years knowing Natalie but not letting myself go there with her. All we can do is move forward. And that's just what we're going to do. Move forward… get there… and get our women."

Letting out a shaky breath, he nodded. Leo returned to looking out his window, and Jeb did the same.

For the rest of the flight, he let Adam coordinate with LSIWC and Logan. Finally, after what seemed like forever, Logan called out, "Approaching the warehouse. I'll circle high to give us a chance to see what's there."

Jeb pressed his face to the window and looked down. The farmland below was mostly brown, and the river was only a thin ribbon running through the area. They were west of Boise, now in Oregon. "I don't see any movement, but two vehicles are parked on one side where a helicopter sets." He had no idea if that was a good sign or not.

"Natalie's and Skylar's tracers are still in the warehouse," Abbie radioed.

Jeb knew that wasn't a guarantee that Skylar would still be there if she were separated from her necklace. *I'm getting her a tattoo as soon as I get her back!*

"How do you want to play this?" Logan asked.

"Abbie, tell us what you've got on the warehouse," Adam requested.

Jeb knew with her background in geospatial photogrammetry, she could pull up the schematics of the original warehouse blueprints.

"The door on the south side leads into the reception and office area. Beyond that is the main warehouse with the loading dock and doors on the west side, closest to the river and the main road. There is a staircase that is on the east side of the warehouse, near where the offices are—"

"Staircase?" Jeb asked. "Is there a second floor of offices upstairs?"

"Yes. There are three floors of offices," Abbie said. "The first two floor offices have windows that overlook the warehouse and have smaller windows overlooking the outside. The third floor has a window that also faces the outside."

Adam whipped his head around, and the three Keepers shared a look. "Fire escape?" Leo asked.

"Yes.

Logan said, "I'll land on the flat land to the northeast. There are no windows on that side. We can separate and move around the building."

"You're going in with us?" Jeb asked, unable to hide his surprise.

"You need every hand until the rest of your crew gets here. Anyway, I figure I'm the one here who knows how to disable their bird."

The tightness in Jeb's chest didn't ease, but an added layer of gratitude filled him at Logan's offer. Jeb and the others were unbuckled instantly as the helicopter set down with barely a bump. They alighted as a group, and then, with a plan in place, they separated and moved stealthily toward the warehouse.

30

As soon as the door had closed, Skylar let out a breath. "He'll let us go?"

Natalie held her gaze, her eyes full of sympathy before she shook her head. "No. He said he'd take care of us. My guess? He'll blow up this fucking warehouse as soon as he gets the contents on their way to the highest bidder."

"O… oh," Skylar choked out, wondering how stupid it was that she'd made the assumption they'd be released.

Natalie turned in a circle, her gaze scanning before she pointed toward the back wall. "Let's move the shelves."

Skylar's gaze jumped to follow Natalie's finger, willing to do anything but sit and wait to see what Gerald planned. Natalie's expression was one of concentration as she grabbed one side, and Skylar grabbed the opposite end. Stunned when they shifted away from the wall, she exclaimed, "I didn't think they'd move."

"I think this was an office before storage," Natalie said.

"What makes you say that?" Skylar asked as she heaved against the heavy shelving unit again.

"Look at the floor. You can see where the feet of a desk or table once stood. The rusty stain at the back looks like a metal filing cabinet once was placed."

Skylar dropped her gaze to the old, stained tile floor. "Good God, you're right." She hated that she had not been more observant.

Natalie's lips were curved in a satisfied smile. Skylar was relieved that Natalie appeared glad of the discovery but had no idea how that would help them escape. With several more pulls, they shifted the shelves away from the wall.

"That's just what I thought," Natalie exclaimed.

Skylar couldn't imagine what was hiding behind the shelves but stretched her neck to see around the shelves and stared with awe. The metal shelving had covered a window leading to the outside. *But we're on the third floor.* She pressed her lips together, battling the urge to ask what Natalie was thinking and already forming a protest that she wouldn't be able to accomplish whatever she suggested.

Natalie's eyes narrowed as she stared at the window, then shot her gaze to Skylar. "We can use the window to get out of here. When we flew in and circled the building, I noticed the three windows connected by a fire escape."

Skylar blinked as she looked up. "A fire escape?" Skylar said, feeling foolish that she had noticed nothing useful while in the helicopter.

"Come on," Natalie urged. "Let's get this window open."

Side by side, the two women strained against the stubborn window. Their efforts met with unyielding resistance. Sucking in a hasty breath, Skylar shook her head. "I'm puny when it comes to strength," she admitted, now hating that she hadn't spent more time exercising when she'd been solitary on the island.

"Never mind," Natalie said, brushing aside her protestations. "We'll get it."

Skylar's chortle of incredulity slipped out. Seeing Natalie's gaze on her, she inwardly winced. A strange feeling moved through Skylar's entire being, so strong that she felt a full-body shiver. Tired of being afraid. Tired of being used by others for their own gain. Tired of letting her destiny just unfold.

She glanced up, having no idea what was keeping the window shut, but if Natalie had an idea for how they could get out, Skylar was all in. "I'm not you, and you'll have to tell me what to do, but if it's within my ability, I'll do it."

Natalie's slow grin morphed into a wide smile. "Girl, there's no difference between you and me other than our experiences. Whatever superpowers you think I have, believe me, they're in you as well."

"All I know is that I'm tired of being used by people who don't have my best interest at heart. So I sure as hell am ready to help us get out of here."

Natalie dipped her chin. "Damn straight."

"What is holding it shut?" Skylar asked as she stared upward again.

"I guess it helps that Gerald's pilot didn't think to search me." Natalie bent over and reached inside her boot, pulling out a thin leather case. As she flipped it, she exposed a knife, a screwdriver, and several other small tools. Pulling out one of the objects, she twirled it between her fingertips. "Voilà!"

Skylar couldn't help but smile at Natalie's smirk. Blowing out a deep breath, Skylar waited to see what would happen.

Natalie dragged the blade of the tool over the glass, and with each motion, Skylar felt a sense of elation when she realized the glass was being cut.

"We'll take these out in smaller pieces," Natalie said.

Skylar followed Natalie's directions at the end of the square cut and kept her fingertips on it before pushing it outward. "Shouldn't I try to get these inside instead of letting them fall so far?"

"Normally, yes. But no one is out there, and I don't want you to get cut."

For the next cut, Skylar pushed against the bottom and carefully pulled the top away, taking it between her fingers and laying it on the floor. Grinning, she remained quiet as Natalie gave a nod of approval. They kept going until the glass was cut away from the base of the window and most of the way up. The hole was large enough for the two women to get through. Both leaned out to spy a small ledge leading to the rusty metal fire escape stairs.

"Not much room," Natalie muttered, then turned to Skylar. "Look, I can go down and find a way back up—"

"I've got this," Skylar assured. "The ledge is wide enough for us to maneuver." Seeing Natalie's assessing stare, she chortled. "Seriously, I have plenty of experience on window ledges and no fear of heights."

Natalie grinned. "Well, all right. Let's get out of here."

They leaned out the window again, and Skylar quickly analyzed the best way to get to the fire escape. "I'll go first. I can scooch along the ledge until I reach the stairs. Then you follow, and I can give my free hand to steady "

"I should go first," Natalie said. "As you admitted, I'm stronger."

"That's true, but I'm smaller. I'll be able to make it the few feet to the ledge easier and then you'll have my hand in case the wooden ledge gives."

Natalie nodded, but her lips were pressed tightly together. Skylar was sure the other woman hated to give up control, but Skylar was so comfortable looking out over the ledge at the same height. She used to as a child. And with the lighthouse.

Inching carefully, she found the wood ledge strong enough to hold her as she scooted to the end, reaching out to grab the metal fire escape rail. Then reaching back with her other hand, she watched Natalie follow her movements onto the ledge. Clasping hands, she helped guide Natalie until they were next to each other.

Shifting her body again, Skylar swung her leg underneath the rail, planting her sneaker foot onto the first rung. She hated to let go of Natalie, so she decided to move on to the fire escape only using one hand. As soon as Natalie was able to follow and grab the railing, Skylar let go.

"I knew you had superpowers in you, girl," Natalie said as she followed Skylar.

Just as they stood on the rung together, side-by-side, the fire escape wobbled precariously, a few bolts coming loose from the outer wall of the warehouse. "Shit!" Skylar cursed, grabbing hold of the rail and holding on.

"Start down," Natalie ordered. "I'm going to stay here while you go down."

"No," Skylar argued. "We need to go down at the same time. If we both lean closer to the wall, our combined weight will give it more steadiness."

"You got it," Natalie agreed.

Determination filled her, and Skylar swung around to the other side of the ladder. "Ready?"

With a nod, Natalie lowered her foot to the next rung and Skylar followed on her side. The ladder shook with each step, but they leaned toward the side of the warehouse to keep their weight from pulling the ladder bolts away from where it was attached. Her arms ached as she held on tightly, noticing Natalie's descent was much smoother. "How did you go down so easily?"

"Pull-ups in the Army," came the muttered reply.

Skylar added pull-ups to her newly formed exercise routine. The ladder was shaking, and their descent was difficult to navigate. Natalie moved slightly lower than

Skylar, still close to the wall. Skylar's foot slipped, and Natalie grunted.

"Oh, God, I'm sorry!" Skylar whispered. "Did I hit your foot?"

"Just my arm. Keep going," Natalie encouraged again.

The rusted rungs and flaking paint showed evidence that the fire escape ladder and the warehouse were relics of the past. It clung precariously to the outside of the dilapidated building. Skylar wished Natalie was above her so that she wouldn't step on her again, but there wasn't enough room for them to change positions. They managed to descend about fifteen feet and came to the second-floor office window. The windowsill ledge was wider than the one on the third floor. Before she had a chance to catch her breath, the ladder groaned once again. Only this time, the sound was accompanied by a shudder and loud creak as it started to pull away from the building.

"Shit!" Skylar cried as she grabbed the window ledge, pulling her body onto the small platform as the ladder leaned farther away.

Natalie cursed under her breath but managed to grab the ledge as well. Skylar reached over and grabbed Natalie's arm. "I've got you."

Natalie swung her leg upward but missed the ledge the first time. Her hands almost slipped, but Skylar hung on tight. "Come on. We've got this."

Natalie caught her gaze, and something passed between the two women. Skylar couldn't define it, but it felt a lot like a sisterhood she'd never felt before. "We've got this," she repeated.

Natalie swung her leg up again. This time, it landed on the ledge. With Skylar's assistance, the two women were soon on the ledge together as the ladder leaned farther from the wall, leaning at an angle that gave evidence it would soon crash to the ground. They shifted to their knees on the windowsill and looked into the empty office.

Skylar was surprised when Natalie stopped. "Aren't we going in?"

"Hear that?"

Skylar tried to listen to anything other than the roaring of blood rushing through her ears. The sound of a loud rumbling could be heard in the distance. Brows lowered, she cocked her head to the side in silent question.

"Transportation must be coming in to move the contraband he has stored." Natalie pulled out her glass cutter again.

Skylar looked at the window, then nervously licked her lips. "We go in here? There's a window on the other side of the room that faces the interior of the warehouse. We'll be visible there."

"No choice," Natalie said as she kept cutting.

"I was afraid that was what you were going to say." Skylar looked upward and sighed, at least glad that they were no longer on the third floor. Looking back at the window, she placed her hands on the section Natalie was cutting. She caught it, but with their side of the building in shadow, it was harder to see the glass edges. "I don't suppose you have a light in your magic case?"

Natalie chuckled and reached inside her case, pulling out a pen light.

Taking it, Skylar chuckled. "Can I get one of those Keeper cases? It might make my life easier."

"Don't see why not. Leo gave me this one when we got married."

As strange as that might sound to some, Skylar thought it was sweet. She wanted to ask if Natalie was afraid of not seeing Leo again, but that only made her think of the possibility of not seeing Jeb again. Closing her eyes for a few seconds, she shoved those thoughts back into a box, determined to lock the lid. Breathing out, she asked, "Okay, I'm ready."

Once again, Natalie cut from the bottom and continued upward until the was enough room for them to slip through without getting sliced on the glass.

Natalie cautiously shifted around to put her feet through the opening first. Her boots landed on the glass but kept her feet protected. She leaned out, grabbed Skylar's arms, and pulled her gently inside. Skylar grabbed Natalie's shoulders and almost fell on top of her as they staggered slightly.

"No points for finesse," Natalie quipped in a whisper. "But that's a full ten for getting the job done."

Skylar snorted, the sound carrying softly in the empty office. "If I have to be trapped in this mess, I'm glad you're with me."

"Same here," Natalie echoed with a smile, her gratitude evident in her eyes. "And thanks, Skylar. Couldn't have done it without you."

Overwhelmed and still reeling from their recent escapades, Skylar could only offer a faint smile in return. They weren't out of danger yet but out of the locked storeroom. She counted that as a victory.

Suddenly, their moment of respite was abruptly shattered by the murmur of men's voices. Instinctively, Skylar rolled to her side to crouch behind the lower portion of the wall so she wouldn't be visible from the warehouse. Natalie mirrored Skylar's movements. The voices were too far away to tell what they were saying, but Skylar's heart pounded. Still crouching, she looked at the inside glass windows of the empty office and realized they might be free of the storage room, but they were now even more susceptible to exposure. Looking at Natalie, she grimaced, feeling vulnerable and clueless as to what they should do. "I don't suppose you have a gun in that little case, do you?"

Natalie's response was swift and silent. Reaching into her boot, she pulled out a small gun with practiced ease and then turned to Skylar with a lifted brow.

Skylar blinked at the weapon and desired to learn how to take care of herself. "Well, looks like I need boots like yours as well as a little case."

"Talk to Jeb… he'll take care of you."

The mention of Jeb stirred a whirl of emotions in her. She rolled her eyes in spite of the continued danger at the idea of seeing Jeb again… and asking him to teach her to shoot. Refocusing on their situation, she glanced around. "We're sitting ducks in this office," she said, gaining Natalie's nod.

"As soon as we determine where Gerald and the pilot are, we can get out of here."

With more courage than she knew she had, she followed Natalie's lead as they raised slightly and peeked out the window. The trucks they heard in the distance hadn't yet reached the back cargo door, but now the large doors stood open.

The sound of a gunshot from somewhere below caused Skylar to drop to the floor, instinctively covering her head. "Oh God, do you think the Keepers are here?"

Natalie reached out and grabbed Skylar's hand. "That's not the sound of their guns."

"Oh…" Skylar had no idea that different weapons made different sounds.

"Hey. We got this." Natalie drew Skylar's attention back to her.

Skylar sucked in a deep breath and let it out slowly as she nodded. "Okay, what's next?"

"We need to see what's happening, then get down to the first floor. We head to the front if Gerald is at the cargo doors."

Nodding, they peered out the window again. Skylar could see movement toward the back of the warehouse but couldn't hear what was being said or who was moving. Natalie headed to the door, opened it a crack, and looked out. Skylar was out of her element and willing to follow Natalie's more experienced lead, grateful that the competent Keeper was with her.

Natalie looked over her shoulder and nodded, then slipped out the door. Trying to walk as quietly as possible while crouching, Skylar made it through the door. Natalie waited on the landing and motioned for Skylar to close the door behind her. Doing so, she turned and tiptoed down the steps to the warehouse floor behind Natalie.

Darting over to the first stack of crates, they hid from view. She looked at Natalie's solid stance with the weapon in her hand. Now, Skylar wished she already knew how to shoot and had a weapon as well.

31

Jeb bent low and raced toward the warehouse. Reaching the back corner, he moved with stealth to the front door. Leo was heading to the loading dock doors at the rear to see if there was an opening while Adam took the windows on the west. Logan was moving toward the helicopter to render it unusable. As soon as he neared the front door, the sound of two men shouting met his ears.

"I told you to get the helicopter ready! What the fuck are you doing?"

"I want more. You said this would be easy. Fly a woman here. I didn't ask questions. I wasn't expecting her to be cuffed to the seat, but if that's what it takes, I was willing. But it was two, and if one of those women was FBI, that changes this shit completely. I'm not going to go to prison for you."

You'll do what I fucking say! With the money you're getting paid, you can't back out now."

Jeb was thrilled to hear the two men fighting. In his

experience, when criminals can't get their shit together, they're so distracted they're much easier to subdue.

With his weapon out, he radioed, "Two men in earshot. One is the pilot. One is lead. Arguing. Position unknown."

From the LSIWC compound, Carson interjected. "Landon is coming with FBI. It seems the black-market tank hulls were shipped out two days ago and headed to Oregon. They may be at your location."

"ETA on other Keepers?" Jeb asked.

Abbie replied, "Ten minutes."

"I'm at cargo doors. No opening. I'll go toward west and meet you at the front," Leo responded.

Jeb wished he could give Leo assurances about Skylar and Natalie's location, but all he knew was that both were brought to the warehouse. "Copy."

He was glad to see Leo round the corner of the building, coming toward him. As soon as the other Keeper neared, he shook his head, mouthing, "Can't determine the location of men."

Suddenly, the shouting started up again, and it sounded closer.

"I'll fucking drop you here, you piece of shit!"

"And then who will fly your ass out of here? Your driver already drove off, so you're down to me. You want my continued services, then pay up."

"Fine. You want to extort a bonus, then you'll get it when we land."

"Window is boarded up," Adam reported.

"Fuck," Jeb cursed. Suddenly, a gunshot rang out. His normal response of heightened danger and caution kicked in, but his heart rate pounding out the rhythm of his fear for Skylar was new.

Waiting was no longer an option. Turning the knob, Jeb slipped through the front door with Leo right behind, their weapons drawn.

The first room was empty but could have once been a reception area. With no furniture, it was easy to see no one was hiding. He darted to the door that led into the large warehouse, filled with crates and large tarp-covered objects. He had no doubt they'd found Alistair's hidden stock of military equipment waiting for sale on the black market.

"The next one goes in you!"

Jeb shared a look with Leo, then dipped his head in acknowledgment of Adam's arrival. The three carefully moved without making a sound, each heading in a different direction in the warehouse. Coming to a large tarp, he bent low and lifted the bottom of the tarp. He recognized the item and radioed, "No sight of men on west side. Tank hulls here."

Dropping the edge of the tarp, he focused on finding Skylar and Natalie, making sure to keep the danger away from them.

"Two men near cargo doors at back," Adam radioed.

Jeb started at the wooden crates he felt sure held military weapons. In truth, he didn't care what was in them, other than they served as an easy cover. When Landon and the FBI arrived, they could sort out the contents.

As he made it past another stack, a male voice shouted.

"Fuck! They're loose!"

"Where did they go?"

"You locked them in! How the hell did they get out?"

"They're behind those crates!"

Multiple footsteps could be heard, and Jeb crouched low as he raced forward, past one set of crates at a time. Peering around each one before continuing toward the offices, he moved forward. A gunshot fired out, and then another one returned. He radioed, "Do you see Natalie or Skylar?"

"Negative."

Another round of fire could be heard, only this time, the distinct sound of a female scream sounded out. Jeb's heart clenched when he recognized Skylar's cry.

"I've got you, bitches. I don't know how you got away, but this ends now. I didn't spend the past ten years kissing up to an asshole to be taken out by you two."

Footsteps could be heard, including what sounded like a scuffle. Jeb had been on many rescue missions, but now, trying to find Skylar to keep her safe, he cursed the massive warehouse. Sounds echoed, making them indistinct as to location. Skylar cried out, she was probably hit. He hated that he couldn't call out to let her know he was there.

Leo radioed, "At northeast corner. Moving to southeast. Coordinate."

"Southwest corner, to east," Adam responded.

"Center. Moving to southeast," replied Jeb, racing forward.

Another shot rang out, and he halted to locate the gunfire.

"She got me. The bitch got me!" More footsteps. *"Where are you going?"*

"I told you. I didn't sign up for this shit!"

Adam radioed, "Smoke 'em out."

Jeb knew it was the best way… hell, they'd done it on many missions. He hated thinking of Skylar's fear but was desperate to get to her. "Copy," he replied, hearing it echoed by Leo.

Abbie radioed, "FBI and Keepers landing nearby. ETA to warehouse, three minutes."

Not willing to wait, Jeb said, "Smoke."

A few seconds later, Adam let off the smoke bomb that quickly filled the air swirling inside the warehouse. Pulling on a mask, he ducked low and raced toward the sound of the woman's scream.

32

Skylar stared at the gun in her hand as she tried to realize what happened. Natalie had shoved Skylar behind some crates when Gerald came around the corner. She shot toward him, but he'd gotten a shot off before racing behind one of the large tarps.

Natalie had jerked back, the gun landing on the floor.

"Shit!" Natalie groaned, clutching her arm, blood seeping through her fingers.

Skylar darted to her side, but Natalie shook her head. "Get the gun!"

"I can't take that," she protested. "I've never even held a gun, much less shot one."

"Put your finger on the trigger and pull," Natalie said, grimacing. But only if you're sure of what you're shooting toward."

Bending, she snagged it off the floor, holding it the only way she could figure out, keeping her finger on the trigger. Adrenaline raced through her blood, and her vision became laser-focused.

She tried not to cough as the smoke drifted their way. She blinked furiously to attempt to erase the stinging in her eyes. Kneeling, she jerked off the shirt she was wearing over her long-sleeved T-shirt and wrapped it around Natalie's arm and shoulder. Using the shirt arms as the ties, she chewed on her bottom lip as she tried to ascertain if the bleeding had slowed. "What else do you need me to do?" she asked in a hushed voice.

"Let's just get the fuck out of here," Natalie said through gritted teeth.

Hauling Natalie to her feet, she took much of Natalie's weight and gave her support. "The only open door I know of is the one in the front."

Natalie nodded, and they slipped around one of the crates, heading in the direction of the offices.

Natalie stumbled, and Skylar tightened her left arm around Natalie's waist. The smoke was billowing now toward the back of the warehouse. While she knew they were close to the front door, she feared that Gerald would be heading that way at the same time.

Suddenly, a lone figure loomed ahead, walking straight out of the billowing smoke. She gasped and instinctively started to raise the weapon. Then her arm dropped as she spied Jeb walking toward her, appearing like an angel with the fires of hell billowing around him. Suddenly, another figure emerged from behind a crate, and she recognized Gerald. Screaming, "Watch out!" she watched as Jeb dropped to his knees and lifted his weapon.

At the same instant, she fired at the man who made her life hell. She had no idea how to aim, but he was so close the bullet managed to hit his arm. He screamed and dropped his weapon as he grabbed his arm, blood oozing through his fingers as he swirled around and stared at her with rage. His expression didn't cause any fear in her. Instead, she matched his anger.

The smoke had now obliterated her sight, and she couldn't see Jeb for a few seconds. A figure loomed to the side, and she screeched until she realized it was Leo. He reached for Natalie, and Skylar released her hold as he swept his wife into his arms.

In the direction she last saw Jeb, he once again raced toward her through the smoke. Stopping just short of her, he jerked off his goggles. "Give me the gun, sweetheart. Adam has Gerald, and the other Keepers apprehended the pilot and guard at the back."

She handed the weapon to him, and he quickly secured it. Then without wasting a second, wrapped his arms around her and held her tight. He picked her up and rushed toward the front door, following Leo with Natalie and his arms.

Skylar thought he'd let her go once they got outside, but he seemed unable to loosen his arms around her, and she didn't care.

Outside the warehouse, the scene appeared to be total chaos as she watched men and women rushing around, some with jackets emblazoned with FBI on the back, others with ATF, and others in military uniform.

If she wasn't mistaken, she even saw an Oregon sheriff and deputies there as well.

"Natalie! We need to see how she is!" she cried.

"I'm heading to the ambulances, sweetheart," he said. "I want you checked out."

"But Natalie—"

"That's where she'll be."

The parking lot that had been so unused when she arrived hours earlier now swarmed with vehicles, including fire trucks and ambulances. "Natalie!" she cried, gaining the attention of the woman sitting up in the ambulance, glaring as the paramedic adjusted her IV.

"Jesus, I just got grazed. In the field, they would just patch me up, and we keep going—"

"Be quiet," Leo said softly.

Natalie turned her glare toward her husband and lowered her brows. "You did not just tell me to shut up."

"No, I didn't tell you to shut up. I told you to be quiet." Before Natalie had a chance to explode, Leo continued. "Babe, for hours, I had no idea if you were alive. And I couldn't get here any quicker. So pardon me if my worry over you getting shot inconveniences you. Let's just do what the paramedic says and get to a hospital. They can patch you up and then we will be on our way. I don't plan on letting you out of my sight."

Skylar watched the tension in Natalie's face melt away. Turning to Jeb, she said, "I had no idea what to do, but Natalie made me feel like we were going to get out of this."

"Don't give me all the credit," Natalie called out.

"You held your own and saved my life at the same time." Natalie's gaze moved to Jeb. "Just saying, man... she's a keeper. And I mean that in every sense of the word."

The ambulance doors closed with Natalie and Leo on the inside, then moved around the other vehicles and headed down the road.

"Ma'am? Let's check you out," another paramedic said, hustling over.

"I'm fine, really—"

Jeb stopped her words with a squeeze. "I'd feel better if you got checked out."

She held his gaze, seeing the worry lines etched into his face. She reached up and gently cupped his jaw, rubbing her thumb over his cheeks. Unable to deny him anything, she nodded. "Okay."

It didn't take long for the paramedic to check her out. He said she was mildly dehydrated but wouldn't need an IV. She took the proffered water and drank gratefully.

She and Jeb walked over to the group of Keepers, standing just to the side. They'd barely made it to them when she found herself engulfed in hugs. Finally getting passed back to Jeb, she smiled at all of them.

"What's going on?" she asked, looking around at the chaotic scene.

"The FBI has Gerald and his pilot, plus the truck drivers who were on their way here. The ATF and military have confiscated the warehouse's contents, and they will take possession of them. They have Gerald's confession on the tape we supplied from Natalie's watch recording."

Her eyes widened as she grabbed Jeb's arm. "He took it… Gerald did. I don't think he noticed it at first, but when he took us to the top office, he suddenly decided to get rid of it. I was afraid when he smashed it with his foot, it would mess up everything."

"Nah, we got it," Bennett assured.

She sighed in relief, suddenly exhausted. Landon walked over and said, "Good to see you, Skylar. I hate to do this, but I need to interview you. You'll be free to go once we finish this initial interview."

She nodded, knowing it would have to happen. Before she had a chance to begin, another man walked over to shake hands with Jeb.

Jeb looked at her and said, "This is Logan Bishop. He flew me, Leo, and Adam here so we could get here quicker."

She rushed forward and clasped his hand with both of hers. "Oh, thank you so much, Mr. Bishop. You all came just in time!"

The dark-haired man smiled as he allowed her to hang onto his hand until Jeb pulled her back into his embrace. "It's my pleasure. And Logan is fine."

She knew he wasn't a Keeper, so she'd probably never see him again, but she smiled in return. "And I'm just Skylar."

He nodded, then made the rounds among the Keepers, shaking their hands, introducing himself to those he hadn't met. He turned to Jeb and Skylar again and said, "I'll head back to Montana now, but Carson is providing your transportation back to California. If Carson and

Mace get their way, I have a feeling I'll be seeing you real soon."

Jeb grinned and nodded before Logan waved goodbye and walked toward another helicopter in the distance.

With the attention back on her, she and the Keepers followed Landon to an area set up by the FBI. She was able to sit down for the interview and was grateful for Jeb's constant presence as he stood behind her with his hand on her shoulder. At times, his grip would tighten, especially when she repeated the threats made against her, how she and Natalie had to go through the third-floor window to get away. And then, when she recounted how the fire escape ladder separated from the building, and they had to hold the window ledge to survive, she grabbed Jeb's hand on her shoulder to get him to ease his grip.

Twisting her head, she offered him a soft smile. "I'm okay, honey." Those words didn't seem to have the desired effect, but she understood it would take time for both of them to get beyond the nightmare of the day.

Turning back to Landon, she explained how she had assumed it was Alistair Montague, but according to Gerald, he was the one behind the military equipment black-market scheme.

"Don't worry about that, Skylar. The Bureau is investigating Montague Industries and Alistair. What you're providing is icing on the cake, but we have the evidence needed to stand up in court."

As soon as she finished his last question, she stood

and was engulfed in hugs again, finally ending in Jeb's arms. "How do we all get back home?"

"Carson has a plane ready to take all of us back to California."

"Whew," she heaved. "I much prefer a plane over a helicopter!"

He leaned down and whispered, "Sweetheart, when we get home, we might never leave again, so you won't have to worry about another helicopter."

She grinned and melted into his embrace. Then as they climbed aboard the plane and settled into their seats, she wondered when she should ask him for a gun and shooting lessons. Glancing to the side, she decided that maybe later would be best.

With a smile, she reached her hand over between them. And just like old times, he rested his palm over hers, and their fingers linked.

33

TWO WEEKS LATER

Skylar walked into the kitchen and smiled as she headed straight to the coffee. One of the delights of being back in civilization was having guilty pleasures at her fingertips again. Her guilty pleasure at the moment was Jeb's coffee maker, which could be set with a timer so she didn't have to wait for her hot morning pick-me-up drink. Next, she pulled down two mugs from the cabinet overhead. One was a Go Navy mug, and the other was a cup with a bright sunflower on the front. She had bought the cup many years earlier, loving the bright colors to start her mornings.

The day after they'd returned from Oregon, Jeb had declared he wanted her to move in with him. So many changes had occurred, but she didn't hesitate. For her, it had always been Jeb. The next day, they drove to her apartment. She wasn't sure if Gerald had emptied it but had breathed a sigh of relief that it was just as though she'd simply been gone a few days instead of over six months.

She'd packed up her clothes and items that had sentimental value. A small, framed photograph on her wall was of her and Jeb sitting on a log, laughing together as their sticks with marshmallows toasted in the outdoor fire. She had spied Jeb staring at it and was mesmerized by the expression on his face.

"I didn't know anyone took our picture that night at camp," he'd said, his face full of wonder.

"I didn't either until I was in college, and the camp counselor who'd taken it sent me an email. She was clearing out some photos and asked if I wanted it."

"And you said *yes*?" Incredulity had dripped from his words.

"Of course." Holding his gaze, she'd said, "Jeb, you might have walked away from me, but I never forgot what you had meant to me growing up." She reached over to the wall and took the frame down.

He'd taken it from her hands carefully, then backed her up against the wall and kissed her. Not a soft, gentle kiss but a hard, possessive kiss that left her breathless and needy. They would have made it to her bed, but the moving company knocked on the door, interrupting their declaration of forgiving the past and racing toward the future.

Breathing heavily, they separated, and Jeb adjusted his crotch, then nipped at her lips. "We'll finish this later," he had promised, sending a tingle straight through her.

She'd carefully wrapped the picture, along with other items of sentimentality. At the same time, Jeb had the movers pack the rest to take to a storage unit near where he lived so that she could go through the furniture and household items at her leisure.

One of the items that she'd brought with her was the cup. "Life's too short not to enjoy the little things that make us happy," she'd declared to Jeb when she carefully wrapped the cup to bring with her.

Now, after pouring two cups, she opened the refrigerator, and another smile slipped over her face. Jeb made sure he had her favorite creamer. Such a simple act yet having someone care enough to know her favorite and make sure she had it at her fingertips made her heart light.

Glad it was a Saturday, she relished the idea of having Jeb to herself for the morning, and then she would attend a "welcome to the family" party. She was anxious to share something with the other Keepers.

Once settled into his home, Carson offered her a Keeper position, having her stay on the investigative and security side of LSIWC's computer systems. She'd spent the past week learning everything she could about their business. One bonus was getting to know the other Keepers, especially the women. She discovered a world of girlfriends that she'd never experienced before. And the bonus… working with Jeb every day.

The hammering sound in the hall jerked her out of her musings, and she quickly set her cup down. She hurried around the corner to see what Jeb was doing. Spying him setting the hammer down, having left a small nail in the wall next to their campfire photograph, he bent to pick up another frame from the floor and hang it on the wall. Her brows lowered in curiosity as she neared, then stared in stunned silence at the new photograph he'd hung.

It was a print of the two of them on the island with the seals sunning on the cliff rocks behind them. The colors were vibrant, and the two of them wore brilliant smiles. The air rushed from her lungs. "Oh my God! I forgot about the selfie you took!"

He turned and wrapped his arms around her, bending to kiss her deeply. "Mmm," he mumbled. "You taste like delicious coffee."

When the kiss ended, she grinned and lowered her heels to the floor. "Got a cup all ready for you. Perfect way to start the morning."

"The perfect way to start the morning was what we did in bed when we first woke up," he corrected.

Her smile widened, knowing he was right. Poking him in the stomach, she nodded before grabbing his hand and leading him into the kitchen.

His phone vibrated with a message, and he looked down, then back up. "Carson says to watch the breaking news." He hit the remote, and the TV flared to life. Standing next to each other, they watched as the newscaster announced that Montague Industries was being investigated for a black market scheme involving military equipment. Gerald Butler, the head of Montague Industries' Cybersecurity Division, had been arrested, along with Colonel Spelling of the US Army. The FBI and the Army were still investigating, but Alistair Montague's attorneys had made a declaration that he had no knowledge of the wrongdoings and would cooperate fully with the investigation. It was noted that Alistair's political friends were taking a step back, declaring they would no longer accept donations from him until the matter was cleared.

Cutting off the TV, he turned to her, his intense gaze assessing. She patted his arm and said, "I'm fine. Really, I am. I know that my name is no longer associated with Gerald's illegal activities, thanks to the work we did. I have no idea what they might pull on Alistair, but he'll get out of it, no matter what." She shrugged. "Having Alistair spinning as he watches his name get dragged through the mud and having Gerald go to jail is good enough for me."

"That's what we tell ourselves with each case," he reminded. "We get the evidence and then turn it over to the authorities. When we can save someone in the process, that's what we're all about."

"And I'm the one you saved," she said, turning to wrap her arms around his waist, smiling up at him.

He slowly shook his head. "No. You're the one who saved me. Back when we were children and you first opened the door to me, then shared your attic retreat. You saved me when you forgave my foolish actions all those years ago. And now… agreeing to share my home and my life."

"I love you, Jeb."

His gaze held her captive as he sucked in a hasty breath. "You do?"

Nodding slowly, she said, "I think I fell for you when I was a little girl and saw you coming up the walk to the Bakers' house."

Jeb bent, taking her lips in a barely-there kiss. "I love

you, too, Skylar. I think I fell for you the first time I saw you sitting on the attic window ledge," he whispered against her lips.

A ribbon of warmth wrapped around her as strong as his arms. Then clinging together, the kiss flamed, consuming them as they headed back upstairs.

That afternoon, she reached into the back of the SUV to grab the large, insulated tote. A presence at her back sent a smile over her face as Jeb's front pressed over her back, and his long arm grabbed the tote. Twisting her neck, her eyes were filled with his face so close to hers. "I can carry that, you know."

"Yeah, you could if I wasn't here. But since I am, then I'll carry it."

Before she could utter another word, he erased the scant inch between their faces and kissed her. As he pulled back, she sighed, blinking her eyes open. "Keep that up, and we might not make it to the party."

He laughed, then straightened, linking fingers with her. "Come on. You've got something to show off."

They walked into the large house and found the party already in full swing. The rooms were filled with friends. Some were setting food on the kitchen table and counters, and others set up folding chairs around the large dining room.

While Jeb carried the tote to the kitchen, Skylar made a beeline to the family room where most of the attention was centered… Hop and Lori, each holding a twin baby. Skylar's heart melted seeing the two adorable bundles. Jeannie handed off her and Carson's five-month-old son to Rachel, so that she could get closer to the newborns.

Rachel bounced the little one with Teddy standing close by, his hand on her back. Shaking her head, Rachel bemoaned, "This might be the closest I get to a grandchild."

Carson looked over at Jeannie, cooing over the twins, and sighed. "She's going to want another one soon."

Hop laughed. "Then you'll just be catching up to me."

"And we won't be too far behind," Leo said, with Natalie tucked under his arm.

It took a few seconds for the group to realize what he'd said. In deference to the babies sleeping, soft cheers of congratulations rang out.

"I'm three months along," Natalie said, her smile softer than Skylar had seen.

"Oh my God," Skylar breathed, realizing Natalie had been pregnant during their kidnapping and escape. It seemed to hit the others as well.

Carson's jaw tightened. "No more fieldwork for you for a while," he ordered.

"Don't worry, boss. The big guy here has already laid down the law," she said, patting Leo's stomach.

As Leo and Natalie beamed at each other, Skylar noticed glances between Chris and Stella, Rick and Abbie, and Dolby and Marcia and wondered if more announcements would be forthcoming over the next few months. With smiles between Ian and Vicki, Poole and Tricia, along with Bennett and Diana, she felt sure their ranks would be growing.

"And in other good news," Leo continued. "My brother, Oliver, is getting out of the Rangers."

Natalie offered a shaky nod. "After everything he's been through, he's finally coming home."

"And will have a job waiting for him," Carson pronounced.

Skylar had heard that Oliver had been in a helicopter accident while in training. No one on his team had been killed, but several of them had been injured.

The group soon moved to the food, finding more than they could eat. The conversation flowed between good friends and coworkers.

Before dessert, Jeb tapped his fork on his plate, gaining everyone's attention. Reaching his arm around Skylar, he said, "While we're celebrating, I wanted you all to see Skylar's newest decoration."

She laughed and pulled up the sleeve to expose the still-reddened tattoo of a lighthouse on her shoulder. The whispered cheers and gentle clapping resounded again. "As soon as it heals, I'll get the tracker embedded," she said.

"While she's waiting on that," Jeb continued, "I wanted to give her something else. And since you all are our family, it's only right that you witness this, as well." He reached into his pocket while dropping to one knee.

She gasped, staring wide-eyed at the perfect diamond ring before her gaze moved back to his.

"Skylar, we share a past. And I want us to share a future. Will you be my wife?"

She dropped into the chair in front of him, bringing their faces closer. He filled her vision as everyone else in the room faded away. All she could see was the boy who shared her little ledge and her heart. Nodding, she choked back a sob. "Yes. It was always you. It will always *be* you."

Watching as he slipped the ring on her finger, the others filled the room with hearty approval and congratulations.

But she only heard her heart beating in time with Jeb's.

Are you ready for Logan, the start of the Lighthouse Security Investigations Montana series?
Click here! Logan

And for Leo's brother's story, click here!
Oliver's story: Time for Home (LSIWC crossover novel)

You do NOT want to miss these other Lighthouse Security Investigations books!

Lighthouse Security Investigations West Coast

Carson

Leo

Rick

Hop

Dolby

Bennett

Poole

Adam
Jeb
Chris's story: Home Port (an LSI West Coast crossover novel)
Ian's story: Thinking of Home (LSIWC crossover novel)
Oliver's story: Time for Home (LSIWC crossover novel)

Lighthouse Security Investigations

Mace
Rank
Walker
Drew
Blake
Tate
Levi
Clay
Cobb
Bray
Josh
Knox

Keep turning the page to discover all the Maryann Jordan books!

ALSO BY MARYANN JORDAN

Don't miss other Maryann Jordan books!

Baytown Boys (small town, military romantic suspense)

Coming Home

Just One More Chance

Clues of the Heart

Finding Peace

Picking Up the Pieces

Sunset Flames

Waiting for Sunrise

Hear My Heart

Guarding Your Heart

Sweet Rose

Our Time

Count On Me

Shielding You

To Love Someone

Sea Glass Hearts

Protecting Her Heart

Sunset Kiss

Baytown Heroes - A Baytown Boys subseries

A Hero's Chance

Finding a Hero

A Hero for Her

Needing A Hero

Hopeful Hero

Always a Hero

For all of Miss Ethel's boys:

Heroes at Heart (Military Romance)

Zander

Rafe

Cael

Jaxon

Jayden

Asher

Zeke

Cas

Lighthouse Security Investigations

Mace

Rank

Walker

Drew

Blake

Tate

Levi

Clay

Cobb

Bray

Josh

Knox

Lighthouse Security Investigations West Coast

Carson

Leo

Rick

Hop

Dolby

Bennett

Poole

Adam

Jeb

Chris's story: Home Port (an LSI West Coast crossover novel)

Ian's story: Thinking of Home (LSIWC crossover novel)

Oliver's story: Time for Home (LSIWC crossover novel)

Hope City (romantic suspense series co-developed with Kris Michaels

Brock book 1

Sean book 2

Carter book 3

Brody book 4

Kyle book 5

Ryker book 6

Rory book 7

Killian book 8

Torin book 9

Blayze book 10

Griffin book 11

Saints Protection & Investigations

(an elite group, assigned to the cases no one else wants…or can solve)

Serial Love

Healing Love

Revealing Love

Seeing Love

Honor Love

Sacrifice Love

Protecting Love

Remember Love

Discover Love

Surviving Love

Celebrating Love

Searching Love

Follow the exciting spin-off series:

Alvarez Security (military romantic suspense)

Gabe

Tony

Vinny

Jobe

SEALs

SEAL Together (Silver SEAL)

Undercover Groom (Hot SEAL)

Also for a Hope City Crossover Novel / Hot SEAL...

A Forever Dad

Long Road Home

Military Romantic Suspense

Home to Stay (a Lighthouse Security Investigation crossover novel)

Home Port (an LSI West Coast crossover novel)

Thinking of Home (LSIWC crossover novel)

Time for Home (LSIWC crossover novel)

Letters From Home (military romance)

Class of Love

Freedom of Love

Bond of Love

The Love's Series (detectives)

Love's Taming

Love's Tempting

Love's Trusting

The Fairfield Series (small town detectives)

Emma's Home

Laurie's Time

Carol's Image

Fireworks Over Fairfield

Please take the time to leave a review of this book. Feel free to contact me, especially if you enjoyed my book. I love to hear from readers!

Facebook

Email

Website

Made in the USA
Middletown, DE
01 May 2024